Our Summertime Secrets

Victoria Jane

Copyright 2025
Victoria Jane

The right of Victoria Jane to be identified as author of this work has been asserted by her in accordance with the Copyright, Designs and Patents Act 1988.

All Rights Reserved

No reproduction, copy or transmission of this publication may be made without written permission.
No paragraph of this publication may be reproduced, copied or transmitted save with the written permission of the author in accordance with the provisions of the Copyright Act in 1956 (as amended).

Any person who commits any unauthorised act in relation to this publication may be liable to criminal prosecution and civil claims for damages.

ISBN   9798280588769

This is a work of fiction. Names, characters, businesses, places, events and incidents are either the product of the author's imagination or used in a fictitious manner, any resemblance to actual persons, living or dead, or actual events is purely coincidental.

First published in 2025 in Great Britian
Independently Published by Victoria Jane

Dedication

*For anyone that thought a situation was hopeless…
there's always a chance.*

Our Summertime Secrets

Contents

Prologue: Jake (One Year ago)	9
Chapter 1: Lexi	13
Chapter 2: Jake	21
Chapter 3: Lexi	29
Chapter 4: Jake	38
Chapter 5: Lexi (One year ago)	47
Chapter 6: Lexi	51
Chapter 7: Jake	65
Chapter 8: Lexi	75
Chapter 9: Jake	86
Chapter 10: Lexi	100
Chapter 11: Jake (One year ago)	122
Chapter 12: Jake	126
Chapter 13: Lexi	139
Chapter 14: Jake	148
Chapter 15: Lexi	162
Chapter 16: Jake	190
Chapter 17: Lexi (One year ago)	201
Chapter 18: Lexi	204
Chapter 19: Jake	219
Chapter 20: Jake (One year ago)	233

Chapter 21: Lexi	238
Chapter 22: Jake	256
Chapter 23: Lexi (One year ago)	273
Chapter 24: Lexi	279
Chapter 25: Jake	295
Chapter 26: Lexi	310
Chapter 27: Jake	320
Chapter 28: Lexi	339
Chapter 29: Jake (One year ago)	355
Chapter 30: Lexi	361
Epilogue: Jake (six months later)	374

A note to the reader

First of all I wanted to say an enormous thank you for picking up my book and giving Jake and Lexi's story a chance. You are helping my dreams come true and it is incredible.

Before you start reading, it is important to note that while this book is full of teasing, flirting and lots of romance, it does also discuss some serious topics with mention of abuse, drinking and swearing. While I hope you read and enjoy the story, I do advise readers to be mindful for any moments that may be distressing.

I hope you love reading Lexi and Jake's story as much as I loved writing it and to stay up to date with all new work and announcements please follow *@victoriajanewrites* on Instagram.

Happy Reading!

Our Summertime Secrets

Victoria Jane

Prologue: Jake (one year ago)

Sometimes when you're drunk, there's no power on earth that can stop you from making the phone call you know you shouldn't.
"Hey!" I yelled into the phone.
"Jake?" the voice on the other end questioned, "where are you?"
"You know what Lexi; you are such a good friend. Sometimes I wish you were mine instead of Cassie's so I could have you all to myself!" I heard her sweet giggle and felt light about being the one to get her laughing.
"Okay, Jake, where are you?" she asked again, growing serious.
"Hmmm wouldn't you like to know," I slurred, "coming to join the party?"
"No Jake, I'm going to come and get you so that your parents don't find out. They have enough going on now."

*the humour from her voice suddenly disappeared...
classic Lexi, always thinking of others.
"Right, I'm at Michael's." I muttered.
"I'm on my way." she replied, and the line went dead.
Shit! Her sadness and irritation immediately make me
regret calling her. I tried to stop myself, but something in
me just needed to hear her voice. Load of good that
would do now.*

*My desire to get wasted evaporated like it was never
there in the first place as I flopped onto the sofa. Sinking
into the pillows, hiding from reality, and trying to stop
the room spinning.*

*Michael had asked if I wanted to come round for a few
drinks and with everything going on with my parent's
separation; I needed to get out of the house. Cassie had
escaped to summer camp for the month, my little brother
Bradley was off at football every day and my little sister
Hailey was pretty much too young to have any idea about
what was going on. But me? I was the third parent. While
the others were off with various summer activities, I was
rowing a sinking ship trying to stop the family falling
apart. I left home a few hours ago, exhausted and in
desperate need of a distraction which is how I found
myself at Michael's house. He took one look at my
haggard face and the pack of beer under my arm and
knew exactly what I needed. Within half an hour the*

house was full of drinking, people and music… the perfect distraction.

But it was short lived, as I drank more it only served to make me think more. It was my thinking that caused me to grab my phone and call Lexi, the only person I wanted around me. I heard a car horn outside, with a quick glance out the living room window, I saw Lexi's car. I rushed out, not even stopped to say goodbye, and stumbled towards her car.
"Hey," I grumbled as I slid into the passenger seat.
"Hey there," she said as she smirked back at me, "not looking too hot are we."
"I guess anger and beer don't mix."
"Alright then." was all she said and peeled away from the curb.

As I sat there next to Lexi, my heart was racing. My anger had disappeared and now replaced by nervous energy. Over the summer Lexi had been around whenever she could, trying to help and spending time with Hailey. She had taken her shopping, to the cinema and anything she could, helping with dinner and keeping the house clean. She saved me this summer and in my inebriated state, I wanted to show her how much she meant to me.

I knew she talked to Cassie while she was at camp and knew how bad things were with my parents. But never once did she try to push me to talk to or to do anything really. She had filled the house with laughter when it was a doomed silence, had put smiles on all our faces when we had no hope and made the house feel like a home when I thought it had become impossible. She was a ray of sunshine in my ever-cloudy world.

The car stopped and I noticed we had pulled up to my house. I suddenly felt empty at the idea of saying goodbye to her.

"Right, well, there you go." she said as she put the handbrake on.

"Wait Lexi," I said and grabbed her arm, "I'm really sorry about tonight." I replied, wincing at the slur on my words.

"It's alright, I know things have been difficult lately," she answered, "come on let's get you inside." I nodded and let her lead me towards the front door. I would follow her anywhere.

Chapter 1: Lexi

Why do first dates have to exist? A mind-numbing experience where you pretend to care about things you really don't, and this one is a train-wreck… which is no exaggeration. Here I am sitting in this posh, stuck-up restaurant at a small, impractical table, in an uncomfortable, wooden chair across from this pompous, preppy boy who is droning on and on about how great he is! Talking about all his no carb diet and fantastic workout scheme. To make it worse, his name was Hugo, I mean I don't usually judge, but what the hell kind of name is that?

I was staring at him unable to comprehend how a person can be so utterly dull and self-absorbed yet not stop speaking for a second. I checked my watch and realised that I had only been here for forty-five minutes, we hadn't even got the starters yet and I was already losing the will to live! On top of that my stomach was starting to sound like an angry gremlin wanting to cause mass destruction! I looked back at the menu as Hugo continued about his personal best at the gym. I was seriously concerned that he was about to strip his top off to prove it!

To make matters worse, the menu was filled with dishes as pretentious as the guy sitting across from me. Most of it I couldn't even understand, and no chicken nuggets in sight. It was at that point I knew that I couldn't take anymore. I decided that drastic action was needed, and I pulled out my phone under the table.

Lexi: S.O.S

                                            Cassie: Is it that bad?

Lexi: Worse

                                            Cassie: Emergency call?

Lexi: Duh.

I placed my phone back on the table and waited for my escape plan.
"Oh, I need to take this," I told my date pointing at my phone as he was mid-sentence, but he didn't seem to care. He simply just nodded and continued talking.
"LEXI, I NEED YOU!" Cassie screamed down the phone.
"Woah, woah, what is it?"
"I THINK I'M DYING." she wailed, I turned to the side and looked out the window to stifle my laugh.

"Oh no, can I do anything?" I replied, desperately trying to avoid cracking up at the drama show on the other end of the line.

"YES, YES, SAVE ME BEFORE IT'S TOO LATE!" oh she wasn't making this easy.

"Okay I'll be there as soon as I can." I told her, now covering my face.

"QUICKLY, I DON'T THINK I HAVE MUCH LONGER." she screeched, and I could hear her laughter, I hid my smile and turned back to Hugo. *Still a dumb name.*

"Hey," I interrupted him as he was still talking about himself, "sorry I need to get home, there's a family situation." I stood to flee from this trainwreck as soon as possible.

"Oh, what a shame, shall we split the bill and be on our way?" he said, I looked down at the table at my one glass of house wine that I had barely touched- which I now regretted- in comparison to his three beers he had consumed and raised my eyebrows.

"Yeah, sure. How much is it?" I asked. I couldn't be bothered to fight him on this, I needed to get out of there as soon as I possibly could.

"Well, it will be around £21 plus a tip so shall we say £12 each and call it even." he said, and I raised my eyebrow even higher. *At least he tips.*

"Yeah whatever," I sighed. I put the money on the table, "well bye." I said to him and almost ran out of the restaurant.

We'd arrived in his car, which had been an event in itself. We spent the ride over with him talking about how beautiful his car is, even getting mad at me because I apparently shut the door too hard. While I was thankful, I didn't have to hear more about my fingers smudging the finish, I suddenly realised I was stranded. I walked down the road to avoid him when he came out of the restaurant and called a cab. Within five minutes it had pulled up outside and I was on my way home, luckily having avoided Hugo. *Hugo!*

As I sat back in the cab with a sigh, I felt my phone buzz in my bag. I pulled it out and checked the caller ID, answered it and raised the phone to my ear.
"So good save?" Cassie asked.
"Did you have to be so dramatic? I was sitting there trying not to laugh at your ridiculousness!"
"Aw come on, it was funny! So, tell me about the date." She encouraged.
"Oh no, this was such a bad date that I am in desperate need of ice cream, alcohol and a movie. I'll be over in 15 minutes." I told her.
"I'll get the ice cream." she replied and with that we hung up.

Cassie was my best friend, there was a group of four of us, Connie and Lottie too, but Cassie and I gravitated to each other.
She is my person, the moon to my sun, the Christina to my Meredith. I don't know how I would have made it through some days without her. Although her new obsession was finding me a boyfriend so we could double date. She had met *her* boyfriend, Noah, at a summer camp last year and they had been sickeningly sweet and happy ever since. He was so good to Cassie, particularly when her folks had separated for a while last year.

I on the other hand had never found my prince charming and trust me not from lack of trying. I had found a lot of frogs and had certainly attempted at making them my prince, but still no luck yet. There had been a few guys that didn't make me run for the hills, but no one I could have imagined a future with. Perhaps I was destined to be the fun wine aunt.

The cab pulled up outside Cassie's house, I handed him some cash and got out. I started towards the house and knocked on the front door, there was no response, I knocked again louder this time. I heard some muffled yelling from inside the house and recognised it as Cassie and Jake, it was too loud and deep to be either Bradley or Hailey, Cassie's two younger siblings. Being around siblings always made me laugh as I was an only child with very serious corporate parents. Cassie always managed to include me in everything and sometimes her mum would even joke about how she had three daughters.

The yelling had finally stopped inside the house, and I heard footsteps, after a minute Jake opened the door. Cassie's big brother, three years older and the object of my teenage fantasies. He used to play rugby at our school and when we were about twelve, I would go with their family so I could see him play. He was my first love, but I was never seen as anything more than his little sister's friend.
When he opened that door, I realised that I hadn't seen him in so long! Pretty much since last summer, damn… He had gotten even hotter which I didn't think was possible. He was tall, with hair I just wanted to run my fingers through and had clearly caught some early summer colour.
He was always so busy and seemed to constantly be hiding whenever I was around. I had been busy with my first year of university too, studying to become a lawyer. But I was home for the summer now and ready to have some fun.

Jake had definitely grown-up handsome. I quickly figured it out in my head and realised that he was 22 now, I had turned 19 late last year, I was a winter baby. He was quite

similar to Cassie, but his hair was a little lighter. Where Cassie's hair seemed brown, Jake's was definitely a dirty blonde, he had these delicious chocolate eyes that I couldn't help but fall into. His shoulders were tight and broad, and he certainly towered over me. At that moment I couldn't help but think of those arms around my body, holding me tight, pressing me against his chest…
"I didn't know we were expecting you," he commented and interrupting my thoughts, I shook myself out of my fantasy.
"Cassie invited me round." I told him.
"Any reason?"
"Total crash of a date." I answered.
"Ah…" was all he said.
"Yeah, I got there and could already tell that he was a fool. He was such a snob, and I couldn't make it past drinks." I didn't know why I was telling him all of this, but I just couldn't stop, "Well he then made me pay half, which I'm fine with but he had three beers, and I only had one glass of house wine so, you know…" I rambled on while Jake just looked at me with an amused smiled and his arms crossed over his chest, causing his arms to bulge.
"Wow, he sounds like a true Prince Charming," he joked.
"You have no idea, want to know the best part?" he nodded his grin growing wider, "his name was Hugo!" I told him and he burst out laughing.

"Hugo and Alexis, seems like a great couple." he said over his laughter.

"Oh, shut up and don't use that name you know I hate it, *Jacob.*" This caused his laughter to stop, and his face turned to surprise.

I always used to call him Jacob when I was younger because it annoyed him, and I thought it would be a great way for me to flirt with him. Over the years it had just stuck whenever I wanted to annoy him, I always called him Jacob. But this had repercussions as he now used my full name to annoy me. He looked down at me and I stared right back, challenging him. Staring into those delicious eyes put me under a spell and one I never wanted to break. Unfortunately my best friend also had terrible timing.

"Hey!" she came bounding downstairs, "Sorry, Noah was on the phone." she explained breathlessly.

"No problem," I smiled, it was nice to see her so energetic and happy.

"I need details now!" Cassie demanded I nodded in acceptance as she began dragging me upstairs, "the ice cream and alcohol is waiting upstairs, let's go!"

"See ya Jacob." I called over my shoulder as we made our way to Cassie's room.

"Good luck on the next date Alexis!" his words chasing me up the stairs.

Chapter 2: Jake

"Are you serious guys," I called through my mic, "that was a rubbish shot!"
"Come on Jake don't be such a sore loser," Michael laughed at my failure.
I was sitting in my room on my computer gaming with my friends, which was how a lot of my evenings passed. I had been working ridiculous hours recently, just starting a new job as a digital designer and it had been stressful as hell! It was at this small start-up called SureShot. I really wanted to start designing my own games and I hoped this job was a step in the right direction.
 I was trying to balance life and the job but for the meantime I'd given up on the former. I had my gaming time, and I assumed that once I had settled into the new job then things would start to calm down and I could get back to actually living my life. So far? No such luck.

Our Summertime Secrets

I had been working for just over a month and was exhaustingly satisfied, I loved the team I was working with. There were a couple of cool guys similar to my age that I seemed to get on well with and a couple old dudes that seemed like they were on their way out. I'd gone out for a few rounds of drinks a couple times with some of the boys from work but that was as far as my social calendar had reached. The company was successful but still small which meant that I had very long hours and heaps of work.
"Yo Jake watch out, behind you!" A voice came through my headset, and I tuned back into the game just slightly too late.
"Wait wha- oh damn." This sniper had come out of nowhere and shot me.
"Tough luck Jakey," James, another friend from school, laughed.
"Well, that's me for the night then gents," I sighed in defeat, "I'll talk to you guys tomorrow." I heard a chorus of responses and switched off my monitor.

I stood from my seat and went over to my bed. I was exhausted. It was a Friday night and here I was at the ripe age of twenty-two and nearly passed out from exhaustion. I shouldn't be like this, surely, I should have more energy to be able to do something after work. I grabbed my phone and began scrolling through it, nothing of interest.

Victoria Jane

My phone had been depressingly quiet since I finished university last year.

I had rather struggled in the female department. Not trying to sound modest, and it wasn't for lack of interest. I went on dates, had a few girlfriends too, particularly at university. But I got to the point where small talk was a rather tortuous activity. I couldn't be bothered to ask how many siblings a girl had anymore or what her favourite colour was. The questions that, for most girls, I would forget the answer to at the end of the date. So, let's just say that for now I had given up on trying to find anything. I had previously searched for that desperately, particularly when everything happened with my parents. Last year they had decided they needed some time apart from each other, dad moved out for a while and mum was a wreck, it only lasted for about six months, but it was the worst. Cassie had been okay because she had Noah, he really helped her with our parents' separation and had been there through the rocky path of them getting back together. I had to keep it together for myself and everyone else. I couldn't show weakness because everyone else needed me to be strong.

I checked my phone once again, it was only 9:30pm and I could already feel my eyes drifting shut, unfortunately I had too much work for that to happen.

I closed my eyes momentarily and sat back desperate for a slither of relaxation. It was a glorious relief to just not think about anything even for the shortest time. I drifted into a comfortable silence, but life clearly wasn't going to let that happen and a sharp thump disturbed it. KNOCK KNOCK, echoed from downstairs, my eyes sprung open and I glared at my door. I was met with silence, so I closed my eyes once again. KNOCK KNOCK KNOCK! Again, the loud thuds carried through the house and this time I sat up. *Who the hell was that?*
"JAKE!" Cassie yelled from somewhere in the house, "get the door!"
"Why can't you!" I replied.
"I'm busy, come on please." She whined and with a groan I rolled off my bed and made my way to the front door. *I can't wait to get my own place.*

I reached the bottom of the steps and opened the door.
"I didn't know we were expecting you." I commented as the door swung open.
Lexi stood on the other side of the door looking exhausted, but incredible. I hadn't seen her in so long, she had really grown up gorgeous! She was wearing a tight black dress that hugged her hips and stopped midway on her thighs. It showed off each of her curves. Her silky blonde hair was down and flowed softly light beach curls and she had a light dusting of makeup on her face.

I never thought she needed makeup; her face was so naturally beautiful. I could see the constellation of freckles that she always got in the summer under her makeup. Her glistening green eyes stared back at me, twinkling underneath her lashes that were clad with mascara. She wore a pair of heeled, strappy sandals and I noticed how tanned and slender her legs were under that dress.

I my mind flash to how it used to be when we were kids with her enormous crush on me. *Always* trying to talk to me, *always* showing up at my rugby games, *always* around our house; yet Cassie never seemed to go to hers. The memories made me chuckle at how she used to be because that didn't seem like the girl standing in front of me right now, she oozed confidence and seemed to have total disregard about me standing right in front of her.
"Cassie invited me round." her voice flowed like smooth chocolate, and I was hanging off every word, I was desperate to hear more.
"Any reason?" I asked pushing for more detail just to extend this interaction and have her standing in front of me for longer.
"Total crash of a date…" she told me, the idea of her being with a guy that didn't treat her with complete adoration made my blood boil. I tried to tamp down the jealousy, blaming brotherly overprotectiveness. I couldn't deny how attractive she was, but I had known her whole

life and she was my sister's best friend. She was like a sister. Nothing more.

"Ah," was all I could think of saying.

She started speaking again, clearly spurred on by my awkward response and the silence around us. She proceeded to spout on about the date, he sounded like a total twat. Part of me was glad that it didn't go well because a guy like him doesn't deserve such a stunning girl like Lexi. I stood there with a small smile hinting on my face at the thought of her sitting on that date, the idea that she would have tried to be as nice as possible. How it would have ended with Cassie calling with an emergency and that was why she was at my house.

"He sounds like a true Prince Charming," I sneered. Thinking of him sitting there with a pompous look on his face sitting opposite Lexi and not realising how incredible she was. She told me his name and I could no longer hold in my laugh. *Hugo*? What kind of name was that?

"Alexis and Hugo," I said to her, "sounds like a true love match." I teased, I knew how much she hated her full name being used.

"Oh, shut up and don't use that name you know I hate it, *Jacob*." she replied with a grin on her face. She raised her eyebrow trying to challenge me. *I had missed her*. I couldn't remember how long it had really been but between my job, finishing university and her being in her first year at university and so busy with her work, it meant she hadn't been over in a while.

We stood opposite each other and just smiled. I was in a daze, a dream, a fantasy. Until my dear little sister chose that exact moment to bound in. I loved my sister but siblings knew exactly how to wind you up.
"Sorry Noah was on the phone." Cassie's voice shattered the spell. I silently cursed my sister as she appeared then, desperate for more time to see this new Lexi.
"No problem," Lexi smiled past me. I couldn't tear my eyes away from her as she smiled at Cassie, it lit up the whole hallway and lightened my dark mood.
"I need details!" Cassie insisted and I watched as she yanked Lexi away.
"See you, Jacob!" she called as Cassie dragged her upstairs, she turned back to me flashing me a quick grin and she disappeared with Cassie, the echoes of giggles trailing behind them.
"Good luck on your next date Alexis." I called, grinning at the evil glare she returned with. I shared a low chuckle with myself and thought about the countless times I had seen Lexi run up those stairs giggling with Cassie.

Once they had disappeared, I finally turned back to the front door and shut it. Cassie and Lexi had completely vanished now and all I could hear was the distant sound of music and laughter echoing from Cassie's room. I inhaled deeply and started back to my room. Leaving my work sitting and staring at me on my desk. I removed my jeans and my t-shirt and slipped between my sheets. Sleep greeted me as soon as my head hit the pillow.

Chapter 3: Lexi

I slumped on Cassie's bed, the interaction between Jake still lingered in my thoughts. Cassie sat there desperately trying to conceal her laughter at my dating failures.
"Cassie, come on!" I complained.
"Alright, I'm sorry, it's just pretty funny," she admitted.
"Well, we can't all be lucky enough to find our prince charming at 18 and stay with him forever." I teased. Trying to keep the bitterness from my voice.
"Okay, okay so it was bad, and he wasn't the right one for you," she rolled her eyes, "and your version of Noah is waiting out there, we just need to find him."
I sighed at her eagerness, but it was only because she wanted me to be happy and I wanted that too.
"How would you feel if I maybe set you up with one of Noah's friends?" she asked with uncontained excitement.
"Hmm." It seemed like a good idea, but I knew that things could get complicated if it was one of Noah's friends. If it didn't go well then, I would feel awkward

with Noah and his friends, but if it went well with the other guy and something happened with Cassie and Noah then that would be even worse. I tended to overthink a lot with this stuff.

"So?" she asked keenly.

"Ugh okay fine, I will go out with *one* of Noah's friends, but this is one time thing so if you mess this up with the wrong guy then I am *not* letting it happen again." I warned. She let out an ear-splitting squeal and I flinched. "Damn Cassie you're going to deafen me." I scolded as I covered my ears.

"Sorry Lex, I just want you to be happy. I've been talking about this with Noah, and I think I've already found the perfect guy for you!" she grinned. But if the devious smile that crept onto her face told anything then I knew I had something to worry about.

"Well, let's hope he is as perfect as you think because I'm tired of all of these frogs and I need my Prince Charming," I joked. She began rambling about this friend of Noah's, apparently, he was called Tate, and he was just amazing for me. As she kept on about him, I couldn't help my thoughts drifting to Jake and that sexy smirk he always had plastered across his face.

The rest of the evening passed with no further digging into my love life. I asked about how things were going with Noah and if the loved-up smile and blushing cheeks were any sign then I knew it was just as perfect as it always had been. I still envied what they had together.

Cassie deserved it so much, but it made me desperate to experience the happiness they had.

We opened the bottles of wine that Cassie had managed to retrieve in the short space of time between my disaster date and my arrival, rose for herself and I had a bottle of red. She'd grabbed two spoons from the kitchen, and we cracked open the pint of Ben and Jerry's. Much like the classy women we were, we sat there eating with a spoon in one hand digging into the ice cream. Whilst the other was holding our wine glasses that were generously filled with our choice of poison.

I knew I would feel this in the morning but after my disastrous evening, I couldn't care less. It was exactly what I needed after such a failure of a date and Cassie always knew how to cheer me up. These dates had become so repetitive, and all these terrible events just merged together into one major wreck that I had the displeasure to call my love life.

With a big gulp of wine, I pushed all the failed attempts out of my mind and focused on the movie that way playing. I had lost track of what was happening but all I could tell was that it was some kind of horror. Clearly, Cassie was going full anti-romance tonight to save me from thinking about my failing romance!

In no time the wine was truly taking effect. I could feel my mind going dizzy and my troubles feeling far less important. Soon the empty glass was discarded on the floor, and we finished the movie, my phone read 1am and my eyes started growing heavy.

"Hold on, I need a wee." I told Cassie as I stumbled off her bed. Focusing on my feet I tried to get to the bathroom without falling over. I leant against the wall and let my eyes focus again, but what I had thought was a wall had turned out to be a door and it started to swing open. I could feel myself falling back, until two warm hands grabbed me and kept me upright.

"This is a welcome interruption." Jake teased.

"What d' you want'" my words now sounds rather than anything recognizable.

"Well, I heard a pretty loud disturbance outside my room, and I came to check that it wasn't a murderer or robber." he smirked.

"Did I wake you?" I slurred.

"Just a tad."

"I need a wee." I told him as I leant towards him smelling that scent that always reminded me of Jake.

"I think you'll find the bathroom is that one." he said as he pointed to the door opposite his room, "no toilet in here I'm afraid."

"I know that." I told him as my head started to sway and I reached out with a hand on Jake's chest to steady myself.

"You need some help?" he asked, he held my hand against his chest whilst his other hand found my hip to help steady me.
"I can pee on my own dank you." I slurred and spun around walking towards the bathroom.
"Well that really is a shame," he called to me as I turned away, "I'm always happy to help."
"I do *not* need that kind of help." I said with my hands on my hips, looking as frightening as I could.
"Whatever you say…" he said with a laugh, "good luck with the wee Alexis!" he said and turned back into his room. I rolled my eyes and stumbled into the bathroom.

Five minutes later I made my way back to Cassie's room with no further accidents or interactions. Cassie was already passed out in bed hugging her empty wine bottle, the credits of the film playing on the TV casting the only light into the room. I stumbled to the other side of the bed, grabbed the remote and switched the TV off swallowing the room in a comforting darkness and settled into bed next to Cassie.

"I am *NEVER* drinking again." Cassie groaned as she sat up. We'd both fallen into a deep sleep and the clock was now reading midday. The memories of last night came flooding back, Hugo, Jake, wine. Lots of wine. It was Saturday, I remembered my terrible Friday night and was happy to start over on the weekend.

My body felt achy, and my head was spinning but as I looked over to Cassie, I could tell that she was doing much worse. She'd never been able to hold her drink very well and the ice cream with wine clearly was not the best combination for her. I was still slumped on the bed and wasn't even attempting to sit up yet.
"I need water." I groaned but made no attempt to move and as if by magic Jake appeared at the door holding aspirin, water and toast.
"I think you guys will be wanting these." he said as he placed the toast down on the bed and passed each of us a glass of water with two tablets each.
"Oh, big brother, I have never loved you more than now." Cassie said as she grabbed the tablets and a slice of toast.
"Cassandra take small sips," Jake instructed as he noticed her starting to gulp down the water, "big mouthfuls are going to make it worse." he continued but it was too late, Cassie had finished her glass of water and a slice of toast in record time and was soon grabbing her stomach covering her mouth and running for the bathroom.
"Oh go-" she started as she raced out the room, Jake watched her go and with a chuckle turned back to me.
"I tried to tell her, please learn from her errors." he walked forward and plumped down on the end of the bed. He leant back on the bed and his arm was dangerously close to my bare leg and I couldn't help the rush of excitement at the possible contact. He wasn't even

touching me and he worked up a storm in me, just by being close.

"Hey, I am an expert at nursing a hangover, this is not my first evening of drunken antics." I assured him looking over at him as I took my tablets with small sips.

"I'm sure you are," Jake replied, "however, if last night was any sign, then I would beg to differ." he chuckled as I looked at him with a puzzled glance at him.

"Well last night you seemed to have confused my room with the bathroom," I just stared, "any recollection?" he looked at me quizzically waiting for any indication and that was when things started to fall back into place, my trip to the toilet and my run in with Jake, the feel of his hand holding me steady. Oh god I felt dizzy again.

"Ah that little incident last night." I said and I could feel my cheeks heating from the memories. "Well don't you worry I'm fully recovered and will not be adorning your bedroom door any time soon, I have a grasp on where the toilet is now." I joked.

"Well at least there's that," he said still with a sly smile, but it almost seemed that his smile had faltered slightly at my words. I averted my gaze from Jake and focused on grabbing a slice of toast from the pile on the plate, taking a tiny bite and waited for it to go down first before I attempted another bite. The buttered toast was delicious, and I suddenly felt starving, so I took a bigger bite and enjoyed the saltiness of the butter and started to feel less like a zombie.

"I swear to you both, mark my words, I shall never drink again!" Cassie declared as she wobbled back into the room and laid back down on the bed. Jake quickly lifted himself up and returned to his position of leaning against the door frame looking slightly disappointed.

"Oh, sweet Cassie, you say that every time until there's alcohol involved again, and the drinking begins." I laughed.

"Ugh your right," she said to me with a sigh of defeat and closed her eyes laying back on the bed, "but honestly this just so isn't worth it. I apparently called Noah whilst you were in the bathroom and I can't remember anything I said, but according to him it was a very interesting conversation."

"Ha!" Jake let out a deep laugh from the door frame and glanced over at me.

"Why are you still here?" she sat up and glared at him, "I'm too tired to deal with you!"

"Ah come on, I was the great big brother that brought you the aspirin and the water and the food," he said with a gesture towards the toast that was still on the table.

"Well, *I* appreciated it Jake," I added just to flame the fire, their sibling disputes always made me laugh.

"See Cassie, Alexis was happy. I was just being a big brother for you guys," he teased. I felt an odd weight in my chest at the idea that he put us both in the little sister category. At least he cared.

"I take it back now; you called me Alexis." I retorted.

"Ouch, I'm wounded." Jake grabbed his chest.
"Well then loving big brother, would you take your wounded heart and mind leaving me alone so I can change and talk to my best friend please." Cassie said to him, and I join in giving him a flutter of my hand shooing him out of the room, with a roll of his eyes he turned around and walked out the room.
"Farewell you hungover monsters, don't kill each other!" he called down the hall.

Chapter 4: Jake

I slowly made my way back to my room while the encounter with Lexi last night and this morning swirled in my head. If I focus hard, I could still smell her enticing aroma dance around me from when she leant into my chest. This wasn't the first hang over Cassie had suffered with and I would usually just leave her to it, let her come down in her own time and nurse her hangover. But the thought of Lexi being there flared something up inside of me and I had to go and see them, luckily Cassie seemed too hungover to notice any odd behaviour. I'd been far too brave with it when I'd gone into Cassie's room and sat next to Lexi, but I couldn't help it.

I reached my room and walked painstakingly slowly to my desk. I loved my job but the amount of work I had was absolutely insane. Particularly after having left all the work, I had intended to do yesterday, it all just added to the load. I mean it was a Saturday morning and here I was about to start all the work I needed to catch up on ready for Monday. Everything got shoved onto me because I'm the new kid and they know they can get away with it, but I promised myself I wouldn't let it stop me.

Two hours into the tedious grunt work and I had made a small dent to the pile of papers and emails. With a sigh I decided that I needed some sustenance. I'd stolen a few slices of toast from the girls but that was hours ago, and my appetite was relentless. With a groan I stood up, moved away from my desk and started towards the kitchen to hunt for food.

The house seemed oddly quiet which meant that either Cassie and Lexi had already gone out or they were passed out in bed once again. I hoped for the former as I was anxious about any further run-ins with Lexi. My stomach began to rumble pulling me away from my thoughts and I sped down the stairs to where a kitchen full of food waited for me. This is a true perk of living at home...the free food! After hunting around the cupboards for a while I decided on a ham and cheese sandwich. Simple and quick. I sank down at the table and inhaled my food.
"Oh god that is good." I said with a moan.
"Well, that is an interesting noise," I heard, I looked over and noticed Lexi leaning against the door frame. I almost choked at the sight of her, with the glorious sun behind her she looked like an angel, blessing my life with every

moment she looked in my direction. The shock of her arrival had caused some of my sandwiches to become lodged in my throat.

"I- I thought you and Cassie had gone out, the house seemed suspiciously quiet." I grabbed my glass of water off the table to prevent the coughs that were building up in my throat. I moved from the table to the sink and stared out the window as I pushed my thoughts away, that was Cassie's best friend, practically my little sister!

"Oh no, not yet, we're going but Cassie is taking ages," she told me with a roll of her eyes. I turned to watch her and smiled knowing how my sister can be getting ready after a big night of drinking.

"Where are you going?" I asked her, trying to keep the conversation light. My stomach was still rumbling so I wandered over to the fridge to keep myself occupied.

"Um, shopping I think," she told me, "Cassie wanted to grab some stuff, and she thinks that I need a few new outfits for my future dates."

"Ah," was all I could muster, overwhelmed by irritation.

"Yeah, it wasn't my idea, but Cassie is relentless and thinks more options to add to the rotation as she said," she paused, "she's trying to set me up with one of Noah's friends or something, it's crazy."

"Uh huh." was all I said.

"It's not my choice," she started, "it's Cassie."

"Yeah, you said," I said shortly and turned to her. She seemed nervous but I couldn't understand why. I didn't know anything about fashion, but she looked amazing. She was in a pair of acid wash ripped jeans and I could see her tanned legs through the gaps. She was wearing black boots that must have been some kind of magic because her legs looked incredible. She also had this weird cross strapped black crop top, one that sloped slightly lower in the front. All I could think about was all of the guys they were going to pass in the shopping centre that would get to see her out in that outfit, watch her, admire her. My blood began to boil. *Just brotherly protection.* I had to remind myself.

She waited for Cassie to come down while I grabbed the stuff from the fridge to make another sandwich. My stomach continued to growl, and I finished making my second sandwich as I tried to focus on the food rather than the girl that kept stealing my attention. I probably cost my mum a fortune in groceries.
"Hungry, are we?" Lexi teased, clearly trying to downplay the awkward silence that had fallen over the room.
"Always." I replied, covering my mouth. Lexi just looked back at me, flashing me a polite smile as I carried on eating.
"So-" Lexi began to say but I was silenced by the sound of footsteps approaching and soon Cassie came bombarding into the kitchen.

"I have finally pulled myself away from the bathroom," she said facing Lexi, "and I'm ready and not feeling nauseous anymore so let's go."
"Uh" Lexi said, and I was sure that she looked over at me almost as if she was hesitant to go, I tried to ignore the way my heart soared at the thought... I was unsuccessful.
"What?" Cassie looked at Lexi confused, waiting expectantly for Lexi to turn and walk out the house.
"N- nothing, let's go." she mumbled and gave Cassie a weak smile, with one more glance at me and a quick smile at me she turned and walked out the room, I couldn't help but watch her go.

I heard the door slam shut with a chorus of giggles and with that they were gone. I turned back to my sandwich and a packet of crisps; with a sigh I started towards the stairs. It was the weekend, but I knew that I had mountains of work waiting for me, maybe if I just didn't go to my computer then I could ignore it...right? I passed mum and dad sitting in the lounge on the way to the stairs. They were sitting together on the sofa with my mum reading a book and dad watching one of his old shows on TV.
"Hi sweetie." my mum said as she noticed me loitering in the doorway.
"Hi," dad mumbled without turning his attention away from the TV. He had become a lot more closed off since last summer, he had come back to the house and things

seemed better with my parents but definitely not how it used to be.

"Hey guys, just wanted to show you I'm alive before I disappear all day in my room getting my work done." I told her.

"Those people work you so hard," mum added, concern laced her voice, "you need a break from it, you got in so late yesterday and are still working today." she continued, but I just rolled my eyes and smiled. Ever since I started my job mum had been worried about the hours I worked.

"Mum," I interrupted her, "It's fine I'll get a break, it is just a busy time for the company and there aren't many of us, so we all need to pick up some slack." I assured her but I could still see the worry in her eyes, "please mum this could get me to where I want to be, I'll be okay, I promise."

"Okay," she sighed, "you're just like your father you know, so headstrong and independent. I don't know what I am going to do with the two of you." she said, dad was still facing the TV, but I could see the small smile creeping on his face at her words.

"I know mum," I said with a smile as I walked towards her and planted a kiss on her head, "I'll see you later." and with that I left her to her book, shot dad a quick smile and nod of my head and made my way to the work that awaited me.

Our Summertime Secrets

Six hours of tedious typing and a few conference calls later I decided that I'd had enough for now. I knew I would still be working late into the evening but for now I needed a break.

With a stretch and a groan, I stood from my desk and made my way downstairs feeling like a zombie as I walked, my legs aching from disuse and my mind foggy. Mum and dad were no longer on the sofa, so I assumed they had probably gone out for dinner with Hailey and Bradley and seeing as Cassie and Lexi still weren't back from shopping it seemed that I was eating alone tonight. What a life! I realised that I was far too tired to even attempt cooking something edible, so I decided to order a pizza for myself. I sat down at the table and pulled out my phone scrolling uselessly through Instagram trying to kill time while I waited for my food. Twenty minutes later I heard the doorbell and nearly toppled my seat over in my attempt to get to the door, yes, I was *that* hungry.

"You're not pizza." I said feeling saddened, looking at the person on the other side of the door that didn't seem to be holding any kind of food.

"Well hello to you too," Lexi said as she stood there, her hands full of shopping bags.

"Do you ever go home?" I asked her bitterly.

"Wow, someone's stroppy." she teased as she wrestled with the bags she was struggling to hold.

"I'm hungry," I told her, "I thought you were pizza."

"Oohhh, you ordered pizza?" Cassie called from her car as she grabbed her bags from the back seat.

"I didn't get enough for you!" I told her with a scowl. I looked back at Lexi and saw her mimicking my face and I just rolled my eyes.

"Is there enough for me?" she asked me, now looking sweet and innocent. The way she looked up at me through those long lashes made my words catch in my throat.

"No," I growled and stormed back to the kitchen.

"JAKE!" Cassie yelled from the hallway a few minutes later, this must be the fateful food I hoped for.

I once again stood up and made my way to the hall and to my joy there was the scent of pizza and a teenage boy standing there in that blue cap that read Dominos holding two boxes and a bag clearly holding my drink.

"Not enough for us huh?" Lexi commented looking at what he was carrying.

"I'm hungry Alexis," I commented.

"Are you going to eat all of that then Jacob?"

"I like it reheated, anything left, the small amount that might be left, will be my lunch tomorrow so I was telling the truth, there isn't enough for you two." I told her as I grabbed my pizza and stalked back to the table, my mouth watering at the smell. As soon as I sat down, I opened the box and began to devour the pizza.

"And you got Pepsi?" Lexi commented.

"Of course, Pepsi is the best," I scoffed.

"No, Diet Coke wins out." she replied.

"Oh, I can't believe you would offend my ears like that," I said disgustedly, "you really have no idea."
"Well maybe you'll have to change my mind." she teased, and I read far too into that simple comment.
"Wow, that smells good." Connie commented as she walked over to me.
"Go away." I said through a mouthful of pizza.
"Okay," she said sweetly, she walked over, grabbed a slice of pizza, kissed me on the cheek and ran out the room, "thanks Jake, best brother ever!" she called, I looked over my shoulder as she ran out scolding her existence.
That was when I felt a hand on my shoulder and Lexi appeared on the other side, she bent down, her hair brushing past my face, I could smell the glorious scent of her shampoo. She grabbed another slice of pizza and followed Cassie's suit, kissed me on the cheek and ran out the room.
"Yeah, thanks Jacob," she called back with a laugh and I rolled my eyes at the two of them. I turned back to my food and took a drink of my Pepsi trying to ignore the burning feeling I felt on my cheek where Lexi's lips had just been.

Chapter 5: Lexi (one year ago)

My heart skipped when I saw Jake's name flash up on my phone, I hardly ever heard from him and still each time I did. I would always react in the same way, it was embarrassing.

I had tried to distract myself this summer, but it made no difference to how I felt about him, not that he would ever care. It was already 1am so I had no idea what he would want either, but my confusion quickly vanished when it connected, and I could hear the music blaring through the speaker. He was drunk. After a matter of minutes, I ended the call having found out the state he was in and where he was. I grabbed my shoes to go and get him. Luckily my parents were away again so I didn't have to worry about asking anyone, I was home alone, as usual. I grabbed the car keys and headed towards Michael's house.

Jake was out the door immediately and I could tell by his unsteady steps that he wasn't in good shape. Even in his current predicament, I could help but admire how he looked in those snug jeans and white striped shirt. Once he was comfortably secured in the car and I was sure he wasn't going to be sick, I quickly made my way back to his house and pulled up in front of the drive and shut off the engine.

"Right well there you go," I said as I removed the key from the car and sat fiddling with the keys, scared to look at him for what my eyes may reveal.
"Wait Lexi," Jake said as he grabbed my arm drawing my attention to him, "I'm really sorry about tonight." I could hear the slur in his words.
"It's alright, I know things have been difficult lately," I answered, "come on let's get you inside." he nodded in response and helped him out of the car and towards the front door.
"Key?" I whispered, knowing Brad and Hailey would be asleep. I knew they were deep sleepers so it should be fine, plus Cassie was off at her camp so I didn't need to worry about her. He rummaged around in his pocket, proudly produced his house keys and dropped them in my hand. I slowly unlocked the door, shushing Jake as he stumbled in.
"Come on," I ushered him upstairs to his room. I knew this house so well that I walked past Cassie's empty room and led Jake to his, "wait there." I told him as he fell

back onto his bed, and I sped to the bathroom to grab some painkillers and a glass of water.
When I got back to his room he was sprawled out on his front, changed into his pyjamas. I couldn't decide if I was relieved or disappointed.
"Come on, drink this." I said as I coaxed him to sit up, handing him the tablets and water, he downed the glass at once and I went back to refill it.
"Thank you," he whispered as I was creeping back from the bathroom with a freshly filled glass.
"Okay so you have everything next to you, make sure you drink more and take those when you wake up okay?" I gestured to the stuff on his bedside table. I started back towards the door but was halted by his mumbling.
"What?" I asked.
"Don't go yet." he repeated, stronger now.
"Okay, I'll stay here a little longer," I replied, stumbling over the speed of my answer and trying desperately to recover from my excitement. I perched on the end of his bed becoming very aware of the fact it was just us.
"Come here," he said in a slightly sleepy tone and my insides began to melt. I shuffled closer to him.
"I'm here." I replied.
"Why is it that you are always saving me from my screw ups?" he asked. I looked slightly perplexed, "you always show up at the right moments when I have no idea what the hell I'm doing, and you make things look so easy."
"Hey, come on, you do pretty well on your own," I joked.

"Not like you," he replied, *"I don't know what I would do without you."*
"Well good thing you won't have to, I'm here for you," I replied before adding, *"and Brad and Hailey. I'm like a replacement for Cassie for the summer, just consider me another sister."* I was trying to make the situation lighter, but the way Jake was looking at me was making it increasingly harder each minute.
"Don't." he said, his tone suddenly harder.
"Don't what?" I asked.
"Don't tell me to think of you like another sister." he replied, his mouth just a breath away from me.
"W- why not?" I was desperate to know, my dreams were going wild.
"Because the way I feel about you would be illegal if you were my sister." he murmured and with a final glance at his lips I couldn't help but lean him and meet his lips.

Chapter 6: Lexi

"Oh, I can't be bothered to get ready!" Cassie groaned from the bathroom as she attempted to apply makeup to hide the tiredness from her hangover.
"Aww poor baby." I replied to her with mock sympathy. I received a groan from the bathroom in response.
"I'll be downstairs then." I told her and ran out the room to try and save myself before I heard her complaints. As I began downstairs, I heard a groan coming from the kitchen that only acted to confirm my suspicions and hope, Jake was sitting on his own in the kitchen digging into his lunch.
"Well, that's an interesting noise." I commented as I entered the kitchen leaning against the door frame simply watching him.
"I- I thought you and Cassie had gone out, the house seemed suspiciously quiet." Jake said as he recovered from the initial confusion. He looked cute and hot somehow simultaneously. He was wearing a pair of tight

grey joggers that deliciously hugged his thighs paired with a simple white t-shirt. It was such a basic outfit but damn he managed to make it look delicious.

"Oh no, not yet, we're going but Cassie is taking ages." I said as I shook out of my daydreams and admirations of him.

"Where are you going?"

"Um, shopping I think," I replied, "Cassie wanted to grab some stuff, and she thinks that I need a few more options in my rotations as she worded it."

It was kind of weird talking to Jake about my dates, but I guess over the years he was just like a big brother. *Ignoring last summer of course.*

"Ah." was all he replied with, his face now looking annoyed and bothered.

"Yeah, it wasn't my idea, but Cassie is relentless," I paused, "she's trying to set me up with one of Noah's friends or something, it's crazy."

I continued to ramble on about my dates and shopping not wanting there to be any awkwardness, but it seemed that all of my attempts were rather useless, Jake's face had grown dark.

"Uh huh." was all he said. What was up with him? It didn't have anything to do with him anyway, but I couldn't help continuing.

"It's not my choice," I blurted, almost trying to assure him that it wasn't what I wanted. "It's Cassie." I said with a weak laugh.

"Yeah, you said," he grumbled, looking even stormier now. *What the hell is wrong with him?* He was absolutely fine not two minutes ago; I scrambled for something to say. His eyes trailed up and down me. I had my favourite ripped jeans on with a black crop top, it was just a normal outfit, but he made it seem like the most outrageous outfit ever.

"Hungry, are we?" I said, the silence that had fallen upon the room became unbearable. He was leaning against the kitchen counter finally having stopped judging my outfit and now enjoying his second sandwich.

"Always." was his reply, he looked so tense, and I was so desperate to move closer and ease the distress, I had become so used to doing that. But I was waiting for Cassie, and I knew it wasn't my place anymore.

"So-" I began but my words were drowned by Cassie's entrance.

"I have finally pulled myself away from the bathroom!" she was clearly feeling much better than the mess I had left in the bathroom 15 minutes earlier, she could never handle her drink well, "I'm ready and not feeling nauseous anymore so let's go."

"Uh-" I paused, scolding myself for wanting to stay with Jake.

"What?" Cassie asked, looking confused at my hesitation and hopefully not noticing the small glance I shot at Jake. Also hoping Jake hadn't seen me glance at him, the last

thing I needed was him knowing that he was the root of my hesitation.
"N- nothing, let's go." I smiled, as convincingly as I could, and herded her out of the room.
I trailed behind Cassie towards the front door, and we headed out the house towards Cassie's car.
"Ugh, I've needed a shopping day with you." Cassie smiled.
"Same." I smiled and distracted myself with the aux.

Twenty minutes later we turned into the car park, I jumped out and paid for the parking while Cassie was busy talking to Noah, well I assumed by the wide grin as she stared at her phone that she was. I ran back with the ticket and placed it in the car before we made our way to the shops. Connie and Lottie joined us and after a chorus of 'hellos' we started to Starbucks.
"Okay, where do we start?" I asked, sipping my overpriced drink.
"You need a new outfit for your hot date tonight, so we need to find something." Cassie said, but I just rolled my eyes.
"It's not a big deal." I said.
"How do you know?"
"It's just another guy online, I've been talking to him for a little bit, but I don't know…"
"You never know, he could be the one you're waiting for."

"How many painful first dates do I need to go through? This is torturous."
"If we can't control the type of guy you're stuck with. We can control the outfit to make you feel good." Cassie smiled.
"What about this?" I suggested, "I can pair it with these jeans or something." I suggested but she made a disgusted face and shook her head. We had gone to three different shops with no luck and now I was desperate.
"Where is he taking you anyways?" Connie asked. Lottie had managed to find a seat by the shoes and had pulled out her book.
"Er I think he mentioned a fancy restaurant, but you never know what fancy really means to certain people." I commented.
"If he at least said fancy then you need more effort than just a pair of jeans. So come on!" Cassie insisted.
"Okay what are you thinking then, seeing as my suggestion was so terrible." I teased. Cassie paused for a moment looking deep in thought and soon made a choice.
"Okay," she started, "I'm thinking of a skirt or a dress. Needs to be nicer for the restaurant, we aren't doing jeans. You have the little black dress, but you wore that yesterday so let's try something else...what about red?" she asked excitedly, I realised it wasn't the worst idea, plus my wardrobe could use more red.
"Okay fine you've sold me, let's look for a nice red dress." I agreed, with a squeal she dragged me out of the

shop while calling Lottie from where she had her nose buried in her book, she glanced up and soon scuttled over to us. Three shops later Cassie seemed satisfied that she had found me a good enough outfit. She had landed on an off the shoulder red body con dress, which I would style with Cassie's leather jacket, and I would wear my favourite pair of black shoes to not make it seem too fancy. Plus, I always worried that guys wouldn't be the height they actually were, and I am not the shortest girl, so flats were the easiest option.
"What about makeup?" Cassie asked.
"I need more mascara actually." I admitted.
We went to Sephora and found a few new products as well as my favourite mascara too.
"Well, I think this has been thoroughly productive." Cassie noted.
"Me too," I agreed, "and with a big dent in my purse and only a little while until my date, I think it is time we head home."
"Let's do it."
"Can I come and get ready at your house? My parents are home, and I can't deal with them." I explained.
"Of course, babe, my house is basically your second home. You need to get my jacket anyway!"
"Thanks, love you Cas." She really was one of the greatest friends ever. It was all I ever wanted, just to be Cassie's real sister. I practically was and spent so much

of my time at her house, I should have convinced her parents to adopt me.

"Okay to our house it is!" Cassie said as she took a left towards her house, or our house as she liked to call it. We turned onto her driveway, parked the car and both got out. Cassie pulled her phone out of her pocket and checked it. I assumed it was a message from Noah, but her face looked horrified.

"Cassie, what- what is it?" I asked her as she froze, and I was now panicking.

"It's bad Lexi, really bad." she told me.

"Oh, for goodness sake Cassie tell me!" I moaned

"We only have like an hour until your date!" she burst, my face dropped, and I looked at her.

"Really?" I asked her.

"Yes! Come on Lexi, we need to get you ready!"

"An hour is plenty of time Cassie, please chill." I said, but she was already yanking the shopping out of the boot and dragging me into the house. Oh boy was I in trouble. She shoved open the door and burst through making the door slam against the wall, I was honestly worried the hinges were about to break off.

"Let's go!" she said to me, and she dragged me upstairs. As we reached the landing, Jake poked his head out of his room, he looked really tired.

"What the hell are you two doing?" he asked, leaning on his door frame stifling a yawn.

"No time to talk," Cassie called, dragging me to her room, "date prep, Lexi has another hot date in an hour!" I looked at him and just shrugged with, what I hoped, was an apologetic look on my face.
"Oh...whatever." Jake grumbled and walked back into his room, shutting his door much harder than he needed to.

"Okay so clothes or makeup first?" she asked, "Because I don't want to get makeup all over the dress, but it might be hard to put it on after the makeup is done." she rambled on and I just sat quietly fully aware that she would be making this choice, not me. I assumed that she had decided as she began to pull the dress out of the bag.
"Go change!" she ordered, I nodded and saluted as I walked into her bathroom and slipped on the dress. I stood looking in the mirror and realised how well Cassie had done with this dress actually.
I did a quick spin checking out the full fit, then emerged from the bathroom.
"Oh, I'll talk to you later bubs, she's just walked out the bathroom... Yes, I love you too." Cassie hung up and threw her phone on the bed.
"SOOO?" I asked her.
"Lex, you look absolutely incredible! Red is definitely your colour." Cassie said which caused me to smile even more. I felt good tonight.
"I really love this dress," I told her.

"Me too, it's giving Taylor Swift at the Grammys with the dress and your hair! Okay so we have like forty minutes now so it's time for some makeup." she told me, and I nodded.

"What were you thinking?" I asked her, slightly nervous at her ideas, in all honesty I was better at makeup than she was. But she was so excited about the date that she wanted to see what would go with the outfit.

"I'm thinking like a smoky look but not too heavy," she said, I nodded and smiled knowing that I was thinking the exact same thing.

"Let's go." I said and turned towards her dressing table to raid her makeup, "you're going to need to help me with my eyeliner Cassie." I said to her as I began to apply some foundation to my face.

"Oh of course, I can do that," she replied. I nodded and turned back to the mirror and moved onto contour, in twenty minutes my face was covered in makeup and my eyes looked smoky and ready for my date.

"Okay I need to go and grab a drink quickly." I hadn't had a drink for a while, and I needed something to keep me awake for this date.

"Oh, damn," I said as I bumped into something tall, wide and hard. Hands reached out to steady me and I realised it was Jake, "woah. Sorry."

"Hey, no problem," he grumbled, "are you okay?"

"Yeah, yeah, I'm good, just going to get a drink." I told him.

"Me too." he said and started walking downstairs, I trailed after him.

"How's work going?" I asked, trying to make conversation.

"Yeah, fine." he said shortly and carried on walking. I was confused but didn't try to overthink it, maybe he was just tired.

"Have you got any plans for the weekend?" desperate for some kind of conversation.

"Nope." was all he said in response, at this point it was starting to annoy me.

"What are you looking for?" I asked him.

"Nothing." he snapped as he was looking into the fridge.

"Woah okay, what on earth have I done to you?" I told him, "You have been short and snappy with me since this morning and I want to know what I did for you to treat me like this because I really can't be bothered to do this!" he finally turned and looked at me, he seemed a little shocked at my outburst.

"Oh er, I'm sorry, I guess I'm not in a talking mood at the moment," he replied, "must just be work, I'm really tired." he added.

"Right…" I replied, I couldn't be bothered to get into it with him, I quickly grabbed a can of coke and walked back out of the kitchen leaving Jake standing there staring and trying to recount what just happened.

I wandered back upstairs to Cassie's room and flopped down at the dressing table in front of the mirror.
"You took a little longer than I expected." she said with a concerned look on her face.
"Oh yeah I just got distracted." I explained to her hoping it sounded convincing, so I didn't have to relay any of the weirdness that had just transpired between Jake and me.
"So, are you ready for me to do your eyeliner yet?" she asked, waiting excitedly. I assessed my face in the mirror and decided that I was happy with how my make up looked so far.
"Yep, you're good to go," I told her, "Then I'll do my mascara, and I shall be ready." I was feeling quite anxious about this date. I just hoped it wouldn't be a repeat of Hugo. I turned to face Cassie, and she shuffled to the end of the bed facing me.
"Okay please don't move Lex." she said as I felt the eye liner touch my eyelids. Cassie had this talent for eyeliner, and I was envious of it really, she always managed it so smoothly, I felt the pen glide over one eye and then move to the next eye and start again there.
"And ... we...are done!" she said triumphantly, and I opened my eyes to turn and look in the mirror.
"Oh wow, Cassie, it's great!" I said to her as I started unscrewing the mascara bottle to apply the final step of my makeup.
"Of course," she replied with a shrug.

"I think I'm ready," I told her, "I just need my shoes and my jacket now."

"Ah," she jumped up and ran to her closet, she rifled through it for a few minutes and emerged with a cute black leather jacket as well as a small black clutch.

"That's so cute," I said to her as she passed them over, I shrugged on the jacket and swapped my phone and cards from my handbag into the clutch. I slid on my trainers that we had agreed on and did a final look in the full-length mirror.

"Lexi you look incredible, this guy would be insane to not want you." Cassie said encouragingly. "You think you'll come back here after?"

"I'm not sure yet, I haven't seen my parents for a while so I might pop in later or tomorrow, depending how the date goes." I told her with a smirk.

"Well good luck then," she told me, "How are you getting there?"

"He's picking me up. I gave him your address, I hope you don't mind." I told her.

"No problem, this way I get a little sneak peek of the guy taking my best friend out." she said.

"Oh, he should be here soon," I told her, "I told him to pull up and beep."

"We'll see if he sticks to that suggestion."

We stayed in Cassie's room for a little while longer than we heard the doorbell.

"I've got it!" Cassie yelled and sprinted downstairs. I followed her a little slower and calmer, not wanting to seem too eager. When I walked down, Miles was standing there chatting with Cassie.

"Hey," I said to him as I approached the pair.

"Hey back." he said with a smile, "this is for you." he said and held out a single red rose.

"Wow good choice, it even goes with my outfit." I commented.

"Well might I say on that note that you look incredible," he replied.

"Thank you, you don't look so bad yourself." I told him, he was in a pair of fitted black jeans with a crisp white shirt and a smart looking black jacket.

"What? This old thing?" he joked, *I already like him.*

"Shall we get going?" he asked and held out his hand.

"Yeah, let's do it," I said, taking his hand.

"Achem." came from Cassie and we both glanced over, "be careful with my best friend."

"And on that note, let's go!" I butted in before Cassie went crazy, pushing Miles out the door.

"Bye Cassie," Miles called over his shoulder as we walked out, "and don't worry she is perfectly safe with me." I shook my head, and we walked to his car, he opened the door for me and waited for me to get in. Once I was sorted, he shut the door and jogged round to the driver's side, I turned back to Cassie's house and waved goodbye to her where she stood at the front door. Miles started the car, and we were off.

But I couldn't help but notice the movement on the second floor of the house, specifically Jake's room where it seemed he was, or had been, standing by the window watching me leave.

Chapter 7: Jake

That guy was the walking embodiment of a soggy lettuce leaf left out in the sun for too long. I wish I was saying that with more evidence than just because he was taking Lexi out. I was, embarrassingly, watching them as they pulled away from our house in his car. It was a beaten up, old Vauxhall and I knew she deserved more. Lexi looked incredible in that dress, when I bumped into her on the landing, I had this immediate desire just to push her against the wall and kiss her senseless. My mind going crazy at the possibilities of everything I shouldn't- no, couldn't do. I thought that my best option was to just walk away and try to keep my mind off the way she had looked. I failed. I could feel her presence surrounding me and suffocating me when I walked downstairs, and I needed to get away before I did something that I knew I wouldn't be able to take back. I should be protecting her from the kind of guys that want to do exactly what I do. I guess it was safe to say that my feelings had far surpassed the protective brother field.

I quickly shut the curtain when I saw Lexi glancing up to my room from the car, fearful that she had seen me and would question it. I scolded my heart for its response to that small glance from her, those little slivers of attention that I could get from her. She started to drive away from the house, and I couldn't help but think that she should be in my car instead! I should be the one taking her out, making her laugh, seeing her smile.
"Hey, you alright?" Cassie asked as she leant on my bedroom door frame watching me with a mixture of concern and intrigue. I grunted in response, unable and unwilling to tell her what was really going on. I could never confess to her so what is the point? Clearly unimpressed by my response.
"Fine, work is just getting on top of me." I was sure that she would believe that seeing as I always seemed to be busy with work.
"You should find a better job Jake, those people don't appreciate you." she said with a sympathetic tone. I felt horrible for lying to her, but it seemed necessary, I just had no idea how she would react. I mean I didn't even know what to say to her right now, I wasn't even sure of *what* I was feeling.
"Yeah, I know, I know." I muttered to her in the hope that she would leave me alone, luckily she believed my

excuse and walked out of my room. I assumed she was heading back to her room and would immediately call Noah, I swear those two are near inseparable. Even when they're not together they're calling or messaging, I'm envious to be honest.

Once Cassie left and I forced myself to stop dwelling on Lexi and what she was doing on her date, I got back to work. My family were right sometimes, this job could be the end of me if the hours and workload didn't ease up soon. I got that these guys were still early on in the game, and I was thankful that I was given the job, but a man has to sleep at some point. I accepted my fate- for now- and began digging into my work once again.
About an hour later, my phone vibrated.

Michael: Hey man, we're going out for drinks, you down.

Jake: Sounds great but got work

Michael: so lame, next time?

Jake: for sure

Michael: Can we at least drag you away for some gaming?

Jake: yeah, why not, you on now?

Michael: Yeah, just get on when you're ready.

Jake: will do

I replied, but I didn't have much hope that I would actually be able to make the next night of drinks, since starting this job I had missed countless pub trips and boys' nights. I finished the table I was working on within five minutes and switched to the game that Michael had started.
"Hey guys." I said as I started.
"Hey, you made it!" Michael said, "I wasn't sure if we would actually see you, it seems that work of yours is the only thing that gets attention lately."
"Oh, ha ha." I rolled my eyes.
"How's work going?" James asked.
"It's there and there is a lot of it." I admitted.
"That bad huh?" Elliot added.
"I mean I hope that it'll get me to where I want, but I guess we'll just have to see."
"How's the gaming going?" Michael asked, "are we going to be playing your game soon instead of this one for the thousandth time?"
"That's the plan." I replied with a chuckle. We continued playing and soon the conversation was limited to our fighting technique and how we were going to win this game instead of anything about my life, or any of the others.
"So, Jake…" Michael started apprehensively.

"Yes?" I asked cautiously.
"I'm thinking that you could do with a date," he told me.
"Oh god not this again." I groaned.
"Oh, come on Jake, you don't leave your house." Elliot chimed in.
"Not you too El."
"Yes, him too, we are concerned for your social life," Michael continued, "so I have a few girls in mind."
"Uh huh"
"Will you go on a date with one of them?" Michael kept on.
"I'm not getting out of this am I?" I asked, already knowing the answer.
"No way, we are stepping in before you become a full-blown hermit." he replied.
"Fine, I will agree to *one* date with one of these girls you have apparently selected out for me." I conceded, "but that is all, one date and if it doesn't go well then you let it rest, at least for a little while."
"Fine, okay, fine," Michael agreed.
"Yeah, yeah." Elliot grumbled.
"James?" I added, "I know you were in on this, say you agree."
"What- yeah okay." James answered. They were always trying to do this. Now I had agreed to a date, all I could think of, once again was Lexi. Maybe this date would be good, seeing as she was off with that Miles guy, maybe I would like this girl and finally stop thinking about her.

Lexi has always been completely off limits, and I knew I could never go there, I wouldn't do that to Cassie, I mean she had never said, explicitly, that I couldn't and in all honestly, I don't think she thought I would ever want to. Cassie was the middle sibling, I don't think she felt like she had things that were truly hers, but Lexi was. Lexi had been her best friend for so long and Cassie needed that. I had my stuff, and I was the oldest, which came with its perks, and I was trusted most and left to do what I wanted to do. Then Bradley and Hailey were younger so they were still treated like they were the babies of the family and could do no wrong. But Cassie? She usually took on a lot of work to help with those two and around the house but was still forgotten. Lexi was her person, the one that she had always had around and never expected anything from her. There was no way I would make her feel like I took that away from her.

"If I 'm agreeing to this date, can I at least have some insight into who you are setting me up with?" I asked hopefully, but knowing my friends it was a long shot.
"Ha! No way!" Michael replied, "there is no way we are telling you anything about her, if we do there is no way that you'll go out with her."
"So-" I began.
"And no!" Michael continued before I could say anything, "not because there is anything wrong with her,

but because as soon as you find out the smallest piece of information about her, you'll find some excuse to not go out with her."
"Oh, come on!" I protested.
"Mate, he has a point." James chimed in.
"None of you are on my side, are you?" I asked but I knew the answer already. A chorus of 'no's' came through my headset. I shook my head and smiled at my friends, I knew they were right. Unfortunately, the only way I could think of to get my friends off of my back was to agree.

The game soon came to an end, and we started up another, in no time two hours had passed and I knew I needed to be productive once again. I said goodbye not before Michael said he would send me the girl's details. I was *really* looking forward to that. With a sigh I switched off the monitor and my room fell into silence, turning away from my games and towards my work instead, I forced myself to work through the new proposals and emails.

It was soon dinner time when I heard the sound of the door opening downstairs and Cassie greeting someone. I desperately wanted it to be Lexi, walking in looking tired and upset saying how bad the date had gone. I glanced out into the hall and saw no one so I made my way slowly to the top landing and glanced down into the entrance way, desperate to hear the melodious hum of her voice. To my dismay Noah was standing there greeting Cassie instead, my face fell. "Hey man!" Noah called up as he saw me standing on the landing before I was able to hide away in my room, I shook off my disappointment and waved back.

"Hey Noah, good to see you." I said with false enthusiasm, knowing there was someone else I would much rather be seeing. At that point, my parents glanced out of the living room as well to come and say hello, while everyone was distracted, I took that moment to excuse myself and disappear to my room. Once safe, I no longer hid my disappointment, and I sat back at my desk and continued my work.

Work had become a necessary distraction and soon I was so busy, the thought of Lexi on her date has lessened from a raging tyrant in my brain to a small nagging feeling which was the best I was going to get. Buried deep in filing and charts I hardly noticed the time passing, I soon realised I was *very* late for dinner and my stomach wasn't happy about it. I shut my laptop and stood from my desk.

"Ah, our son lives," my mum teased as I walked into the family room. She sat next to my dad with his arm around her and Cassie and Noah sat on the other sofa watching the movie with them.

"Ha ha, yes I am still alive, barely, but I'm starving, have you guys eaten?" I asked them and glanced for an answer.
"Sweetie, it's eleven o'clock, we've eaten, but I was worried about you so there is left over chilli on the stove." she replied, the concern inching into her expression once again.
"Ah mother I do love you, garlic bread too?"
"Of course, I know you, Jakey." she replied with a smile and a small shake of her head. I gave her a quick kiss on the head and walked out of the room to go and get my food. On the way out I ruffled Cassie's head from where she sat with her legs over Noah and she tried, yet failed, to whack me in return as I swerved and ran out. As I entered the kitchen my mouth began to water at the delicious scent of the food, I immediately served myself a huge portion and added a few pieces of garlic bread on top and went back to the family room to sit with all of them.
"What are we watching?" I asked them.
"Oh, one of these mystery crime cases that dad is obsessed with," Cassie replied, "this one is actually pretty good though."
"Hey, these things *are* good!" My dad chimed in, and I noticed Noah nodding in agreement not tearing his eyes away from the TV. I settled in the armchair by the window and quickly dug into my meal, my stomach was truly happy at the delicious warm food it was being given, particularly after so long without any sustenance.

"Are you chewing that or just inhaling that?" Mum asked with a concerned look towards me, but I just waved her off with my mouth full. Focussing on food meant not focussing on the one girl I couldn't seem to forget.

Chapter 8: Lexi

"So where did you grow up?" I asked Miles as he sat across from me in the restaurant, smiling at the waiter who had just delivered our starter. I was surprised at how well this date was going seeing how my track record had been. I guess it was about time I had a decent date and Miles seemed so sincere and good. He was tall, tall enough for me to wear heels and still look up at him, he had delicious brown hair that was loosely styled and swooped to the side. He had a gentle smile and beautiful blue eyes, not bright blue more mellow and calming, different to any I had seen before. He has this natural charm, something about him that just made it impossible not to look and listen to him. The only other time I had this feeling was at Cassies, around her, her family, Jake.

"What about you?" He asked, after a moment I realised he had asked me a question.//
"Oh yeah, so I'm an only child and grew up with my parents still together." I told him.
"That must have been nice."
"Honestly?" he nodded "It was pretty quiet, both my parents are in the corporate world which always meant they had long hours. I would usually spend most of my time at Cassie's house, I still do actually." I replied with a short laugh.
"That's the girl I met earlier, right?" He asked.
"Yep, that's the one and she is my sister, in all the ways that count, and her parents practically adopted me into their family. I would usually go round to their house after school, sometimes even before school if my parents had early starts and it wasn't rare for me to stay at their house either."
"Wow" Miles said, "really close then," he said, and I nodded in agreement, "And what about that guy that was there when I came to get you?"
The comment caught me, "what guy?" I asked.
"The one staring out the window as we walked to my car…" he leaded, waiting for me to build upon it. "He seemed pretty mad that you were going out."
"Oh? I mean there's Jake, that must have been who you saw?" I was confused. The fact that Miles saw him confirmed the fact that Jake had been watching me from the window. I ignored the way my heart leapt…

"What's the deal with him anyway?" he asked me, digging further.

"What do you mean?"

"Well… what's the history there?" he pressed further.

"There's no history there," I assured him, laughing off the suggestion.

"Oh, come on, I know this is only the first date, but I hope there will be more and you don't have to keep history from me, the way he was looking at you? I thought he was about to jump through that window and kill me for being near you." he laughed, but there was an edge to the humour.

"I promise you," I began, "there has never ever been anything between Jake and me. He sees me like a little sister."

"And how do you see him?" he asked.

"Okay, I confess I used to have a *tiny* crush on him when I was like twelve years old, but that was just a childish thing and nothing ever happened." I explained, trying to show that it was simply a childhood crush.

"Hmmm, sounds like there might be competition?" he teased.

"Ha!" I burst out, realising my volume I quickly lowered my voice, "I can promise you, if you saw anything it was brotherly protection. Nothing will ever happen between Jake and I," I assured him, "and for the record, I would like there to be more than one date too." I smiled.

"If you say so," Miles sighed, "but I'll be prepared to duel for the fair maiden if it comes to it." he teased and winked.

"Don't worry, you have *no* competition with Jake." as the words left my mouth, I could feel my heart grow heavy at the confession. Yes, I knew nothing would happen but saying out loud, almost cutting off the prospect was a knife to the heart. But I wouldn't let it ruin tonight. The rest of the date passed without any problems or mention of Jake. I only needed to keep him out of my mind now for every other minute of the day.

We spent hours chatting, what he was doing and what I was doing. He was 2 years older, had just finished university and was looking for a job. He was looking at a job in publishing. I told him that I had just finished my first year of university studying to be a lawyer, which he showed true interest in, but when he asked me what I wanted to do in the future I just shrugged.

"I mean that's fair," he assured me, "a lot of people don't know exactly what they want to do. As long as you do what you enjoy doing." he paused, "My mum always says do what you love and you'll love what you do." he smiled shyly at me and reached over to grab my hand across the table, it rested for a moment on the table with his palm up. I was hesitant at first but reached over and slid my hand into his waiting one, the connection was light and sweet. I felt like a giddy teenager sitting there holding hands with a boy and shockingly it was a feeling I had missed.

After we finished dinner, me having a carbonara and him getting a steak, we both ordered a hot drink.
I had a hot chocolate, and he had a latte, and we shared a slice of cake for dessert, but I'm fairly sure I had much more of it than he did. He didn't seem to mind, which gave him more brownie points in my book. We slowly finished our drinks, and I think both of us were having such a good time that we didn't worry about how long we had been out. My phone had vibrated a few times, but I couldn't tear my eyes away from Miles for long enough to check who was messaging me *and* to answer them.
"All finished?" Miles asked, I nodded once I had scraped the final crumbs off the plate. Within a couple of minutes, the waiter had returned with one of the silver trays with the bill and a couple of mints placed on top. Really classy.
"Do you want to halve it?" I asked him, reaching for my purse to grab my card.
"What? Of course not, I asked you out, I pay." he replied as he waved off the card in my outstretched hand.
"Are you sure?" I asked him.
"Absolutely, but if you still seemed so displeased by me paying then you can get the next one."
"Hmmm," I teased as I pretended to think through the idea, "I think I could deal with that." I said with a smile.

Miles laughed and turned his head down. I pulled out my phone as Miles was sorting out the bill and checked my messages. Of course, the onslaught of messages had been from Cassie.

Cassie: How is it going?
Cassie: Is it good?
Cassie: Are you enjoying it?
Cassie: Have you kissed him yet?

There were ten other messages like that, the last few were just a collection of exclamation marks and question marks. I shook my head at her. Glancing at the time on my phone I realised it was nearly 11pm.
"Oh wow, I didn't even realise the time," I commented.
"Yeah, I hadn't realised how late it is." Miles chuckled.
"I'll take that as a compliment." I replied coyly.
"You should." Miles said with a smile as he stood up and offered me his hand. I grabbed my bag quickly and shoved it on my shoulder, standing up I took hold of his hand.

We strode together, hand in hand, towards his car. He walked over to my door and opened it for me.
"Come let's get you home." he shut my door, jogged round to the other side, got in too and started up the engine. We peeled out of the car park, and we started on our way home. I rested my head against the seat and

looked out of the window with a small smile playing on my lips. The drive home was quicker than I hoped, and we pulled up outside Cassie's house. I didn't want to go home and have my mood ruined by what would be waiting for me, so Cassie's was the option, I didn't actually want to say goodbye.

"Well, I guess this is good night." He said.

"I guess so," I sighed, "I had a really good time tonight, Miles."

"Yeah, I had an amazing time too," he smiled, he jumped out the car and jogged round to my side to open the door for me. I slid out of the car, and I started to walk towards the door, but before I could take many steps Miles grabbed my hand and stopped me.

"There is just one thing that would make tonight even better..." he whispered.

"Oh yeah? And what's that?"

"This…" he replied and in no time, he grabbed my face and pulled me close to him, his lips brushed my gently first but once he knew I was happy he deepened the kiss. It was glorious. His hands moved from my face and slid down my body to my hips and pulled me close. My body fell against his. My arms hung loose at my side not sure what to do. He slowly pulled away and looked down at me. "Now it's perfect," he grinned.

"Uh huh," was all I could muster, my mind still going wild at what had occurred.

"Come on, let's get you inside before Cassie comes out and attacks me. From what you've told me, I'm sure she will want all of the information." He joked and pulled me to the door. I pulled out my spare key not wanting to disturb people. She was already expecting me, and she had given me the key so I could just walk in and out when I needed to, I was here often enough.
"Thank you for a nice night." I said to Miles, now recovered from the surprise of the kiss.
"You're very welcome." He replied and with one last smile at him I opened the door and stepped inside shutting it behind me my body falling against the door in awe of the date I had just had.

"So?" Cassie asked as she waited expectantly at the top of the stairs staring at me while I was still leaning against the door. I shook out of my dream and looked up at her.
"It was alright." I shrugged, I was adamant I wasn't going to give everything away straight away and let her suffer for a while.
"Oh, come on, you *have* to give me more than that!" she protested poking out her bottom lip.
"Okay fine, it was really nice." I told her, I could feel the smile on my face growing wider, I don't think I had stopped smiling since we had finished dinner. Cassie let out a deafening squeal and threw her arms around me.
"Finally!" she cheered. "My faith in men can be restored!"

She grabbed my hand and pulled me up to her room, after she had scampered to the kitchen to grab a bottle of wine of course.

"What is going on-" Jake started with his head poking out of his room to see what the commotion was.

"Oh move!" Cassie moaned at him as she pushed him away, back into his room, I made sure that I didn't even look at him as I passed. We dashed into Cassie's room and slammed the door behind us. Not even Jake's foul mood would lessen the smile on my face.

"Okay spill," Cassie said as she flopped down onto the bed, fiddling with the seal on the bottle of rose she had procured. So, I did, I told her everything about the date, from him opening the door to him paying and the kiss at the end.

"But?"

"But what?" I asked her.

"Well don't get me wrong that all sounds super adorable, but it feels like you're leaving something out." she ventured. I could hardly tell her that I had an intense run in with her brother and the crush I tried so hard to expel was slowly creeping up on me.

"No, no 'but' I guess it's just a weird feeling for me to have a date that actually went well you know, not used to success." I joked hoping that it would satisfy her enough to stop asking questions.

"Okay," she replied, still hesitant but I could tell she was going to let it go. "Well come on then, do you think you'll go out with him again?"
"I think so," I assured her, "it would be nice to go out again."
"Yes!" she squealed but then quickly stopped, "Wait so does that mean you don't want to go out with Noah's friend?"
"What?"
"You know..." she began, "You were going to go out with Tate? Noah's friend?"
"Oh right, yeah of course, Tate."
"You forgot, didn't you?" she asked, slightly amused.
"Maybe?" I sighed, "I'm sorry Cassie I forgot, but yes, we can still go out, it was a double date after all?"
"Okay good," she replied, and her excitement returned. "I'll message Noah and confirm it all with him and we'll book it for next week."
"Alright. It'll be good." I assured her, another squeal confirmed her excitement, and I couldn't help but laugh.

We sat with each other, giggling and drinking until early hours of the morning. Cassie was increasingly excited at the prospect of me having a boyfriend, which was when I quickly reminded her that we had only been on one date and of course she waved me off straight away saying it was only a matter of time. As she planned my apparent future with Miles I couldn't help the thoughts of Jake creeping into my mind. I did really like Miles, that is what I needed to focus on now, I needed to ignore Jake, I could do that...Right?

Chapter 9: Jake

I heard the commotion out in the hallway and without even checking I knew the delicious melody of Lexi's laugh as Cassie talked to her about her date with whoever that loser was earlier. I felt a heaviness in my stomach at the idea of Lexi having such a good time on that date with some ridiculous guy that I didn't know. Lexi didn't even acknowledge me, and I couldn't blame her. Seeing how I reacted to her before she went on her date but oh if only she knew, if only she knew the ideas running through my head when I had seen her in that dress…

Cassie slammed the door behind them and their laughter continued to echo through the hallway. With a sigh I turned and walked back into my room, I had done this for too long. I was being crazy about Lexi and I needed to put an end to it. I stomped over to my bed and picked up my phone from where I had chucked it earlier.

Jake: Hey, when is this date going to be sorted for?

Michael: Man, are you serious?

Jake: yeah, it's about time, plus she sounds great.

James: Yes, way to go Jake!

Michael: I'll give you her number.

Jake: cheers

Elliot: Finally!

I knew this was the best thing I could do right now; I needed to move on, and this was something I could do. My phone chimed once again, and it was a message from Michael with a phone number along with numerous emojis that I just rolled my eyes at. My mates hadn't even given me her name so I paused for a while thinking about what kind of message I could send without sounding like a creep. After a while of thinking I started typing out a message.

Jake: Hey!

I erased the exclamation mark.

Jake: Hey, it's Jake. I'm Michael's friend, the one that was set up about the date.

I paused before I pressed send, then it was done. But I then thought that there was no point being cautious now and I quickly typed another message.

Jake: What are your plans tomorrow night?

I sent the message, threw my phone back on the bed and went to sit at my computer scrolling through my emails having a look through to see if there was anything important, of course there wasn't. I leapt up in surprise when my phone chimed and grabbed it.

Unknown: Well hello Jake who is Michael's friend

                                    Jake: Good to hear from you

Unknown: Well, I thought I would reply

                    Jake: So what do you think about tomorrow night?

Unknown: I will need to check my calendar

Jake: Oh really? Busy are you?

Unknown: Just in high demand ;)

Jake: Well, I hope you have space for me

Unknown: If you're lucky

Jake: I hope I will be.

Unknown: I think I can.

Jake: Good, so how does 7 tomorrow night sound? I'll come get you

Unknown: sounds good

Jake: It's a date then
Jake: Want to give me a name and an address

Unknown: oh right! I'm Millie

Jake: I look forward to tomorrow Millie :)

She sent me a message with her address and a kiss. I couldn't help but smile. Millie seemed nice, from the brief messages we had shared and what Michael had let slip. I chatted briefly to Millie for a little while longer after we had sorted out the date. I could feel my stomach growing heavy, as if something was sitting in it, an uncomfortable weight. I thought about them sitting in Cassie's room laughing and chatting about the date that Lexi had been on, and the weight only grew heavier. Did she have fun? Are they seeing each other again? Had he kissed her? I scolded myself again and for letting my thoughts go there. I needed to tune it out, so I switched on my TV, turning on the Big Bang Theory and making it loud enough that I couldn't hear them anymore. After a while I could feel my eyes grow heavy and I fell into a deep sleep. I only wish that Lexi hadn't followed me into my dreams.

I was woken up by a sharp ray of sunlight poking through my curtains, alerting me that it was time to get up, one more day of freedom before the work week started again. With a groan I turned over and checked my phone seeing that there were no messages from Millie but saw that the clock read 10:15am, I knew I was picking her up at seven this evening, so I had all day to kill. I eased myself out of bed and got changed before heading downstairs for some breakfast.
"Hey mum," I said as I walked into the kitchen. She was sitting at the table with a plate of pancakes and a book. Bradley tucked into his pancakes that were covered in chocolate and bananas next to her. Hailey was nowhere to

be seen, but I assumed she had already gone for her
morning activities, I think today was swimming.
"Hi honey, there's pancake batter in the fridge if you want
to make yourself some and I just made a fresh pot of
coffee." Mum greeted me without even looking up from
her book.
"Thanks," I said to her while stifling a yawn, I grabbed
the batter from the fridge as well as the milk. I poured
myself a cup of coffee and added milk and sugar before
pouring some batter into the pan as I sipped my coffee.
"Did you sleep well?" she asked.
"Yeah, not too bad." I told her, leaving out the dreams
that had me tossing and turning all night. "What about
you?" I asked her.
"Oh yes, it was fine." she said to me absentmindedly,
"your father has popped to the shops by the way, buying
more material for one of his little projects."
"Of course," I replied as I flipped the pancakes over then
turned to the cupboard to retrieve the peanut butter.
"What are your plans today?" she asked me.
"Um not much today I don't think, going to take a break
from work, I'm going out this evening." I told her,
bracing for the questions.
"That sounds nice, you need some time for yourself," she
replied. I looked at her curiously, thankful for the short
reply.

"Morning mum," a low grumble came from the hallway, and I turned to see Cassie enter the kitchen, Lexi followed close behind looking slightly better than Cassie but still very rough. Her hair was placed in a messy bun balanced on top of her head, her cheeks looked paler than usual, but her lips were as full as ever. There has always been something about her lips, looked almost like a heart, plump and rosy.
"Morning, " Lexi murmured behind her. She glanced my way quickly but turned away as soon as she saw me looking at her, not even daring to meet my gaze. Even that small glance formed something in the bottom of my stomach, I had never been affected like this. I turned back to the pan to quickly scoop up my pancakes, cover them in the peanut butter and decided to add some bananas on top.
"Ooo pancakes." Cassie said, becoming rather chipper since seeing the pancakes.
"Make your own." I grunted as I walked over to the table carrying my plate and my coffee.
"Someone's happy today," Cassie mocked, as I walked over to the table I passed straight in front of Lexi. Her scent teased me, urging me to wrap her in my arms. I wasn't complaining, it seemed to be the closest I was going to get to her. I watched her as she and Cassie made their own pancakes with the batter. Cassie stood with a cup of coffee and I watched Lexi head over to the kettle and fill it up. I had forgotten for a moment about her

hatred for coffee. This morning she seemed to settle on green tea, guess it was too early for hot chocolates. Turning my attention away from her every move, I slumped down into my seat and dug into my pancakes. The girls ended up with us at the table, Cassie slid down opposite me, next to my mum, Bradley and Hailey on either end, which left Lexi forced to sit next to me. I could feel her hesitation at first but clearly not wanting to show that something was wrong she soon sat down. The proximity was intoxicating. She was wearing a pair of criminally short jersey shorts, borrowed from Cassie I assume, as well as a sweatshirt that seemed far too big for her and oddly familiar.
"Is that mine?" I suddenly exclaimed, shooting Lexi a questioning look.
"Oh right yeah, sorry I let her borrow it yesterday, she is getting too tall for my stuff and that was all I could find," Cassie chimed in before Lexi could answer, I noticed her looking vaguely uncomfortable next to me.
"Right." I muttered, "ask next time alright."
"Sorry," Lexi mumbled, "there wasn't much other choice."
"Dude what's your problem?" Cassie asked, "It's just a sweatshirt."
"You can have it back," Lexi offered, already grabbing the hem.
"No!" I burst out, knowing that if she removed that sweatshirt, I wouldn't be able to keep composure when I

saw what was underneath. This unfortunately earned shocked looks from those around the table, even Bradley looked up in shock, "just…whatever it's fine, put it in my room later."

"Right." Cassie said. The thought of my sweatshirt being covered in Lexi's smell not only thrilled me but also horrified me. Why, all of a sudden, was she making me feel this way? I tried to focus on what Cassie was saying, something about a trip with Noah for their anniversary coming up. All I could focus on was the fact that Lexi was so close to me, in *my* clothes. I shifted in discomfort, but that only made matters worse as now my leg was pressed firmly against hers. She was swallowed by my sweatshirt, but then those tiny jersey shorts drew my attention to her olive legs disappearing under the table. I knew I should move, but my mind and my body weren't working together and my desire to be close to her won over the logic of moving. I knew I needed to get away while I could.

"I've got to- uh -uh go," I said abruptly, interrupting Cassie, "sorry." I muttered as I knocked Lexi's arm in my speedy attempt to leave the table. I sped out of the kitchen and rushed upstairs, I shut myself in my room and took a deep breath. My arm tingled from our brief touch. *Why the hell did she have to be wearing my clothes, and why the hell did they have to look far better on her than they ever did on me.*

I went to my computer and started working. Hours slowly passed by as I was glued to the screen getting through as much work as possible. After checking my phone briefly and quickly replying to the message I saw from Millie about tonight, I headed downstairs to relax for a while before the date. I passed Cassie's room and saw her and Noah cuddled on her bed watching something on TV. I said a quick 'hi' but swiftly continued my decline downstairs. As I reached the bottom, I heard the TV blaring in the front room playing the Great British Bake Off and noticed mum quietly snoozing on the sofa, an open book laying on the sofa next to her.

I went hunting for dad and knocked on the door of the garage in case he was working with some sort of power tool.
"Hey dad," I said as I walked in. I noticed he was using a hammer; I waved my hand in his direction to let him know I was here.
"Oh, hey son." he said, putting his tools down, "how are you?"
"Yeah, I'm good, just thought I would come and say hi," I told him, "What are you working on?"
"I'm not sure yet, we had some spare scraps so I thought I would see what I can do with it and right now I really don't know what it is." He told me in a slightly distracted voice.
"Seems like a good idea. Are you alright?"

"Wha- oh yeah I'm great," he said but I could still see that he was distracted.
"Do you know if mum is okay?" As soon as I asked that question, I could see his head snap up in realisation of my question.
"Yes, she's fine. Why do you ask?" he rushed to say suddenly, seeming rather skittish.
"Oh well she just seems a little preoccupied, that's all." I replied suddenly feeling rather awkward under the intense stare coming from my dad.
"Well, it must just be work getting in the way then. I can't think of anything else it could be," he assured me before he snapped his gaze back to what he had been fiddling with in front of him.

I left my dad alone a little while after and decided to go for a drive. I was on autopilot while I was driving around until I reached the McDonalds drive thru.
"Hi, what can I get for you?" a voice suddenly squealed through the intercom machine.
"Oh hi," I said, shaking myself from the shock of the sudden voice, "can I get 6 chicken nugget meal with a large chocolate milkshake."
"Yeah," they replied, "next window." I drove on, unsurprised by the flat tone of voice. I was, however, slightly impressed by the fact that their face was even flatter than their tone of voice. I pulled up to the window, paid and then got my food. I stayed in the carpark for

about an hour when I realised it was nearly six and I needed to pick up Millie at seven. I only had about an hour before I needed to pick up Millie.

I called out to my parents when I got home, although I'm not entirely sure they even realised I'd gone out. I went up to my room and got ready, realizing I didn't have long before my date. I quickly jumped into the shower before changing, I landed on a pair of blue trousers with a striped shirt and my vans. I fixed my hair to make it look acceptable, sprayed a little cologne and I was ready to go. I checked my phone one more time and noticed a mix of messages from Michael, James and Elliot and noticed the time (6:43) I sped downstairs and grabbed my jacket, keys and wallet. I called goodbye and sped out the front door. It's never good to be late on a first date…

I had a few minutes to spare as I arrived at Millie's, grabbing the bouquet of daisies I'd bought earlier, I went to knock on the door. A small, smiling woman opened the door, she was blonde with a slightly plump and aged face, and she had one of the biggest smiles I have ever seen. When I saw her, I couldn't help but smile.
"You must be Jake," she announced.
"Er yeah that's me." I said, still slightly baffled by the meeting.

Our Summertime Secrets

"Oh, call me Judie, I'm Millie's mum, I bet Millie didn't even tell you my name, please come in, come in." she ushered me into the house.
I stood patiently, yet awkwardly, in the hallway.
"She'll be down in just a minute, those flowers are lovely, dear." her mum told me. I smiled and nodded; it had been a long time since I had stood in the hallway of a girl's house with their parents before a date.

After a few more minutes Millie finally made her way down the stairs and I had to do a double take, she was absolutely stunning. She was tall and slender all wrapped up in a tight blue dress matched with a pair of heels. She had silky blonde hair, a similar shade of her mothers, and deep emerald, green eyes. She descended the rest of the stairs, and I could smell her perfume surround me. As she got closer, I noticed her dress was decorated with sweet small flowers and ended just above her knees. I was in utter shock at how amazing she looked, and I knew that Michael had made an excellent choice with the blind date.
"Hi," she said quietly, looking at me through her eyelashes.
"Hey, you look nice," I replied, "uh these are for you." I told her, handing her the bouquet.
"Oh how… sweet," she replied as she took the daisies from me and lifted them to her nose, "thank you."
"We should get going if we want to make our reservation." I told her.

"Yes. yes, you two get going." her mum chimed in. I had been rather aware of her watchful gaze as Millie had come downstairs. Millie passed her the flowers and started towards the door. I led her to the car making sure I opened the door for her before going round to my side of the car. I got in my side of the car and turned on the engine, the radio came to life playing soft music and I drove away. Here we go…

Chapter 10: Lexi

I left Cassie's house in what I can only describe as a complete state...well mentally anyway. I hid it from Cassie for the most part but after breakfast I made my excuses rather promptly and got myself out of there. This morning, I thought I'd be able to face Jake and expel the odd behaviour from him last night. But as soon as I walked into the kitchen, I could feel my heart rate pick up. I had given so many years to that boy and all he saw me as was Cassie's dumb little friend, yet here I was excited at the possibility of seeing him. The whole situation was made even worse when we went to sit down, and I was forced next to him. I was addicted to his smell, Rosewood mixed with something inherently Jake. As soon as I had his scent wrapped around me, I knew I was gone, his frame took up so much space on the small bench that any movement would have caused me to be pressed against him. Something that to my embarrassing

joy he seemed to initiate as he shifted in the bench and
my leg was soon flushed against his.
To my dismay, Jake's food seemed to be eaten in record
time and I couldn't help the wave of sadness that washed
over me as he fled as quickly as he could. Before I could
get the chance to see if he had been as affected as I had,
he was gone.

My hunger left the room with him and I spent the next 10
minutes pushing my food around my plate hoping that
Cassie wouldn't question my sudden silence. Once she
finished her food we made our way back upstairs, she
walked ahead of me and headed into her room. I couldn't
stop myself from glancing towards Jake's room to see if I
could hear anything, but I was only met with silence.
"Come on," Cassie said and yanked me into her room.
"Are you alright?" she asked, the one thing I truly hated
was that I was scarcely able to hide any of my feelings
from her. Any sort of expression I had, she was able to
decipher and interrogate.
"Wha- oh yeah, yeah I'm fine, just the effects of last
night getting to me." I confessed, hoping it was enough of
an excuse.
"Yeah, I guess last night did get pretty heavy," she
agreed. After the date we stayed up all night. I *was*
honestly exhausted, that part wasn't a lie, it just wasn't
the entire truth. But how are you supposed to tell your
best friend that you have an extreme crush on her brother

and have practically loved him since you were like eleven years old? Answer? You don't.

"I think I'm gonna head home actually," I told her, "I'm just so tired and my parents should be home today so I should make an appearance."

"Okay, I get that, message me if you need anything." I could see the worry in her face and immediately felt guilty.

"Of course," I assured her, "I just need some sleep I think." I explained. She nodded and with a hug I grabbed my clothes from my date yesterday and left.

"Are you leaving, love?" Claire called from the kitchen, Claire had always felt like my second mother (sometimes more like a mother than my biological one) and I loved her like family.

"Yeah," I replied, "my parents are going to be home today, so I thought I'd go and spend some time with them."

"Okay sweetheart, well I'll see you soon alright?" she replied with a worried smile, "do you think you'll be here for dinner?"

"I'm not sure, I need to check with my parents first," I replied apologetically.

"Not to worry, just shoot a text if you know," she replied and smiled. "Goodbye love!"

"Bye," I called back and shut the door and rushed out to my car.

The drive home was done before I even realised, I had been so zoned out on the way back that at one point I had almost steered into another car. I pulled into the drive quickly and started towards the house.

"Hello?" I called in no particular direction as I opened the door. "Hello!"

"Oh, good evening Alexis." I heard as my dad walked out of his office downstairs.

"Hi dad, how are-" I began.

"Alexis, I do not understand why you feel the need for that shrill." My mother scolded me as she walked down the stairs.

"Sorry," I mumbled, "I just couldn't hear where anyone was."

"Well, please refrain from screeching like that again, it was completely embarrassing on my business call. You know your father and I are very busy at work and you screaming in the back of my call makes it seem very unprofessional!" she scolded.

"Sorry. Mother." I could hear my voice becoming smaller and smaller and I was reminded how much I hated being at home. Dad had already disappeared back into his office and I could hear the noises of the keyboard telling me that he had already gone back to work.

"Where have you been anyway?" she asked me.

"I was with Cassie; I stayed with her last night as I didn't know when you and dad would be back."

"Ah," my mum answered. She had never been the biggest fan of Cassie, even though I had been friends with her since we started school together, almost 10 years ago. Comically it wasn't even because she had done anything wrong, it was simply because Cassie and her family weren't the kind of people they liked to associate with. Cassie and her family were warm, loving and chaotic whereas my parents couldn't stand it if anything was even slightly out of place and there could be nothing askew in the house, including me. That was why I never let Cassie come to my house, I knew she wouldn't judge me, I just didn't want the sympathetic looks from her.

"How was your meeting?" I asked. She had been away for the past few days on a business trip. I had stopped asking where a long time ago. It was all too hard to keep up with, but I was partially surprised she was even home today anyway, she's usually away most of the summer.

"Yes, fine." she said in a non-committal tone indicating that the time for conversation had swiftly passed and she isn't interested anymore.

My parents had always been hard workers, when I was younger, I attended an after-school club everyday so my parents could work longer, and then usually I would get dropped home by Cassie's parents. I was hardly one to complain as my parents were still in fact together and they didn't argue, but they also never seemed to smile or laugh together either. In all honesty they didn't seem to do much of anything together. The family meals were sparse, and the only TV I ever used was in my room, there wasn't one downstairs as my parents didn't agree with them. It felt like three strangers sharing a roof sometimes.

Mum walked back up the stairs and I followed her silently, only changing direction to head into my room as she went towards her office. Collapsing back onto my bed I felt the events of last night finally settle on me, the date with Miles had been an unexpected pleasure. I still had the date booked with Tate, Noah's friend, but I had a good feeling about Miles. While stretched out on my bed I heard my phone chime.

Miles: So, I already want to see you again, last night was amazing. Could I see you tomorrow?

I couldn't help but smile at the surprise text.

Lexi: I think that could be arranged, what were you thinking?

Miles: Well, we've already done dinner, so I was thinking coffee.

Lexi: only if you won't judge me if I get a hot chocolate.

Miles: not a coffee drinker, are we?

Lexi: Er no, you see I actually have taste buds.

Miles: oh okay so it's like that, I did wonder on our first date. Don't worry, you can get your hot chocolate :)

Lexi: Okay good, well in that case I will see you tomorrow.

Miles: Good, would 12 be okay? I'll come and pick you up again.

I sent him back a thumbs up and chucked it back on my bed. I couldn't help but smile, Miles seemed to be a really nice guy and it was about time I found myself someone I deserve.

I spent the rest of the day in my room, the house was blanketed in an eerie silence and I knew I would rather stay in my room with my music (turned on at a respectable noise as per my mother's orders) and pretend to be productive, rather than sit in the rest of the house and be around my parents. Their judgments follow all aspects of my behaviour, what I eat, what I wear, what I do. The day managed to pass shockingly quickly and soon I was being beckoned downstairs for dinner.
"She finally appears," my mother commented as I walked downstairs.

"Good evening mother, would you like me to lay the table?" I asked, ignoring the not-so-subtle dig.
"Yes thank you Alexis." I nodded, grabbed the cutlery and began to lay the table. Within five minutes, my mum had placed three plates on the table for each of us accompanied with three glasses of water.
"So did you manage to get all your work done today?" I asked them both.
"Hmm?" my dad replied without even looking up from his phone. I just shook my head and looked at mum.
"Well there's always more to do," she told me and with that the conversation was done. The rest of dinner passed in an uncomfortable silence. It was a rarity for us to have a family dinner, usually one of them was still working or they were away. On the odd occasions where we did sit down and have dinner together (usually after one of them had returned from a business trip) it was just an awkward wreck, hence why I spent so much time at Cassie's. I sat there in silence through the rest of the dinner while my dad was occupied on his phone and my mother sat and calmly ate her food. Once everyone had finished, as per the rules, I asked to be excused and with a curt nod from my mother I stood from my chair and dashed out of the room. It was already half nine, as my parents liked to eat late due to their work schedule, so I jumped in the shower and got ready for bed. My parents didn't tend to do much else than work and sleep so I knew they would be in bed and gone by ten. Once ready for bed, I laid down and

switched on the TV. An old episode of *Friends* was playing and I fell asleep to Chandler's contagious sarcasm.

I was woken by my alarm at 8am. That was another thing with my parents, even though I was on summer holiday and didn't have any work or university for the next few months. They still insisted on me getting up early and being productive, if I didn't I was disappointing and a failure, not much new there. My mother insisted on my maintaining a steady routine through the summer as well, Cambridge could be extremely competitive which meant that it was required for me to stay on top of work, even when there was no work for me to be doing. I couldn't tell you the specifics of what my parents did in their jobs but they somehow managed to have something to say about everything. I finished my first year of university and mother was already making sure that I was keeping up with things for second year, no matter my protests she would always make sure that I was ahead of everyone else.

I dragged myself out of bed and made my way downstairs. I thought I'd be more rested after such an early night, but something about this house sucked energy from me.
"Good morning," I called.
"Wow, she is finally awake," my mother sniped.

"Morning mum, er mother." I corrected as I accepted the bowl of yoghurt and granola that she thrust towards me and sat down at the table.
"What do you have planned for today?" she asked.
"Er I have to tidy my room and do some work," I told her and then remembered the plans I had made with Miles, "Oh and I am going to pop over to Cassie's later. I left something at her house yesterday and I need to go and pick it up, we might get a drink." I told her.
"Right," she replied shortly, "well don't stay there too long, you know that you have your university revision to do."
"Yes mother, I will make sure I get today's work done, don't worry." I dug into my breakfast to ignore her glare.
"Alexis, you know I only do this because I want you to be successful, you need to get ahead in life. None of this is going to work for you if you keep on running around with your friend and ignoring all of your responsibilities, okay?" She lectured, my mother had become quite a broken record when it came to Cassie and my university life.
"Yes mother." I said, stopping my eyes from rolling into my head. I was worried one day they would roll all the way back.
"Alexis, I do not need to tell you how crucial these years are for you do I? If you do not put in the effort now, then the rest of the years are going to be pointless, and you might as well just leave university now. Your father and I

pay a lot of money for you to go to Cambridge and I will not have it all wasted because you decide to mess around!" she shrieked. I squeezed my fists at my side and simply nodded back, not trusting myself to respond calmly.
I turned back to my food and finished my breakfast silently before calmly excusing myself heading upstairs to change and get ready for the day. I quickly got ready then sorted out my bag.
"Mother, I'm going to go out now, I'm taking my work, and I am going to go to the library to get some of it done. I will be back later this evening in time for dinner."
"Thank you Alexis, see you this evening." she replied curtly and turned away as I went through the door. As usual, dad was nowhere to be seen.

I stopped off at the library first to make sure that I would have some work done for mum when I got home later. I let a couple hours pass before I finally decided that I'd done enough. Miles messaged a few times to confirm that I still wanted to see him. I had promptly said yes. So, as I packed up my stuff in the library I let Cassie know that I was making my way over to her house, seeing as that was where Miles was picking me up from, within 20 minutes of sending the text I had pulled up outside. She greeted me, still looking pretty sleepy.
"Why the hell are you here so early?" She groaned.
"Cas it's midday, how are you still in bed?" I asked.

"Hey Noah stayed over and we were watching movies late, not my fault."
"Ah watching movies…" I replied.
"Hey shush," she wacked me, glancing behind her towards the kitchen, worried her parents were eavesdropping on the conversation.
"Okay, just let me in, I promise I'll stay down here and leave your sleeping boyfriend to his business upstairs." I said.
"Well not to sound rude or anything, but why are you here in the first place?" she asked me.
"Miles asked me out again and don't get excited yet, let me finish." I told her as I could see she was losing it, "yeah so he messaged yesterday and said he already wanted to see me again and asked when he could and suggested going to get coffee."
"But you don't like coffee."
"Wow helpful, thank you Captain Obvious. I will not be getting coffee; I will be getting hot chocolate and don't chime in about my childish choice of drink either. Thank you, not all of us are caffeine addicts like you."
"Okay fine." she grumbled.
"But" I continued, "mum was in fine form so I didn't really feel like telling him to go there and having to tell my parents all about him seeing as this is only our second date. Plus, they'll probably question all of his career choices and then still look down on him. No thank you. So, I thought he could pick me up from here."

"Yep. make sense." she replied.
"That's it?" I asked her, confused about the lack of attacking.
"Well, I know how your mum can be, I also know that you don't want pressure on things before you know what they are, so yep, this time that's all. It makes sense."
"Thank you."
"But I do expect a full rundown of the whole date later, okay?" she demanded, I nodded along with her and let it rest.
"Hey Lex, I didn't know we were expecting you." Noah said still half asleep as he walked downstairs in his pyjamas, rubbing his eyes.
"Yeah, sorry to intrude on you lovebirds but I'm meeting someone and he's picking me up here." I explained.
"He?" Noah questioned, suddenly seeming increasingly alert.
"Yep, our little Lexi here has booked herself a date." Cassie explained to Noah as he made it to the bottom of the stairs and wrapped his arm around Cassie's waist and kissed her on the head.
"Wait a second," Noah paused, "if you're going on a date now, why are we fixing you up with Tate?"
"Hey, there is nothing wrong with a lady having options. This is only her second date with this guy!" Cassie defended, scolding Noah as he stared down at her watching as she challenged him.

"Uh babe, if I remember correctly, the last time you were given options, it didn't exactly end well." he said smirking at her. I knew he was referring to the time they met last summer, Cassie had been at camp and found herself in a rather uncomfortable love triangle consisting of Noah and another camper.

"You're never going to let me live that down, are you?" she asked, and his response was a smile shake of his head with his smile growing even bigger.

"Never," he whispered against her neck. I cleared my throat to remind them I was still here.

"But if you'll remember," Cassie began, "that worked out for everyone involved *and* Dean and Emma are doing really well together so…"

"Right, it worked out for everyone in the end. You are a true cupid." Noah nodded with a teasing look on his face.

"*Anyway* lovebirds," I started, "I do have a date today and I did still agree to go out with Tate and yes Cassie is right, there is nothing wrong with a few options. But Noah, don't worry I will not let it get as messy as it did last summer with you guys."

"Hey!" Cassie protested at the same time Noah thanked me. "So, when is Miles coming to get you anyway?"

"Er," I said, checking the time. "Around 20 minutes." I confirmed.

"Great," she replied, "Noah can go and shower while you and I chat."

"Ah, so I'm being sent away, am I?" he asked.

"Yep, glad you understand, it's girl talk time." Cassie said

"But I'm usually allowed to be involved in girl talk time," he complained.

"Not when you have a competitor in the race, you could use it to help Tate, I can't have that." Cassie explained.

"Hey," he defended, "Tate doesn't need an inside scoop, he's great on his own."

"Well, do you want to date him?" Cassie questioned.

Noah paused as if considering his options.

"Na, I'm pretty happy with what I have thanks." he said before kissing her again.

"Aww love you," Cassie replied, going all gushy, "now go away, it's still girl talk time."

"Fine, I'm gone." he surrendered and started upstairs and Cassie dragged me to her room and Noah went to sort out stuff for the shower.

"Oh, that's him!" I informed Cassie ten minutes later, just as I heard Noah leave the bathroom.

"Yay, okay let's go." she said and practically dragged me from the room.

"Hey, hold on, I want to meet this guy, see what Tate's competition is." Noah called out.

"Well hurry up then," we called simultaneously. As we started downstairs, I heard a knock on the door.

"Wow he came to greet you, classy," Cassie approved. I went first and opened the door to find Miles standing there in a fitted T-shirt, blue jeans and a pair of boots.

"Hey," I said, stunned by the way he looked, yes he looked good for our dinner date, but somehow seeing him in his casual outfit was even better.
"Hi, how are you?" he asked.
"Good, good. You?"
"A lot better now," he answered. "Oh, er this is for you." he said as he pulled out a single red rose from behind his back. "I wasn't sure if a whole bouquet was slightly overkill on the second date so I thought I'd stick with one."
"Wow this is beautiful, thank you." I replied. I was so transfixed by this simple and beautiful act that I hadn't noticed Noah joining up by the front door until he cleared his throat to make his presence known.
"Hey, I'm Noah," he said in a shockingly deep voice, and I assumed a threatening tactic. Both Cassie and I sent him a questioning look.
"Right, hi, I'm Miles, good to meet you." he said and held out his hand to shake Noah's.
"I'm Cassie's boyfriend." Noah confirmed, shaking his extended hand.
"Ah right, I was wondering as I knew you weren't her brother." Miles said.
"How do you know that?" Cassie chimed in looking rather perplexed.
"Oh er, I saw your brother when I came to pick up Lexi last time, he was watching out of the window."

"Right," was Cassie's response, seeming slightly suspicious.
"Well, we should be going, hot chocolate to drink and everything after all." I said and started to pull Miles up the driveway.
"Yeah, yeah, you guys have fun!" Cassie called while Noah stood behind her, clearly still sizing up Miles. Once we got to his car, he opened the door for me before sliding into the driver's seat.
"Okay why did that feel like meeting your parents." he joked as we drove away.
"You practically did, Cassie's over-protective and Noah has adopted a big brother stance when it comes to dating so you're not far off." I informed him. "That was probably harder than when you meet my actual parents."
"When?" he asked, "You're confident."
"You never know," I replied with a slight smile.
"I hope I didn't mess it up too much." he joked.
"Eh," I replied and laughed at the frightened look on his face as he drove towards the coffee shop.

"So what can I get you?" The barista asked as we approached the counter.
"Hi, I'll take a white americano please," Miles requested, "and? Hot chocolate?" he looked to me for confirmation to which I smiled and nodded.
"Thank you," I said to the barista, and we turned away to find a seat. We managed to secure a couple comfy seats

near the window at the front of the shop, and we each sat down on either side of the table, facing each other.
"So, how are you doing?" he asked me.
"I'm not too bad, how are you?"
"Very good, how 's your hot chocolate?"
"Hey! Don't mock me, you're sitting there with your bitter drink. Truly you're just jealous." I told him.
"Oh come on, I do actually like coffee." He assured me.
"And what do you like about it? The bitterness? The off flavour? You like coffee because it's a grown-up drink."
"No way, I enjoy it." I laughed as I watched him add sugar.
"You enjoy it so you have to make it sweeter?" I questioned.
"Oh, come on," Miles groaned, "that doesn't prove anything people add sugar to a lot of things." he bargained.
"Like what?" I asked and was greeted with complete silence. "Ha exactly."
"Okay look, yes I like a little sugar in my coffee, but I do still like the flavour of coffee, it is nice and not too creamy and sweet."
"But you didn't like it in the first place." I argued.
"Well… no. Okay it did make me feel grown up at first, but now it's just what I like to drink. Come on, why don't you try it?" he said and held his cup towards me.

"Er no," I said, trying to hide my grievance at the drink in front of me, "I'm good with my hot chocolate thank you." and to prove my point I took a sip.
"Please, just try it." He repeated and I paused for a moment.
"Okay, but what will you give me if I do try it?" I asked.
"Well, what do you want from me?" he returned.
"What are you offering?" I teased.
"I have some ideas." he stated and offered his hand
"Fine." I said and grabbed his coffee, raising the mug to my lips to hide the smile on my face. As promised, I took a small timid sip of the coffee.
"Ugh, no thank you." I replied and winced at the taste. Shaking my head I passed back Miles' drink to him.
"Still not a fan I guess." he laughed and I just continued to shake my head. I picked up my hot chocolate to try and remove the taste in my mouth.
"I will certainly stick to my hot chocolate, thank you." I assured him.
"Very well, at least you tried it, which means that I owe you something for your efforts it would seem." he murmured.
"Care to share your ideas?" I said to him, leaning over the table closer towards him.
"Well, what about this?" he whispered and gently placed his fingers under my chin to tilt my face closer to him.
"Hmm?" I murmured, my mouth now mere millimetres from his lips. I shifted the last small space towards him

and our lips had that one gentle touch. His lips grazed against mine and his hand slid from chin to the back of my head and pulled me closer. I let my hands rest on his knees to stop me falling over the table. His hands were soft as they ran through my hair and I felt the smile spread while we kissed. Before things could get too heated, I placed my hand on his chest and pushed him back.
"Wow," he breathed.
"Yep, and as much as I enjoy the reward for my efforts, let's not give the whole coffee house a show now." I teased and leaned back in my seat, picking up my hot chocolate, the hot drinking matching the heat in my cheeks.
"Okay, maybe you have a point." he agreed and followed me by leaning back and grabbing his drink.

We stayed in the coffee shop for a few more hours, me going through three more hot chocolates and Miles having another coffee, he shared some of my hot chocolate too. We managed to talk non-stop for the whole time learning about his family and his life. He was still on the job hunt and getting a little disheartened by it apparent. Covering a few things that we hadn't talked about on the first date, it all just seemed a lot less stressful now.
"Oh crap, I need to get home." I blurted out when I noticed the time.

"Really?" Miles asked, obviously upset.

"Yeah I'm really sorry, it's my parents, they can be a little… strict sometimes and I have some work I need to do, plus I need to pop back to Cassie's first to grab some stuff, but I really would want to stay here if I could." I assured him.

"How about we just continue this tomorrow then?" he asked.

"I would really like that." I said and smiled at him.

"Really?" he questioned.

"Yeah, I mean constant supply of hot chocolate and a cute little shop. Spending a day like this couldn't get much better."

"Oh, is that all?" he asked.

"I guess the company isn't too bad either." I teased.

"Well, what about we forgo the hot chocolate tomorrow and actually do something together instead?" he suggested.

"I hope you're ready for it because I certainly have a competitive streak on my side." I teased.

"Oh, I am definitely ready."

"Let's do it then." I agreed, "pick me up from Cassie's tomorrow?"

"That sounds like a plan." He agreed.

"But now I *really* have to go." I explained.

"Okay," he said, "let's get you home then shall we. I want your parents to like me so I can actually stick to our plans for tomorrow."

"Let's go."

The drive back to Cassie's house was brief, while we were driving Miles reached over and took my hand, only letting go to change gear when he needed to. We pulled up outside the car and I could see Cassie watching me from the living room. I turned to him briefly and gave him another kiss, his hands left the steering wheel and snaked around my waist pulling me closer to him, my arm looped around his neck and the kiss deepened.
"Okay," he breathed against my lips and pulled away slightly, "as much as I really enjoy kissing you, I can see Cassie watching us from her house and I know I will get grilled for it. So I am now going to walk you to the door and then run far away before Cassie can get her claws in."
"Maybe that's a good idea," I agreed. I jumped out of Miles' car, we both walked towards the front door and after a brief goodbye, before Cassie could invade them, he quickly rushed back to his car and drove off.
"Well, he left in a rush," Cassie observed.
"I wonder why…" I joked.

Chapter 11: Jake (one year ago)

 The moment Lexi's lips met mine, I knew things could never be the same. I had fantasised about this moment for longer than I would ever care to admit, and it still felt like a dream. I leant towards her and could feel her move closer to me as the mattress dipped with our weight. I put my hand on her back and pulled her closer to me, she let out a giggle and all her resolve vanished as she lifted herself and slipped into my lap. I pulled my mouth away from hers slightly.
"That was better than I ever imagined." I stated.
"Hmm?" *her eyes hardly opening, her hands sliding underneath the collar of my t-shirt, they felt cold against my back and I could feel a shiver creeping down my spine.* "What was that?" *she asked again, sounding slightly dazed.*
"Doesn't matter." *I murmured against her lips and I pulled her back closer to me, I could feel her chest pressed against mine and my hands snaked from around*

her waist to hold her thighs lifting her closer. Her hands move over my body and it felt as if it was on fire, but if this were how I would die then I would happily go burning. As long as I could take Lexi with me.
"Wait," she said, panting, "wait, maybe this isn't a good idea."
"Come here," I replied, reaching for the side of her face and trying to capture her lips again.
"No, Jake, wait a second," she said again, pulling my hand away and sliding off my lap. I shivered with the sudden absence of her warmth.
"What?" I mumbled, leaning towards her as she sat next to me, I leaned over and planted soft kisses along her neck and earned a groan that I felt rather than heard.
"What are you doing?" she asked, no longer trying to pull away as her hands found themselves in my hair, tugging at the strands.
"I'm kissing you," I replied, "what does it look like I'm doing?"
"Well, I can see that thank you," she answered, "but I'm asking why you're doing it? Why now?"
"Why not?" was all I could say, it was all I could think really. Why not? Why had I not been doing this for much longer? Why had this taken me so long? Why would I ever stop now?
But as she said it, I realised I had been thinking the same thing, I don't know why I had chosen tonight to suddenly do something. When I had seen her in the car coming to

get me, something in me had changed and I couldn't hold off any longer. I feared Cassie would go crazy if she ever found out, but I didn't care anymore. Lexi had been my rock over the summer, my air supply. I was dizzy around her, but I'd suffocate without her.

"Jake, that's not an answer, what about Cassie?"

"What about her?" I asked and managed to catch her lips in a deliciously slow kiss.

"She would be so mad." Lexi answered as she pulled away.

"I don't want to talk about my sister at this exact moment." I replied with my mouth against her throat.

"We shouldn't be doing this." she whispered but as I moved my face and her lips now hovering over mine, I could tell she was trying to fight it just as much as I was.

"We should."

"You're drunk," she reasoned.

"Not anymore!" I protested, but by the look on her face I could tell she didn't believe me at all, couldn't blame her really.

"Uh huh." she replied, clearly not convinced.

"Okay, yes I was earlier, but I sobered up, all of my focus is on you now, I promise." I saw the look on her face and could tell she was still unsure, so I did the only thing I could really think of doing, the only thing that I knew would show her how much I meant it.

"Please, come here sweetheart, I don't think I can stand not kissing you anymore."

"Jake…"

I pulled her back to me and showed her exactly how I was feeling, a growl rumbled in the back of my throat and that confirmed how much I wanted her. She seemed to have a renewed sense of excitement after that, and both of us forget any reason why we shouldn't spend the rest of our lives in each other's arms.

Chapter 12: Jake

"So, what do you do?" I asked Millie, as the waiter walked away with our dessert order, well my dessert order and Millie's coffee order. I couldn't stop thinking of Lexi, the fact that she hates coffee and definitely would have picked the chocolate brownie instead, possibly even shared one with me. Although I know she would have ended up eating most of it and I would have happily let her.
The date had gone surprisingly well, we enjoyed our dinners, Millie getting a cocktail with her dinner.
"I'm in recruitment."
"Ah right," I replied, "so what does that mean *specifically*?"
"Oh all sorts, but essentially I help find and select new team members that I think would be a good fit for the company, and I work with a range of companies. Anyone looking to hire really." she explained.

It has been really easy really, I was unsure about how things were going to go when I went to pick her up earlier. But it improved once we arrived at the restaurant, and she *did* seem like a really nice girl, I guess.
"Wow so you've got to show them that you're the best company to get into business then right?"
"Yep," she confirmed, "it can get pretty competitive with the top employees, so it's got to be efficient."
"Must take a lot of persuasion."
"I think you'll find I can be *very* persuasive." she winked.
It was at that moment the dessert arrived.
"Wow that looks amazing," she said as my dessert arrived at the table. I had gone with the strawberry cheesecake, desperate for some sugar but not too much.
"Oh yeah," I commented, "it's delicious."
"Makes me wish I had gotten something now." she urged.
It was clear that she was fishing for some and wanted to share. The moral debate in my head was brief but intense.
"Well, do you want some?" I asked through gritted teeth.
"Oh well only if you're offering." she giggled and reached over to steal a bite of the food, the grasp on my fork tightened.
"No problem," I replied as she reached over for another spoonful of cheesecake. It wasn't long after dessert, her eating the majority, that I asked for the bill and we left. The way home was spent with Millie doing most of the talking, I claimed I was just tired.

"So here we are." I said as I pulled up in front of her house.
"Well thank you, thanks for such a good date," she said and slowly leant towards me.
"No problem, it was a good time." I agreed, I could tell she was leaning in for a kiss, I moved towards her. She seemed to smile against me and was about to deepen the kiss but I pulled away before it could become heated.
"Er sorry, I need to get home," I tried to explain, but I could already see that she had been hurt by my hesitation.
"Oh yeah right, I guess I should get inside too."
"Hey," I said and grabbed her arm stopping her before she could get out of the car.
"What?"
"I'm sorry, maybe we could do this again? Soon?" I asked her.
"Uh, maybe." she said, sounding quite non-committal.
I knew I needed to get Lexi out of my mind and I hoped Millie would want another date. Before she could pull away again I gave her another kiss on the cheek, hoping to convince her that I wanted the second date.
"Good night Jake." she said.
"Night," I replied and watched her as she headed towards her house. Once I saw that she was safe inside, I pulled away and started home.

I was relieved when I arrived home, scanned the driveway and noticed that Lexi's car wasn't there and that

I wouldn't have to see her. But my mind wandered somewhere else and a lump formed in my throat at the realisation that she was probably out with that dumb guy again doing God knows what, my revulsion at the thought kicked in before I could fight it. The idea of Lexi out with that guy, frankly the idea of her out with any guy, filled me from revulsion to rage. I felt so deranged when I was around her and the feeling was only amplified when she was gone. I had been outrageously optimistic to think that the date with Millie was going to change that in any way. I pulled into the empty driveway- my parents must have gone out- and started for the house.

The only noise I heard when I entered was the calm chatter from Cassie's room of her and Noah, clearly spending their evening inside. I headed straight to my room and immediately collapsed onto my bed. That date had taken a lot more energy than I had been expecting and it made me realise why I had been so opposed to dating for so long. I quickly pulled off my jeans and top and laid down, sleep couldn't arrive quick enough.

I was woken up to the disgustingly bright sunlight shining through my windows due to my idiocy in not closing the curtains last night. I rolled over to grab my phone and noticed a message from Millie and then another on the group chat asking how my date had gone. I opened Millie's first.

Millie: Hey, still up for a repeat of yesterday?

Jake: Yeah, sounds good.

Millie: How about tonight?

Jake: I'm really sorry but I have work and a family thing tonight.

Millie: right.

Jake: how about tomorrow night?

Millie: Okay, looking forward to it.

Jake: Me too :)

Once we had arranged what we were going to do and when, I shut the chat and tapped on the one with my mates. There was already a steady stream of messages from them, 90% of them were speculating about what had happened on my date.

Jake: guys, everyone calm down. The date was good and we're going out again tomorrow night okay?

Michael: yes man, that is great

James: yeah, way to go

Michael: What about after the date?

Jake: Like I would actually tell you, but all you need to know was that the date went well.

I thought I would let them simmer with that one for a bit. I locked my phone, leaving it on my bed and then heading downstairs for some breakfast. While walking downstairs I could hear Cassie and mum.
"You know how they can be mum," Cassie started. I crept down trying to hear what they were discussing.
"But she looked terrible when she left yesterday, I'm really worried." I immediately snapped to focus when I realised it was Lexi they were talking about.
"I know, she's been acting a little off for a few days." Cassie worried.
"She's been around here a lot too, now I love having her here, but I want to know her parents are okay with her being out so much." mum said.
"Honestly, I don't think they even care." Cassie confessed.
"Oh honey, they're parents, of course they care."
"Well if they do, they have a weird way of showing it." Cassie mumbled.

"Sweetie, all families are different." Mum seemed to reason.

"Mum, they're barely even home! If Lexi isn't here, usually she's at home on her own, when she left yesterday, it was the first time she had seen them in ages! How can you say they care about her when they treat her this way?"

"They provide for her and they do what they can." My mum reasoned.

"But surely there's more to it than just providing for her? What kind of life is that if there's no love?"

Hearing about the neglect that Lexi had to endure just made my heart swell with upset and anger. How could they treat her like such a second-class citizen?!

"Well…" mum started, but she paused, "Jake?" she called out. Damn, she must have heard the stairs. For a minute I debated pretending I wasn't there.

"Yeah?" I called and continued downstairs, hoping to play it off like I hadn't been listening.

"Morning darling," she said and smiled as I turned the corner and came into view.

"Just came down for some coffee." I announced.

"Here you go love," she said as she poured a cup from the pot for me and handed it over.

"Thank you," I said and headed to the fridge to grab the milk.

"Are you working today?" Cassie asked.

"Unfortunately," I confirmed with a nod, "day off tomorrow though."
"Well that's good sweetie," mum commented, "what about this evening?"
"What about it?" I asked.
"Are you around?"
"Err, possibly?" I questioned trying to not confirm yet to see what she was going to ask.
"Well, can you be free? I want us to spend time as a family."
"Oh, right well I do have quite a bit of work to do…" I started but as I saw the disappointment in her face I stopped. "Yeah, sounds good mum."
"How wonderful! So, Cassie you're around too?"
"Mmhmm," she confirmed while taking a sip of coffee.
"And of course Noah is coming?" she asked to which Cassie nodded again. "Good, good. And what about Lexi?" mum asked.
"Lexi?" I interrupted before Cassie had answered.
"Yes Jake, my best friend. The girl that is around all the time. The girl that mum and dad practically adopted because her parents never show up-" Cassie answered.
"That's enough with the dramatics Cassie." Mum interrupted. I saw Cassie roll her eyes and continued.
"But she isn't family, I thought this was a family evening." I said.
"Hey, she is practically family, she's like a sister." Cassie protested.

"She definitely isn't my sister; I have two and she is not one of them." I insisted.

"Come on Jake, you know what Cassie means, Lexi is here all the time."

"Oh, I know she is." I muttered.

"What is your problem? Why are you being such a jerk?" Cassie complained.

"I just don't see why she needs to join us."

"Okay, Jake. I know work has been stressful, but Lexi could do with some support now and she is coming, so wherever this is coming from, it needs to stop now."

"Fine, I've got work so I'll see you later." I sighed and headed upstairs to work. I knew I was being ridiculous, but I hated when people equated Lexi to family. She just *couldn't* be my sister.

I got to my room and shut the door before settling at my desk and laying into the work that had accumulated. In no time I had reached a steady rhythm and begun laying into all of the emails from last night and this morning. I checked the clock and noticed it was the afternoon. I commended myself for the amount of work I had done and pushed away from my desk to take a break. Reaching my arms to stretch out my back, I knew I was getting old by the number of times my back cracked when I stretched. As I leant back, I glanced out the window and an overwhelming feeling of irritation engulfed me…

That absolute tool was here again! I know Lexi was getting picked up from here because of how her parents would be if they knew she was going out with a guy they didn't know. But did they really need to stand there and completely fawn over each other right outside the house? I mean there was a limit, right? Maybe I should say something, that was certainly something that Bradley and Hailey didn't need to see, they were too young!

She had been dropped off here again last night after her date before heading back home to see her parents and he clearly picked her up again from here this morning too. Maybe that is what had spurred on the conversation between mum and Cas this morning. I could see them loitering in his car on the road. She was laughing. Why was she laughing? What the hell could he have said to make her laugh so much. *That should be me making her smile like that.*

She wandered away as he watched and as far as I was concerned, his eyes should have been shut permanently or removed from his head after the way he looked at her. Jesus. I mean it was just so rude of him, to look at her like that, disgusting. This had been like the third date they had been on now in a week, slight overkill if you asked me, they didn't even know each other!
Trying to subdue my irritation I got back to work and continued to work for as long as I could. Unfortunately, I

was a people pleaser and it was never something I would refuse as I knew I needed as much support as I could get. I knew that mum didn't mention the time for us tonight, but it would usually be around 5pm and as it was only 2pm so I still had a few hours before that. I could feel my hunger, so I started downstairs to grab some food and maybe another coffee to help me get through the rest of my work. I started downstairs and could hear them talking in the kitchen.

"So how did it go?" Cassie asked.

"Well, we went for a game of mini golf," Lexi laughed, "he was so sweet because he pretended to let me win at first."

"Oh, I bet that didn't go down well." Cassie commented and I couldn't help but laugh. Anyone that knew Lexi knew that she would rather lose than have someone let her win. She'd be in a bad mood either way, but she always would rather lose honestly that a cheating win. It was one of the things I admired about her.

"Yeah exactly, so as soon as I told him off for it, we played a normal game." She replied.

"Of course, and who won?" Cassie teased. I already knew that she had won, it was obvious, I could tell by her mood.

"He did actually." She laughed. That caught me off guard, usually whenever she lost, she would go into a proper rage. Lexi wasn't one that was happy to lose.

"Okay, so why are you in such a good mood if you lost?" Cassie asked, clearly on the same level of confusion as I am.

"It was quite sweet actually; he promised to get me hot chocolate after and invited me over to his place for a drink."

"Oh, come on!" I blurted out and then cursed myself for it. I had completely given myself away and now I either had to confess or create an excuse.

"Jake?" Cassie called out, "are you listening to us? Ew!" I ignored her and stormed in.

"You can't actually get swept away by that line? I mean come on." I said.

"What do you mean 'that line'?" Lexi asked incredulously.

"That guy is just playing you, trying to get in your good books and get you to his place, and I think we all know what for."

"Well, it's working," she replied with a smile floating over her face.

"Wow I thought more of you Lexi, I didn't think you would get so swept up with that. You shouldn't settle for that." *When I could give you more* was what I left out.

"You know what Jake, I was in a good mood after my date and now you've just managed to put a downer on it and make me feel bad. Screw you!"

"It's better that you know the truth." I replied. "Guys can be jerks."

"Yes, they can." Lexi agreed, "but in this case it isn't Miles being the jerk, it's you." She said and with that she got up and started to walk out of the kitchen.

"Lexi please, don't be like that. Jake was being an idiot." Cassie explained and shoved me, clearly attempting to get me to apologise but I was steadfast on my opinion.

"Yeah he was being an idiot, but that's how he always is. Always mean what you say don't you Jake?" she said looking at me with a pointed glance and I know she was thinking about last year.

"Yes, I guess I do." I muttered.

"Look Cassie, I need to get home and see my parents before they head off on business again. I'll talk to you later." Lexi said.

"Wait, what about family night?" Cassie asked.

"I'll see how I feel." She said and quickly left. I heard the door slam shut and my heart sank. I knew I had broken her, but I couldn't help it.

"Jake, I can't believe you!" Cassie yelled after the door had shut, "why the hell would you say that to her?"

"Well, it's true, he's using her and she should get out before it gets too deep." I hoped that sounded convincing and not just because seeing her with any other man was driving me mad.

"Get over yourself Jake, not everyone is a douche like you when it comes to girls." and with that she stormed upstairs.

Chapter 13: Lexi

I didn't want to go home. But I couldn't go back to Cassie's house either. After what Jake had said I didn't want to be near him. I don't understand how he could say those things about Miles, seeing how he treated me last summer and the way he messed me around. It's really rich coming from him. Oh, how that boy enraged me.
I decided to wander around the local duck pond for a short while just to clear my head before going home. It was rare for my parents to ask me questions to do with anything other than uni at this point, but I couldn't arrive home seeming distracted, they would pick up on it immediately and be annoyed at me. Accusing me of doing something wrong and attacking me for it, often blaming things on me that were far out of my control. There was a quaint cafe by the pond where I grabbed a hot chocolate before heading to a bench beside the pond. I had always loved coming here just to think, I had been

here a lot last summer when everything had happened with Jake and Cassie's parents.

I knew they needed me to be strong, so I needed somewhere to go to let my feelings out, this place had been perfect. The ducks had never seemed to judge me. I used to go round their house constantly last year, not to see Cassie, but to help with anything I could. Jake took on a lot of responsibility with his family and I knew he needed help so I would take Hailey to the shops and go swimming and anything else that I could think of to distract her. When her and Bradley didn't need me, I was either helping Jake or just keeping things up around the house.

But as I brought myself back to the present, my thoughts had begun running wild, things with Miles had been incredible. But every time I saw Jake, my mind was torn back to our times spent together last summer, the moments we had shared while Cassie had been away. The nights spent talking on the sofa in front of the fire when Hailey and Bradley had gone to sleep, the afternoons spent with Hailey and Bradley taking them out and the mornings spent having breakfast with the family, a sense of normality. I had craved the sense of family that Cassie and Jake had always had and I always loved being around them, feeling like family.

I did like Miles, I really did, but there was something about Jake and being with him and I couldn't shake it. I had tried, desperately, but I had never been able to let go of that. Maybe I didn't want to anymore...

As I sat there, I was so confused of how I was feeling, I had literally just had an argument with Jake and here I was considering ending things with such a sweet guy. Miles had done nothing wrong at all, but I guess with the right person things don't need to be wrong with someone else for you to realise that you want to be with them. Maybe that was just the thing with people, they have a place in your heart and you just can't let them go. Realising that I was just going round in circles and I was solving nothing sitting here, I decided I couldn't put off the inevitable any longer and started the fated walk home. Both of my parents had been home for around three days now, which recently was a record, both of them were never usually around for long and would often be in their offices when they were home. That is why I was met with a shocking surprise when I walked inside and saw both of them sitting in the kitchen at the dining table. Given they were both there on their own phones and an espresso sat in front of them, clearly just taking a break from work for a short while. I walked in rather timidly and tried to sneak upstairs before being dragged into a conversation with them.
"Alexis." My mother beckoned coldly.
"Hello mother, how are you?" I asked curtly.
"Your father and I are well, thank you." she replied.

"Great, well I'll be upstairs." I told her and turned on my heels.
"No. I don't think you will be." My father interrupted.
"Huh." I asked.
"I have just gained access to your grades from this past year and if you think that is acceptable then you are sorely mistaken." he continued.
"Wait, what are you talking about?" I asked them.
"Alexis, you received 70% over the past term." my mother informed me.
"Yes I am well aware of what I received, I am the one studying the law degree trying to pass my work."
"It is just not acceptable." my dad explained, "you should not be getting anything less than 90% and if you are then maybe we need to reevaluate the way you are spending your time outside of university."
"What are you talking about?" I asked, "I'm doing well! Do you know how hard my degree is and how challenging law can be? I am trying my best."
"Well clearly your best simply is not good enough." My mother snapped.
"Hey, I am doing all I can while trying to keep up with everything else in my life." I tried to reason.
"Well clearly the other things in your life are taking a higher priority to your degree and we simply can't have that-" my father started.
"Oh, come on." I muttered.

"DON'T YOU DARE INTERRUPT ME." He yelled as he stood and slammed his hand down upon the table, the coffee cups spilling their contents slightly. I took a step back. He pushed his chair away from the table and both nearly tipped over, he walked around until he stood right in front of me, his face mere centimetres from mine.

"I better see AT LEAST 90% in your final grade or I will be doing something about it." he claimed and stormed out of the kitchen. I was frozen in place and was unable to move, I was so scared of doing the wrong thing that I thought it would be best just to do nothing at all than to risk making any mistake at this point. With a sigh my mother rose from her place at the table too and came over to me where I still stood, completely stunned.

"I really hate the way you make him so angry Alexis, if only you could do what we ask, then he wouldn't get so annoyed. He is only trying to do what is best for you. Please try not to aggravate him Alexis. We do not ask for much." My mother said and walked out of the kitchen too.

With a few deep breaths I calmed myself and kept the tears burning my eyes at bay. I went along to clean up the spilt coffee on the table and washed up their cups before drying them and putting them away. I slowly made my way to my room, making sure to not disturb my parents in their respective offices. I rushed inside and softly shut the door behind me before quietly putting on my TV and climbing into bed. I curled up on my side and finally let the tears flow.

I was awoken by a soft tap on my door and my dad walking into my room. I quickly sat up and drew my knees into my chest.

"Hello," he says. He has clearly calmed down and gestures to the edge of my bed, I nodded slightly. I don't say anything.

"I am sorry about yelling at you, and I am sorry for the way I treated you." He starts. "I just want to help you, and you know how upsetting it is when you go against what we have planned for you."

"It's okay." I muttered.

"It will never happen again, I promise," he said to me. I nodded again, "Look your mother is sorting dinner, it will be ready in ten minutes, how about you get cleaned up and join us." I nodded once again and a look of irritation flew over his face. He paused for a moment as if he was about to say something else, but the look was gone as soon as it arrived and he stood. He walked out of my room and left the door wide open; it always annoyed me. I heard his footsteps retreat back downstairs and let out a sigh of relief. He always said that he was sorry, he always said that it would never happen again, and he ended up screaming in my face once again. All the time. God, I hated being at home.

After everything happened with my parents, I knew there would be no way for me to get out and go to Cassie's house for their family night. I was desperately jealous at the idea of them sitting there together playing board games with the music on in the background and all of them laughing together. I craved to be there with them, feeling light and happy, knowing I was cared for and appreciated. Instead of being stuck in this house, scared to step out of line, to say or do the wrong thing. There's nothing I can do until I escape this place.

Once I composed myself and made sure that my parents wouldn't be mad at me for how I looked then started downstairs to endure the painful meal I was about to suffer through. Dinner passed in the strained silence that it usually did. Mother had made an insufferably plain meal full of the latest health kick she was into, this time it was quinoa and some other roots and plants that I didn't even recognise. Seasoning was not something my parents knew about either.

The simple clinking of cutlery and the sporadic work questions that my parents asked each other were the only tool used to slice through the silence. As soon as I had choked down as much of the plain dish that I could, my parents' conversation turned to me discussing how I was intending to improve my university results.

"Well, is there any additional help we can get her?" My mother asked my father.

"And show other people that she needs the help? No, she got herself into this mess, she can get herself out of it." My father replied.

"What about a private tutor? They can come to the house and no one needs to know that she is failing." my mother suggested. I was so tempted to turn to them and say that I was regularly getting 75-80% on my exams, I didn't understand how that made me a failure but I knew that it would just result in me getting yelled at. My parents had always believed that anything below the best was a failure and they saw me not being at the top of my class as a failure. Me? I was just glad that I was still getting through uni, but here we are.

"No absolutely not, there are very influential people around this part of town, if they find out then it'll be an embarrassment." my dad responded, disgusted at the idea of my needing him.

"Gee thanks, I love being an embarrassment." I muttered; my mother shot me a withered glare at my comment.

"What was that?" My father asked.

"Nothing." I mumbled, scared for him to lose it again.

"Yes exactly, nothing." he agreed and turned back to my mother. "You are right, she needs to do something. This is just unacceptable. We never had these issues. Why can't you follow our example, is it so hard?" He questioned while my mother just sat there and nodded then turned to me.

"Alexis, you have this summer to prove to us that you can improve your grades when you go back to university in the autumn. If you are unable to do that then we will stop supporting you."
"What?!" I yelled, shocked.
"Yes, we will not be wasting any more money on your education there if you cannot turn it around. You have only done the first year, you can improve it or you can find something else to do with your life."
"But mum-" I started.
"That is final." my father said and stood from the table, pushing back his chair and leaving the dining room.
"Please Alexis, just be better, why do you keep disappointing us and making your father angry. Do we really ask that much?" I opened my mouth to reply but I could tell by her face that it was rhetorical. She soon followed my father out of the kitchen and I was left standing on my own once again. I started my regular routine of cleaning up after dinner and placing everything in the dishwasher before walking to my room and taking up my old spot on my bed curled up in a ball. I didn't bother changing, and I closed my eyes, wishing for this day to be over and counting down the hours to when they would be leaving again for another business trip.

I woke the next morning with mascara smudges under my eyes and my clothes wrinkled. I turned over and grabbed my phone to see seven messages from Cassie asking if I was okay. She had asked if I was coming over last night for the family night, then the last one just hoped if I was okay and to call her. I refrained from telling Cassie everything, I could deal with this on my own and I would. I told her I was fine, apologised for missing family night yesterday and that I would maybe be over later. Once I had replied to Cassie, I then checked Miles' message and saw that he was asking when I wanted to go out again. I swiped off the chat before I could answer, not knowing what I wanted to say. Then I saw that I still have one more message. I had deleted his contact after last summer so I was never tempted to call him, but I still knew it was his number. All it said was:

Unknown: Sorry.

Jake. I was surprised I got an apology from him. After last summer I had told him I was tired of his apologies for the way he treated me and if he meant it at all then why couldn't he just stop doing it in the first place. But in all honesty, I was annoyed that the apology was even needed. I had deleted his messages and contact from my phone last summer, after everything had happened, desperate to erase any existence of him. I knew the message was from him as soon as I saw it, unfortunately my ridiculous teenage mind had memorised his number and part of me had always clung onto it.

I locked my phone and didn't answer him either, it was too much. I needed to work out what I wanted to do and I needed some space to do that.

Chapter 14: Jake

I messed up with Lexi, I texted her last night after everything that had happened and I didn't even get a response from her. I knew she was tired of my apologies, she had told me that much last summer, but I couldn't help it. I knew how much I had hurt her but I also knew that I couldn't talk to her in person, so what else was I to do? Just seeing her with someone else drove me mad. I wasn't going to bombard her, she needed her space, but every bone in my body was protesting. To get my mind off of things I grabbed my phone and messaged Millie.

Jake: So, are you still up for our date tonight?

Millie: wow I was waiting for you to message, yes definitely, what were you thinking about?

Jake: Well, how about we do something? We could go for a walk. And then there's this secret movie theatre happening in town too.

           Millie: Ugh not sat in a room for hours in the dark.

Jake: Right. Any suggestions?

           Millie: Let's go and get a drink.

Jake: Okay sure, I'll come and get you at 8pm

           Millie: Cool

I rolled my eyes, I loved the cinema and loved going to the underground cinemas but clearly that was not her idea of a good time. Lexi had always loved it, last summer we used to take Bradley and Haley there all the time. They loved it too. We used to make it seem like a sort of secret and they felt so special. But I knew I couldn't compare them; this was a new thing and I had to give her a chance. I got up and got dressed before heading downstairs for a cup of coffee.
"Morning," mum said to me as I walked into the kitchen.
"Hi mum," I said between my yawns.

"How are you?" she asked. But before I could answer Cassie walked in and rolled her eyes. She walked past me and grabbed her own coffee.

"What is with you two today?" My mum asked me.

"Why don't you ask *him*." Cassie muttered. My mum looked at me expectantly and I had no other choice but to explain.

"Okay well that is… something. Look Jake you need to talk to her; Lexi is like family. And I understand why you would be defensive. She's like a sister to you-" my mum started.

"She is not my sister." I growled.

"You need to stop this hostility towards her and you need to make it up to her." she informed me.

"Exactly," Cassie agreed.

"Right. Fine." I said, "I'll be upstairs." I told them and went back to my room. Mum was only doing what she thought was right at the time but she could not have said anything worse at that moment. The constant reminder that Lexi was like family just showed I couldn't feel how I did. Things have only recently gotten back to normal after the whole separation, and here I was causing rifts. It was the weekend and I had no urgent work so I switched on my game and switched off my brain. The morning flew by in record time and I soon decided I needed to get up and move so I changed, grabbed my stuff and headed to the gym.

The gym was always the perfect way for me to clear my mind. Something about pushing all of my energy into weights and running; I knew that being here was the best thing I could do for my mind right now. I had soon been in the gym for nearly 2 hours before my stomach started to disturb me. I decided it was an opportune time for me to head home and get some food.
"Hi," I called when I got in.
"Afternoon darling," mum called from the lounge. "How was the gym?" she asked. I walked in and noticed that she was watching TV and relaxing with my dad who only greeted me with a small grunt of acknowledgement. I glanced over to see what was playing.
"Yeah, yeah it was good." I told her. "Oh, and I messaged Lexi." I informed her.
"Yes, Cassie told me, thank you for that." she replied, "she's on her way over." My head snapped away from the TV.
"She's what?" I asked.
"She's coming over, honestly Jake, why are you being so odd?" She questioned, clearly concerned by my reaction.
"No, nothing." I assured her with a smile, "I'm just going to grab some food, I haven't had a chance to eat yet."
"Okay well there are some cookies in the kitchen, you're welcome to help yourself." she told me.
"Thank you," I replied and walked out, heading to the kitchen.

I made myself a sandwich, grabbed an apple with a plate of cookies and settled down at the table. I was digging into my sandwich when I heard the door open.

"Oh, wow that smells amazing, what is it?" Lexi asked as she appeared in the doorway of the kitchen. I glanced at her and I saw her face slightly falter before she quickly recovered.

"Mhm, Mum's been cooking," I told her as I sat at the table with the full plate of cookies and just finished off my sandwich. I stood and went to her as she walked into the kitchen before Cassie entered the room.

"Hey, I know I messaged, but I wanted to say in person too that I am really sorry." I said to her in a hushed voice just in case Cassie heard me. I stood so close to her that I was almost unable to focus.

"It's okay. I know you meant well. Plus, it did make me think." she told me and I immediately started to wonder what that meant. What had she been thinking about?

"I am *very* sorry." I told her.

"Hey," She whispered, "you remember what I said last year about your apologies." she said with a weak smile. And before I could say anything else Cassie walked into the kitchen.

"What did she cook?" Cassie asked as she came and sat down at the table opposite me, reaching across and stealing some from the plate on the table, "ah her chocolate cookies I love these!"

"Oh yeah me too," Lexi chimed in, "for a minute I was worried they were her oat and raisin cookies." she said with a disgusted face.
"What are you doing?" Cassie asked.
"I went to the gym-" I started
"Not you," She interrupted, "her." she said with a nod to Lexi still in the kitchen banging through the cupboards.
"I'm getting a plate of cookies to eat." she explained as if it was the most obvious thing ever.
"Uh, there's a plate right here." Cassie said from the table.
"HA!" Lexi exclaimed, "you may not care about your life, but I know how Jake is with his food, there is no way I am risking my life when there are plenty of cookies here thank you. Me stealing the pizza was as far as I would have gone. And that was only because I would do anything for pizza."
"Wise choice," I mumbled with a face full of cookies. I was shocked that she remembered, I had always been possessive of my food. Mainly because Cassie was notorious for stealing food, I used to get so mad at her for it. Lexi was really making it difficult for me not to think about her all the time. She was driving me crazy and I couldn't stand it. She settled down at the table next to me with the cookies she had grabbed and tucked into them.
"So, what are you doing today?" Cassie asked me, "besides just scoffing cookies."

"Ha, ha, funny." I told her, "No I've just been to the gym, I did try to tell you and you just interrupted me. I'm going out later."

"No way. Do you and your friends actually go out?" Cassie teased.

"Yes, we do," I told her and rolled my eyes, "but if you must know, I'm not meeting up with the guys tonight."

"Oh really?" she asked, "So who is it?"

"It's a date actually," I confessed, "with someone you don't know before you ask." Cassie tutted. "Well, that's boring."

"Who? Who is she?" Lexi asked. I had almost forgotten that she was there. Almost. I turned my head towards her and her eyes met mine for the sweetest of moments before dropping back to the plate of cookies too quickly for me to confirm my suspicions. Even if my heart did swell at the idea of her jealousy.

"Oh, she is just a friend of a friend." I replied, "Michael set me up with her because he thought I had been too focused on work and it has been so long since I went on a date."

"Right," she said, not even looking up from the plate to look at me.

"Ooo well we won't hold you up any longer, will we Lexi?" Cassie prompted and started out of the kitchen. She seemed hesitant as she rose and looked over, I was so tempted to pull her down onto my lap, trap her with my arms and beg her to stay with me. But I knew I couldn't

so instead I just let her stand up and walk out of the kitchen.
"Have fun on your date." she sounded almost defeated. I saw her eyes once more and the sorrow almost blew me away.

I finished all my food and started upstairs to get ready for tonight. I knew I needed a shower after the gym and needed to change. An hour later I was just finishing styling my hair when my phone buzzed on my desk.

Millie: Hi Jake, sorry, can't make it tonight, something came up.

Jake: Oh no problem, we can reschedule.

Millie: Okay, see ya later.

Jake: :)

There go my plans for tonight it seems, I said and with a sigh I changed into joggers. I sat back down at my desk switching on my computer and at that moment my phone chimed again.

Michael: Yo, I heard Millie cancelled.

Jake: yeah, it's annoying.

Michael: Are you hopping on the game?

I sent him a thumbs up and grabbed my headset. This wasn't the plan but at least it was something.
"Hey guys," I said as I logged in.
"Hey man, you okay?" Michael asked.
"Yeah, yeah I'm good. It was only a cancelled date." I replied.
"Wait Millie cancelled on you?" Bradley asked.
"Yep. like an hour before I was meant to go and get her." I admitted.
"That sucks," he observed.
"You don't say," I chuckled. "You know I wasn't actually bothered about the bluntness of her cancelling; it had only been a little while with her and I wasn't sure about how things were with her anyway."
"Yeah that doesn't sound great." Michael observed.
"So, what are you going to do?" Bradley asked.
"Well. nothing." I told them, "It isn't working out so that it is that."
"Okay well who else is on the radar for you?" he then asked.
"No one…" I told them.
"Oh what about Lexi?" Michael asked.
"W- What. No, not Lexi." I stuttered.
"Oh yeah I forgot she's like a sister, right?" He replied.

"No, she isn't." I growled. "But no, it will not work with her."
"Right." Michael said, sounding disbelieving.
"Honestly, with the stress of work and just being able to enjoy my life, I can't see letting anyone else in my life and having enough time with them to make it worth it. I just can't at the moment." I admitted.
"Yeah, that's fair man, if that's how you're feeling, I don't blame you." Michael replied. "Now come on, are we going to play properly?" he asked.
The next four hours were filled with the occasional noise, instruction or profanity and it was perfect. Yes, I should probably be doing work more than playing with my friends and gaming right now but this was exactly what I needed. However, the calming noise of the guns and the shouting was interrupted by the harsh scream of the doorbell. I glanced outside and noticed the day had gone dark and I realised how long I had been sitting there for.
"Can someone get that?!" I called the rest of the house but received no response. "Hello! Anyone getting the door?" Still I was met with silence throughout the house. Under the assumption that in the past four hours everyone had magically disappeared I sighed, stood and went to see who was at the door. To my surprise I was greeted by Lexi. She stood there shivering, with her mascara running down her face and her eyes red and puffy.
"Damn, Lexi what's going on?" I asked her, now panicked. "I- I thought you were with Cassie?"

"Wait why are you here, I thought you had a date." she observed.
"Doesn't matter. What's wrong?" I asked her again.
"Is Cassie here?" she asked, I could see her lips quivered and her voice was trembling as she spoke as if she was about to start crying again.
"Lex please, are you okay?" I asked again, noticing how her eyes were darting around and she was trying to wipe her mascara away from her eyes.
"Jake. I need Cassie. Is she here?" She asked, her voice now seeming bolder now.
"No, no she's not. I'm not sure where she's gone but I haven't seen her since you two left the kitchen earlier." I informed her.
"Damn, she's out with Noah, I forgot all about that. So stupid." she said, whacking her head, seeming to be speaking to herself more than me. I lurched out and grabbed her arm to stop her and pulled her over the threshold of the house.
"Woah, it's okay, Lexi, stop." I pleaded as she continued to try and harm herself, in the end I wrapped my arms around her and pulled her close to me so that her arms were trapped between the two of us. She tried to push me away, fighting any comfort I could give her.
"I hate him! I hate him!" She thumped my chest punching and hitting.
"I know, shhh, I know."

"I hate them." She repeated over and over again. Her punches became weaker and soon she slumped against me, trusting me to keep her upright. I tightened my embrace and she could no longer control herself, she broke down in my arms.

"Why am I not enough?" she sobbed, "why can they never just accept me? I try my best and still they hate me." she choked out between tears.

"Okay, okay. It's okay. Come on, shhh." I tried to calm her and sooth her.

"I'm sorry, I shouldn't be here, I should go," she said and tried to pull away from my arms.

"Don't. You. Dare." I told her and pulled her closer to me once more. "Come on, let's get you inside."

Chapter 15: Lexi

Jake guided me inside and shut the door, I started to calm myself knowing I was safer now, this house always had that effect on me. After everything had happened with my parents this was the first place I thought of coming to, my feet had taken me here before I could even think about the fact that Cassie wouldn't be here. I just knew I needed to get out of my house and there was nowhere else to go, nowhere else that felt safe. I knew it was a mistake as soon as Jake opened the door, just the sight of him. His relaxed look in his joggers and the way his hair was in chaos from where he had evidently had his headphones on. I knew his protective side would be too overpowering and as soon as he saw me in tears he wouldn't let me leave. Sure, he could be an ass sometimes but when it came down to it, he would walk through fire to help those he cared about.

He ushered me straight upstairs, moving towards his room instead of Cassie's. I had only been here once before and that was last summer, but I remembered every tiny detail. He still had all of his posters on his wall and that small bookshelf that sat next to his bed full of worn-out books, he hardly read so I knew the ones there were only a few of his favourite sentimental ones. I perched awkwardly on his bed, all of the memories of last time I had sat here were coming back and there was a lot swimming around in my head. The tears had subsided and I could feel the puffiness in my face. I knew I looked atrocious; I wouldn't be surprised if I had a terrible case of panda eye either. But I didn't have the energy to care, Jake wouldn't judge me and mum had done far more damage than some smeared makeup.

"Didn't want to go to the boyfriend about this then huh?" Jake muttered as he sat down beside me. While his protectiveness was the reason, he had brought me inside, I knew that his snide remarks were something he found hard to bite back and that I should have expected this from him.

"He's not my boyfriend." I mumbled, "Won't your girlfriend be annoyed that you have another girl in your room?" I had no energy for annoyance at this point, but if he was going to dish it out then he should expect to receive it right back.

"Right." he replied and I could hear the annoyance in his tone.

"Look my parents have already sat there and attacked me and I don't need it from you too so if you are going to be like that when I'm really not in the mood for it, then I don't want to be around you…" I snapped and started to stand from the bed when I felt Jake's hand wrap around my forearm and turned me back to him. He could feel my annoyance and dropped his arms. I started to walk out, happy for the freedom but in misery at the absence of his warmth, that I was really craving right now.

"I'm sorry I didn't mean that. Please I'm here, just talk to me...please," he said and reached out once again. I pulled back and looked at him, I could see that he had such a sadness in his eyes. With a simple nod, I went and sat back on his bed.

"You've always helped me sweetheart, give me a chance to help you now. Tell me what I can do." he pleaded.

"You don't need to worry about me, I'll be fine. I just needed to get away from home for a while." I told him as I wrapped my arms around myself.

"Why?" he asked, pushing for me to tell him but I remained silent, he continued. "Look Lexi, is this about your dad? I heard Cassie talking to my mum about it." he admitted. With that my head shot up and looked at him questioningly.

"What did you hear?" I hated the idea of the poor little Lexi story floating around.

"Not much. Cassie was annoyed at the way your parents treated you. But they didn't say much specifically that I heard." he admitted, "talk to me Lex."

I paused unsure if I was ready for Jake to see this side of me, the damaged side I didn't show anyone.

"Jake…"

"Sweetheart, you don't always have to be strong. let me be strong for you." He placed his hand tenderly on my face. "Talk to me."

So that's exactly what I did. I explained everything. About my parents, about my pressure at university, about being stuck at home. The way they would yell at me for not doing well enough, not being good enough, how it had been going on since I was at school. The way they would punish me if it wasn't perfect. The anger that my dad would show me. The constant comments about how much of a disappointment I was and the way they would regularly ignore me if I had truly been an embarrassment. I explained how I hate being at home and how they never seem to be there so I am constantly on my own even when I am at home.

To his credit, he sat and listened, he was staring so intently at me as I spoke and I could see his spectrum of emotions. From sympathy for me to anger towards my parents.

"So yeah… that is that." I told him, "My sappy little life."

"Oh Lexi," he choked out, his eyes were full of feeling and I could see him working through everything that I had told him.

"So yeah, I guess that kind of explains why I'm around here all the time." I said desperate to end the awkward silence that had descended.

"Have you ever tried to talk to anyone about it?" He asked me.

"Well, I mentioned it to someone in school when I was younger, but I guess no one believed me when I'm the only one saying it. My parents seem perfect and there are no physical signs of it then there's nothing anyone can really do." I admitted. "That's why I am so thankful for your parents, they saw me upset one day and kept asking. They've never made me feel bad for always being here. I've never told them the full extent of things, but even so, they let me stay here all the time and treat me like family."

"But-" he started.

"Yes, but I am not family Jake, I know." I muttered, "don't worry, you keep reminding me." Honestly, as much as I felt like I needed this boy in my life sometimes, he really did know how to kick me when I'm down. Constant rejection and yet, I'm still here.

"No, Lex you don't understand." he said, grasping my hands and drawing my attention back to him. "You *can't* be family."

"Why not?" I demanded, I was exhausted at this point and I just wanted to feel like I could belong somewhere. "Because…" he started. I waited in silence, not allowing him to get away from it this time. He released one of my hands and brought his hand up to run it through his hair. I sat in expectant silence waiting for whatever excuse he was about to offer. Until it was too much.
"You know what Jake, fine. I am not a part of your family, and as that is the case I guess I'll just-" I started to stand but I was encased by his big arms trapping me and yanking me onto his lap. I had no choice but to wrap my arms around his neck and lean into him.
"Screw this." He looked at me with a face of fear, hope and irritation before slamming his lips onto mine. I was in complete shock for a moment before my body reacted, somehow knowing what to do with no help. It was like coming home.

Last year it had been incredible, but I never thought I would ever be able to kiss those lips again and to be able to sit here and do exactly that was an absolute dream. His arms snaked around me, pulling me tight against his chest, my hands reached for his hair and was gifted with a soft moan from the back of his throat as I tugged on his thick locks. I was falling, I was floating, I was free. His scent invaded every sense while his hands explored my body, reaching down and latching under my thighs to pull me closer and higher so our faces were at the same height. When his tongue greeted mine, I thought I was about to combust, I had never known something this perfect, I had always seen Jake as the protective older brother. As I sat on his lap, any brotherly thoughts of him were the furthest thing from my mind. His movements became frenzied as he grabbed my legs and helped me swing them round so I was now straddling him and I was able to wrap my legs around him to get as close as I could. Before it could go any further he pulled away. I could feel his chuckle as he heard my whine at the distance now between us.

"Now do you see why you can't be family?" he panted.

"Well yeah, I guess, if we were then what just happened there would be pretty illegal." I giggled.

"Not that it would necessarily stop me." he murmured against my lips as he came closer again.

"Okay, now I know that was meant to be romantic. But it was just weird. On so many levels," I replied with a slightly concerned look.

"Umm, yeah not the best line I've ever used. Clearly when it comes to you I just don't think straight." he admitted.

"Now *that* was a good line." I replied. He smiled back at me and leant in for another kiss but I stopped.

"Wait, I can't." I looked at him. "Miles."

"No sweetheart, I'm Jake." he replied.

"Haha yes, classic dad joke, nice." I shot at him. "No, I can't do this to him. I need to end things with him first, he doesn't deserve that."
"But you're not even together though right?" he said, slightly confused and seemingly jealous.
"Well no, not technically, and we're not exclusive either. But as much as I want to, it would feel wrong." I told him, "When I'm with you, I want to only be with you Jake."
"You have no idea how long I have wanted to hear that," he confessed.
"You have no idea how long I have wanted to tell you that." I teased.
"But you're right. I don't want any other guy in your head when I finally get you in my arms." he told me.
"Not in your heart?"
"Oh, Lexi you've been in my heart for years, it just took this long for me to realise." he replied.
"I was foolish to think I could ever walk away from you. I tried to get rid of you, but you're rooted in my mind, my life my heart." I shook my head, "it seems I'm stuck with you."
"Good sweetheart, I don't want to do life with anyone else." Jake's hands moulded my hips. "But as much as I love where you're currently sitting, I can't have you on top of me if I am not allowed to do anything about it."
With a sigh I climbed off his lap and sat back on his bed,

he captured my hand once again and laced our fingers together.
"Thank you for listening to me." I said.
"Always," he replied.

After a little while of talking and relaxing, I needed to head off and deal with the carnage left at home. He was unsure about letting me go, but once I agreed to call him if anything happened, he finally walked me to the door. That goodbye was one of the hardest things I have ever had to do. But this was my chance with Jake and there was no way I wanted to ruin that. With one last kiss I tore myself away from him.

I got in my car and couldn't help myself drifting back to what had just happened with Jake, after all this time. Kissing Miles had been nice; it was sweet and gentle, but kissing Jake was in a whole other league. The kiss we had shared last summer had been brief and we both immediately passed it off as a mistake and we had no idea why it happened. He had been so drunk and had been in complete turmoil about his parents. But this time? This was so much more, this was… everything! It felt like I had been sinking my whole life and I had finally come up for air. Like I could finally breathe and my mind had gone from being foggy to feeling clearer than it had in a long time. But as I got nearer to my house, even the thoughts of our kiss and the way he had touched me couldn't pull me back from the worry I felt about arriving home and dealing with my parents.

I'd only been gone for an hour, yet it had changed things completely. The confession from Jake, his comfort, his honesty. Things had changed. After years of following him around and then even more years of trying to hide my feelings and try to get over him, he finally admitted how he felt! But I knew none of it meant anything until I had spoken to Miles. That was a challenge for another day, for now I had to deal with my parents.

I took a few deep breaths and prepared myself before heading into the house. I was greeted with a wave of silence and I didn't know whether to be relieved or scared. I scanned downstairs and it was silent, slightly confused. I started upstairs and checked the office. I could see my dad sitting at his desk typing on his computer, I knocked lightly on his door yet he ignored my presence completely. Not even pausing his typing for a moment.
"Hi dad." I said, he still didn't stop typing. I was receiving the cold shoulder, something I had grown very used to. Usually after I was screamed at and attacked for what I was doing wrong, I was always ignored afterwards, it was the same routine of the punishment. Releasing my attempts of breaking the cold behaviour was futile, I continued on through the house to see if I

could find my mum. I heard her business tone through the door of her bedroom, clearly indicating that she was on a work call, so once again I escaped her too and sped to my room. Shutting the door as softly as I can, I turned and fell onto my bed.

Part of me was relieved at the fact that I didn't have to talk to either of them, particularly after the way they were this morning. The screaming and the door slamming. But now I was dreading them barging into my room and continuing the drama that started this morning, before they told me to leave as I had begun to cry. Desperate to distract myself I grabbed my book and a laptop; I brought up Netflix and started playing 'The Office' knowing that it would help me. I couldn't hear anything else in the house and I made sure that the volume was low so they wouldn't get annoyed. After managing to get through a couple episodes I felt my phone go off on my bed.

Miles: Hey so, how do you feel about grabbing some dinner tomorrow?

Lexi: Hey that would be great :)

I knew this would be the perfect chance but I didn't think a full dinner would be a good idea.

Lexi: Could we make it coffee instead? Get some food too.

Miles: Sounds great, see you then.

Now that was settled and I would have a chance to talk to him I was feeling a bit more at ease. Just as I was putting my phone down, I felt it vibrate again.

Unknown: I hope you're feeling better. Good luck with your parents x

I couldn't fight the smile on my face as I saw the kiss at the end of his text and the way my heart jumped at the fact he was checking in on me. I spent so long trying to get away from him and get him out of my mind, now it was the last thing I wanted to do. I couldn't think of anything better than having him wrapped up in my life and maybe me being wrapped up in his arms.
I didn't respond to him then because I wanted to get things sorted with Miles before I allowed myself to think about anything with Jake. I mean I didn't even want to get my hopes up yet, he did the same thing last year and then turned around and changed after the kiss. I tried to get my mind away from it and turned back to Netflix and grabbed my book to continue some of my university reading. At least that way, if my parents asked, I could show them that I was doing something. After a while I could smell dinner downstairs and assumed that was an indication that I should head downstairs for food. With a

sigh, I dragged myself out of bed and smartened myself up before I started downstairs.

"Hi mother," I said to her as I entered the kitchen.

"Hmm," she replied and did not stop stirring whatever she was cooking on the hob, not looking up at me at all.

"So, what's for dinner?" I asked her.

"Oh. Your father and I have got a steak and potatoes with a red wine sauce, I did not realise that you would be home, I haven't bought you one." she mentioned. I was still standing in the doorway watching her.

"Ah right. Sorry I didn't realise you thought I had plans; I did come back a while ago." I told her. She slammed the spoon down onto the counter and turned to me.

"I am sorry I do not know your exact whereabouts Alexis. I didn't think I needed to cater to my 19-year-old daughter and thought that maybe she would actually be able to sort herself out for dinner." She snapped.

"Yes, of course. I'll sort out some food later." I told her and started turning around to head back upstairs.

"Oh, and here we go now, making me feel like a bad mother!" she said, "I have been working all day and now I am cooking for your father and I too and yet I am now getting moaned at the one thing I didn't do. Honestly Alexis."

"I am sorry mother, I didn't mean that, I will sort something out." I explained.

"Yes." she said and turned back to stirring the pot on the stove. I silently backed out of the kitchen and was about to turn back upstairs when I noticed my father start to descend.

"Did I hear you moaning at your mother?" he demanded.

"No, no I was just asking what's for dinner and she was explaining that you two had steak so I said I would sort something else later." I explained.

"Right so you're blaming her for the fact *you* didn't think about your own dinner in enough time!" he states.

"Um well, I was trying to-" I mumbled.

"You were blaming her?" he repeated.

"Yes father," I replied, scared to look up at him, I kept my eyes glued to the stairs.

"Ungrateful girl." he spat as he walked through the hall and entered the kitchen. I sped upstairs in a way to escape but to ensure that they didn't complain at the speed or volume of my steps. I got to my room and slowly shut the door silently before heading to my bed and slamming my face into the pillow to silence my sobbing.

I stayed there for hours and soon I was too tired to go and get food anyway, with the fear that I would be doing something else wrong and be attacked for it again. I stayed in my room and soon my cries fell silent, the exhaustion took over and I fell asleep.

In the morning, I was woken by my alarm going off at 8am. I was up, dressed and downstairs by 8:30am just to please mum. I knew I had plans to meet Miles today so I made sure to get up and shower, wash my face of the mascara and make up that has smudged all over my face from yesterday. Then I took extra care to make myself look decent today and hide the puffiness from my tears yesterday, just to ensure that no suspicion was raised by my behaviour or demeanour.

Neither of my parents tend to eat breakfast as they usually just had coffee so I grabbed some fruit and an orange juice and sat down. They walked downstairs in close succession, both grabbed their coffee and while my mother sat at the table at her laptop, my dad walked into the lounge with his paper. They were both in absolute silence and I was unsure what to do.

"Hi mother, I will be out for a while today, I'm meeting my friend to study for next year." I explained to her, thinking that it would be better to combine the work with the coffee date so that they didn't get annoyed.

"Good, finally a relief to see you putting in effort to your education." she replied. She said nothing further so I assumed that I was dismissed and I continued back upstairs. I didn't want to be here anymore so I grabbed my bag as quickly as I could, ran back downstairs and started towards the front door. As soon as I got in my car, I started the engine and drove away. I didn't even wait to connect my music instead driving away in silence.

I was at the coffee shop two hours early, but the comfort of the noises around me was far better than the silence of being at home. I headed over to the counter and ordered a chocolate Frappuccino (no coffee) before sitting at a small table by the window. I pulled my books from my bag and started my uni work. The next couple hours went by ridiculously quickly as I blitzed through my work, making notes and reading through all my work.

Miles: Hey I'm outside.

Lexi: Okay, I'm already here.

Miles: Great, see you in a minute :)

I took a deep breath as he made his way inside, I waved him over and started to pack my uni stuff away as he approached the table. He bent down and planted a swift kiss on the side of my head.
"Hey," he said to me. He was smiling so wide and was clearly really happy to see me and I couldn't help but feel a twist in my stomach. It was nice to be around him, but I didn't just want nice, I wanted what I had with Jake. The joking, the teasing, the excitement I felt whenever I knew I was going to see him. I had never found that with anyone else, I doubt I ever would.
"Hi," I replied to him.
"One second." he said to me as he went over to the counter to grab a coffee before coming to sit down next to me.
"So why were you here so early?" He asked me.

"I had some uni work to do so I thought I would come earlier to get it done, my parents were working at home and it was easier to not disturb them." I explained.
"Ah, right. How is it going?" he asked.
"Well, it's difficult and heavy, but I'm getting through most of it so I can't complain." I told him, "Anyway, how are you?" I asked him.
"Yeah, I've been alright. I met my friends yesterday and was hanging out with them last night."
That's good."
"Yeah, and then I was helping my mum with some housework this morning."
Right, that's nice," I was really trying to pay attention but it just wasn't working. My mind was going a mile a minute thinking of all of the work I needed to do, the way to be at home without breaking down every night, worrying about what was going on with Jake and feeling like I had been neglective Cassie for ages. I could tell Miles could see it too.
"Okay Lexi, what's going on?" he asks rather abruptly.
"What?" I replied, shocked out of my thoughts.
"You are so far away right now you might as well be outside." he said with a sense of humour in his tone, but I could tell he was irritated by it too.
"Oh I'm sorry I-" I started but stopped, unsure about how to continue.
"Is this about Jake?" he asked me.
"What? Why do you say that?" I stutter.

"Well because he obviously likes you and I can tell you like him too, I was hoping it was just the end of a crush but I can see that it isn't." he admitted.
"How long have you wondered about him?" I ask him.
"Well since our first date when I asked you." he told me, "From when I saw him watching us as I walked you to my car and the fact that he was then looking again when I brought you back."
"No, he was just protective of me." I said, but I knew that there was no conviction in my voice as that was clearly not the case.
"Come on Lexi, I knew I was already losing when we first went out together. I guess I just liked you so much that I hoped I could change your mind." He confessed.
"I'm so sorry Miles," I said, "trust me I really don't want to like him. He's confusing and it's crazy but…"
"But you can't help how you feel." he filled in for me, completely understanding how I was feeling. I looked at him and just nodded, knowing there was nothing else that I could say.
"I really hope you find someone Miles, someone that actually deserves you." I told him.
"Thank you," he replied, "and I hope Jake knows how lucky he is."
I stood up and drew him to his feet with my and wrapped my arms around his neck giving him a friendly hug. As we pulled away, we both started laughing.

"I must say, it has been a pleasure to know you, Lexi." he said to me, "and maybe we could still be friends?"
"Yes definitely, I mean, who knows maybe I have a cute friend that I can set you up with." I suggested.
"Well, that would be something," he laughed. We sat back down and chatted for another hour or so while Miles finished his coffee and it was surprisingly comfortable. There was no real flirting or any sort of romantic feelings but it was friendly and actually quite nice. After an hour, however, he did tell me that he had to go and that maybe we could meet up another time and that he would talk to me later. Once he was out of sight I sighed and slumped back into my chair. I was glad it went so well, not that I should be surprised, Miles was so sweet that he wouldn't have had any problems with it. In no time I was immersed back into my notes and books for my new modules in September and was making some significant progress on my tasks. My phone had gone off a few times while I had been working, but while I was so focused on my work, I hadn't bothered to look at them as there was no one I was waiting to hear from. However, the persistent vibrations of my phone were making it impossible to focus and I checked who they were all from.

My heart started hammering when I picked up my phone. I noticed I had a message from Miles just thanking me for the coffee and checking I was okay, which wasn't what was worrying me. What truly horrified me was the 3 missed calls I had from my mother and the two messages I had from my father. Now to other people that wouldn't seem too worrying as maybe that was just their parents checking up and wanting to talk to them. But with my parents? That was simply not the case. They avoid talking to me in any way as much as they could. Particularly my father, he never called me if he could help it. So, the fact I had so many calls and messages from them was certainly a cause for concern.

One of the messages from my dad just read 'Answer your mother' and the other saying 'Now.'

I checked the calls from my mother and I saw that she had left a voicemail, which was even more frightening as she usually hated talking to no one and would only say something if she could talk to them in person. Damn! With my hands beginning to shake, I pressed play and lifted the phone to ear.

"Alexis I am completely disgusted and embarrassed by you right now. Not only had you only received 70% in your final term of the year but you also have only received a 2.1 for the whole year? I cannot begin to tell you how disappointed I am in you and how ashamed I am by your intelligence. You know that it is not *acceptable and in this family, you cannot be presenting yourself in that way. How dare you? After everything we have done for you and the support we give you, this is how you decide to repay us. Please do not come home tonight, you have greatly embarrassed us and it is unacceptable, your*

father is entirely outraged and rightly so. Please stay away. We do not want you in the house today, we don't want you here, you have disappointed us immensely."

In utter shock I lowered the phone from my ear and could feel the tears welling up in my eyes already. I didn't even know what to do right now. I had tried so hard this year and it was only my first year, all I needed to do was pass. The rest didn't matter, but it did to my parents. I hadn't gone out often, my parents checked my bank statement and would be outraged at any money spent clubbing or drinking when I should be working. They hadn't let me join any societies either as it was something that would take my mind away from my work and it was absolutely unacceptable and pointless for me to be doing something that wouldn't aid my academics.

But at this point I didn't care, clearly I was never going to be enough for them so why should I keep trying? Right now I am doing what the hell I want and I do not care. With that in mind, I stuffed all my work back in my bag, finished my hot chocolate and stormed out of the coffee shop. Luckily, I had my ID on me and I knew exactly where I was going. There was a bar Cassie and I had been going to constantly since last year, it was this amazing little pub just round the corner from her house and they know us well, I guess it was a testament as to how much we really went there. It was called 'The Lucky Rabbit' and was run by the loveliest couple ever. The guy was called Gary and he was the embodiment of warm and welcoming and his wife, Lara was the perfect mix of cool and strict, able to sit and gossip with us when we went, always offering advice while also making sure we never got too bad when we were just starting to drink. It was exactly what I needed right now.

"Hey Lexi," Gary said as soon as I walked in, he greeted me with a wide smile and beckoned me over to the bar, but his face dropped when he saw how I looked.

"I need a drink," I told him.

"Woah, what's going on?" he asked.

"Oh, just my parents being their ever-pleasant selves," I informed him, "now please I need a glass of wine, and a large one at that, and three shots of vodka." I told him and pushed my money across the bar.

"Lexi, it's midday. Are you sure?" he asked.

"Gary, I know you care about me, but I need this right now." I pleaded.

"Okay," he said and went behind the bar to grab the drinks. First, he poured out a few shots of vodka for me and pushed them over to me before reaching for the wine I always had, it was a delicious and rich red wine that I absolutely loved. He poured the glass out and pushed it towards me.

"Thank you." I said to him as I took a large gulp and set the wine glass back on the bar and looked up at him, his face, often filled with a smile, was now laced with concern for me.

"You want to talk about anything?" he asked.
"I won't lie big-G, talking is the last thing I want to do right now." I confessed. "I really just need to sit here, drink and sort through my thoughts. Is that okay?"
"Of course, but you need to tell me the minute you need someone, I'm here and I will be straight over, or I can get Lara if you'd prefer her. I do love the nickname thank you Lexi." Gary laughed and wandered off.
"Thank you," I said with tears blurring my vision once again, they were so loving and so supportive of me that I didn't know what I would do without them. I sat there staring at my drink for a while before finishing my shots and my wine and asking for another. At that point I pulled out my phone and checked my final exams from uni and all of my email. The irony is that I even had one from my tutor telling me how well I had done this year, clearly not good enough for my parents. Gary did come to check on me a few times. He tried to ask me what was going on a few times but each time he did I just waved off his inquiries and had more to drink.

Very quickly three hours had gone by and I was now down about 5 glasses of wine. Or I think it was that many from what I had left on the bar. Gary was getting more and more concerned and also a lot more uncomfortable with me having no one, clearly knowing he would rather not serve me seeing as I was on my own.

"Lexi, how are we doing over here?" Lara came over to ask me once she had tidied up a table, I envied her and Gary's marriage.

"We're good." I tried to say but the words began to slur together and feel weird on my lips, my tongue suddenly felt too large for my mouth.

"You wanna talk?" she asks.

"Nope! But I would love another glass of wine." I tried to say but I don't know how much of it sounded like proper words.

"Ah you know the rules honey, too much to drink when you're on your own means you get cut off and I need someone to call. So come on, either cough up the phone and tell me who to call or get it up for me, your choice." she told me.

"But I'm fine." I whined.

"Oh yeah?" she asked, "walk in a straight line for me and I'll pour you another glass."

"Fine." I announced and spun around on the chair to stand and start walking. I couldn't even find my feet before I could see the floor quickly charging towards my face.

"Darling, she's down!" Lara called.

"On it." I could hear Gary say and in a matter of moments I quickly felt myself being lifted up and placed back on the seat.

"So, we're going to say no more wine, okay?" Lara said.

"Fine," I grumbled and laid my head on the bar.

"Right, who are we calling Lexi?" she asked.
"Huh?"
"I'm not letting you home on your own." she declared, "you know the rules so call someone or hand over the phone and I will."
"Fine, fine." I conceded and grabbed my phone. I tapped on my contacts and scrolled down to the 'J' names, but I couldn't find what I was looking for.
"Wait! He's unknown!" I shouted and received a very confused look from them both. I ignored their looks and went to my texts to find our text thread. I clicked the call button and waited for him to pick up.
"Hello?" He asked.
"JAKE!" I yelled down the phone.
"Lex, what's going on?" he asked, his voice full of concern.
"You're so good you know. So sweet." I said. "I wish you were here."
"Where are you?" he asked me.
"Others don't see how nice you are, but I do! I've always seen it."
"Lexi. Tell me where you are right now." he demanded.
"Why?" I asked.
"Because I am coming to get you," he states as if it was the simplest question ever.
"Ugh, Gary, he is too nice. I'll tell you because he won't listen to me." I gestured to the phone and turned to him behind the bar to speak to him instead.

"Yeah, yeah of course he is." Gary replied, "Jake it's the Lucky Rabbit, come and get her before she does any damage to herself."
"I'm on my way," he called out so Gary could hear, "Lex, don't move."
"I won't-" but I wasn't able to finish my sentence as he had already hung up and was on his way here, I assumed. I put my head to the bar and closed my eyes.

Five minutes later I felt arms wrap around me and I began to fight them.
"Get off- Jake!" I stopped fighting his embrace and threw my arms around him. "What are you doing here?"
"Lex, I was on the phone to you 5 minutes ago. I said I was coming to get you." he told me.
"Riiiiiiight." I said.
"You don't remember." he stated more than asked.
"Nope! But boy am I glad to see you." I told him and looked up at him watching those gorgeous eyes as they scanned my face to make sure I was okay.
"Thanks Gary, I've got her from here." he confirmed and swept me from the bar stool in a fireman's carry.
"You look after that one," Gary said, "she's a special one."
"Don't worry, I know she is." he confirmed and whisked me out of the bar as I wrapped my arms around him.

"Lexi don't be difficult." he begged as he tried to get me in the car outside the bar and I constantly fought him. I didn't want to go home, why did the night have to be over!

"But the night is young Jake. I want to be outside!" I declared and threw my arms and head back.

"No, we need to go home. Put you to bed." He stated.

"In your bed?" I asked and gave him, what I hoped, was a flirtatious look, but he simply ignored the question and continued wrestling with me to get me in the car. Soon I stopped being difficult and let him place me in the car and do my seatbelt up. He got into the driver's side and started the car.

"So, I guess I'm not taking you home?" he asked.

"Absolutely not." I told him. My head was resting on his shoulder as he drove and he had one hand on my thigh while the other was navigating through the streets back to his house.

"Oh how the turn tables."

"Huh?" Jake asked. I thought as I was cast back to last year as I sat outside his house.

"First of all, the fact you do not understand that reference us a travesty and I will be educating you." I waggled my finger at him, "Second, last summer I was the one rescuing you when you were drunk, seems to be the other way round now." I teased.

"There's only a slight difference between this time and the last time if you remember…" I said coyly as I thought back to when we had sat in the same place last year, but just in my car that time instead of his.

"Hmm, that's true…" Jake pondered for a moment, "well we can easily change that." he said and took my face in his hands and brought my lips to his.

I was hesitant at first, filled with shock at Jake's sudden brazenness but I soon melted to his touch. I wrapped my arms around his neck and realised how desperate I had been to feel his lips once again. I fit so perfectly against him and Jake snaked his arm around my waist pulling me closer. It had been a struggle to reach him but I was determined and I managed it. My hands found themselves intertwined in Jake's hair as I moved from his neck to his head, I tugged it slightly and he released a growl low in his throat.

"Wow, that was better than I remember," I murmured almost giving away that I hadn't been able to get either of their kisses out of my mind.

"Agreed." Jake replied still in a daze from what had just happened.

Chapter 16: Jake

There were no words. No words. I was kissing Lexi! She was kissing me! I had no idea how I had gone so many years without kissing those delicious lips. Now I couldn't seem to get enough. My restraint last summer and for this following year had been impeccable knowing how addictive kissing her had been.
The limits of the car were irritating me but there was no way I was stopping now; I knew that kissing Lexi was my new addiction.
"Wanna go inside?" she asked, pulling away slightly. She looked at me coyly, through those incredible lashes of hers. My words were failing me so instead I just nodded and got out of the car. I raced round to her side and grabbed her as she slipped out of my car, uneasy on her feet from the copious amounts of alcohol still in her system. I didn't loosen my grip on her until I had to when I got to the door to unlock. She made a noise of clear

complaint at the loss of my touch and I couldn't help but smile.
"Hey, give me a second. I just need to unlock it." I whispered to her. But despite my explanation she still proceeded to grab my hand and wrap it back around her waist.
"Better?" I asked her with my arm now tied around her again. She gave a satisfied nod and I pulled her against me to feel her warmth. I managed to slowly open the door, making sure to be as silent as possible. Not that my mum would care about the noise, it was more that I didn't want her seeing Lexi. Tonight was mine and I was spending it with her.
"Where are we?" Lexi slurred. Looking exhausted and disorientated.
"Lex, we're at my house," I explained, "you're drunk and you need to sleep and I am not taking you back to your parent's house."
"Riiiiiiiight," she said, but I wasn't convinced she actually knew what was going on.
"And shush, we don't want to disturb anyone. We don't need awkward questions right now." I told her. Her face changed to extremely serious and ran her fingers across her lips as if she was zipping her mouth shut.

As we, slowly, made our way upstairs, I was impressed at how quiet Lexi managed to be. There were a few times her feet nearly missed the steps; it seemed like I was carrying her more than her actually walking.

As soon as I shut the door and released her, she stumbled over to my bed and collapsed on her back. Her arms and hair sprawled out around her.

"Stay here and try not to fall asleep." I slipped out of the room with a small groan from her, only to come face to face with my mum.

"Hi sweetie, are you alright? I thought I heard you speaking to someone?" she asked, coming upstairs holding a cup of tea and glanced towards my door.

"No, no, just ending a game I was playing with the guys," I lied.

"Ah right." she replied sceptically.

"I'm just heading to grab some painkillers; I have a bit of a headache." I explained.

"Okay sweetie, in the cupboard below the sink in the bathroom." she informed me.

"Great thank you," I replied and rushed to grab them. I then grabbed a bottle of water from the fridge downstairs, thinking a bottle would be better than a glass with Lexi's current state.

Upon my return to my room, I saw that Lexi was still in the exact position I had left her.

"Here," I said to her gently as I coaxed her into a sitting position and popped out two tablets for her, placing them in her hand before opening the bottle and handing it to her. Immediately, her grip slackened and spilt some water over her top.

"Okay," I told her and took the bottle back from her.

"Hey," she protested, trying to grab the bottle back from me.

"You just split it over yourself, let me help." I told her. After she had swallowed the tablets I put the bottle on the bed side table and screwed the cap back on.

"You want to change into something else?" I asked her, glancing at her clothes thinking she mustn't be very comfortable.

"I see," she said coyly.

"No, no not like that," I rushed to explain, "I just meant to be more comfortable, you can borrow a t-shirt."

"Right," she said in a teasing tone. "Well yes please."

"Great," I said to her and went over to my drawers to grab a top, "here."

"Thank you," she said and started to get off the bed to get changed.

"I am just going to stand here and face the wall." I said, I heard her laugh and could hear the rustling of her clothes. It was unbearable to not turn around and take her in my arms, but I knew that it would be the wrong thing to do right now, she needed comfort and calmness. That was exactly what I was going to give her.

"Okay, I'm all good." she announced and I turned around to see her cuddled up in my bed with the duvet up to her chin.

"Good," I said and cleared my throat. The sight of her in my bed, knowing she was wearing nothing but my top, was a fantasy I never thought I would ever have the luck of coming true. I pinched myself. *Nope definitely real.*
"So, are you joining me?" she asked, looking up at me again through her eyelashes.
"Er, yeah." I replied suddenly feeling extremely nervous about being so close to her. "Just one second." She nodded and I snuck out of the room to brush my teeth and get ready. Once I came back I could see her eyes closed, but as I softly shut the door, her eyes fluttered open again and smiled when she saw me. My heart warmed.
I walked over to the bed and got in next to her. As soon as I laid down, she shuffled over to me and settled in against me.
"Goodnight Jake," she whispered and leaned up to kiss me on the lips once more and then tucked her head in below my chin.
"Goodnight sweetheart," I replied and with a kiss on her head I settled down with my arms wrapped tightly around her, I watched her for a moment, her gentle breaths tickling my arm, and a smile stuck on my face. I don't know when it had happened but Lexi wasn't Cassie's annoying friend following me around anymore. She had become my light, my air, my heart. She had become the thing I would never be able to live without. She had become my everything.

Lex was asleep in no time; I checked my phone and realised the whole ordeal had only lasted a few hours and it was still far too early to sleep. I was full of adrenalin and wide awake, but there was no way I was moving while I had Lexi in my arms. YouTube it was.

Light shone through my window without the blinds shut and my eyes squinted at the brightness. I don't even remember falling asleep but I had been out cold. It took me a few short moments for me to adjust to the shocking light and I managed to peel open my eyes. My hand stretched over the bed grasping around for her, but all I could find was rumpled sheets.
"Lex?" I whispered as I sat up trying to work out where she was, but all I received was silence. My room was empty. She was gone. I sank back into my bed and closed my eyes. What had I done? I had made the biggest mistake I ever could. After all these years of fighting my feelings for her I had finally caved and shown her how I felt and now she regretted it. Slipping out in the early hours of the morning before we could even talk about it.
"Shit!" Knowing that sitting in my bed sulking about it wasn't going to change anything, I dragged myself out of bed preparing myself for the moment that I might see her. I rolled out of bed and started towards the bathroom to get ready for the day, but as I passed my desk, a slip of paper caught my eye. Something that hasn't been there yesterday.

Hey, I'm sorry to rush off but I had to get back before my parents noticed.
I can't wait to see you later.
Lexi xx

My heart flipped in my chest. The note, the joy, the kisses. She didn't regret it! And she was looking forward to seeing me! Man, this couldn't get any better.
"You seem in a good mood today." Cassie observed.
"Oh, Jesus you scared the hell out of me Cas." I replied in shock as I turned and noticed her leaning against the doorframe, watching me with a confused and slightly intrigued look on her face.
"Whoops." she replied, yet her inquisitive look never faltered.
"What do you want?" I demanded, "Can I not just be happy for once?"
"Well, you can," she said and paused, "you just never usually are."
"Well today I am then, if that's alright with you." I replied.
"Whatever," she sang and walked away. I rolled my eyes but was glad she was gone. Looking back at the mirror, I felt like an excited schoolgirl. After a whole year of hell, I had finally confessed to her and there was no way I was going to be taking it back now. My phone rang and I dove for it.

"Oh hey," I tried to hide my disappointment as I realised it was my boss.
"Hi Jake, we need you to come in this afternoon for a meeting with a new sponsor," he said.
"Er right, okay. Yeah, sure I can be there in a few hours." I told them.
"Right." He replied and hung up the phone.
"Ugh," I moaned as I fell back onto the bed at the possible delay in seeing Lexi. I got dressed and collected all my stuff for work before heading downstairs.
"Morning mum," I said as I walked into the kitchen.
"Hi honey," she replied. I walked up to her and gave her a kiss on the cheek before grabbing some coffee and going to sit down next to Bradley on the table as he ate his breakfast. "What's your bag for?" She asked, looking at my bag suspiciously.
"I need to head into work quickly." I explained.
"When was that decided? You never told me." She replied, seeming hurt.
"No, it was a very sudden decision. They asked me to come in for a meeting about a sponsor, but I'm not too sure of much else."
"Ah right." she said, "well that's a shame, you'll be missed around the house today. I think Bradley had some hopes that you would be around to play with him for a while."
I looked over at Bradley and immediately felt guilty as he sat there looking down at his food.

"I'm sorry buddy, I didn't realise. How about we sort something next week and maybe you and I can head to the park for a while." I wrapped my arm around him. He softened then smiled up and nodded enthusiastically, before settling into his food again.
"Okay well I'm heading off." I said and stood after finishing off my coffee, "I'll see you tonight."
The office wasn't too far, luckily and within thirty minutes I was pulling into the car park. With a sigh I started inside and immediately heard all of the panic and noise of a startup.
"Jake!" I heard someone call, frantically looking around. I tried to find the owner of the voice but failed. "Hey!" They called again and I finally noticed Patrick walking towards me.
"Ah Pat! How nice to see you."
"Yeah, all great. Now I need some help." he demanded.
"Right, I'm here, what can I do?" I asked and could already tell that this day was going to be exhausting. Immediately Patrick started explaining how he was in and out of meetings today, some of which I was going to be needed in. I immediately got to work, starting by getting the offices organised so that it wasn't too chaotic to start interviewing people. As much as I kept myself working, I couldn't help but imagine what Lexi was doing and where she was, desperately hoping to escape the office quickly so I could get back to her. I must say it was an extremely effective incentive to keep working.

"Hey, Jake, we need you in here." Patrick called from his office, which was still looking pretty cluttered.

"Coming," I called out and with one last look at my handy work, I joined him in his office.

"Okay, so we have a potential employee arriving in half an hour for an interview, and I want you in on the meeting with me." Patrick explained.

"Great!" I replied cheerfully, already enjoying the new responsibilities.

"I see you've done a great job in the waiting area and the conference room is looking good so we'll use that for the interview. Meet you there in twenty minutes."

I nodded and went to my cubicle to sort myself out and make sure I looked presentable. I also checked my phone for any message from Lexi, unfortunately since her note this morning, I hadn't heard anything from her.

"And this is Jake," Patrick introduced me as the meeting began.

"Hi nice to meet you," she said, "I'm Jessica." She reached out her hand and I took it, offering a brief handshake before settling down again.

"Well thank you for coming in," Patrick said an hour later as we finished up the interview, "any further questions you wished to ask?"

"No thank you, this has been most informative and I look forward to hearing from you," Jessica replied sweetly, "nice to meet you, Jake."

"You too," I responded absentmindedly, all I could think about was getting out of the office and getting back to see Lexi. I grabbed my phone and typed her a quick message.

Jake: I can't wait to see you later. Very interesting conversation to be had... xx

After my royal screw up last summer, I knew I needed to make it matter this time around. Lexi had become more important than the sun, moon and stars. She brought light to my life when I had lived in the shadows for far too long. I couldn't live without her light again.

Chapter 17: Lexi (One year ago)

Jake's arms tightened around my waist and pulled me back onto his lap. My heart was a drum in my chest! I knew that the alcohol had worn off a while ago and he was being truthful when he said he was sober, he would remember this as much as I would tomorrow. Still, none of it made any sense.
I couldn't believe that after all the years of making sure I was around when he was, trying to create 'coincidental' meetings, trying to make myself look as good and grown up as possible around him. It was now that he chose to make a move- when I was dressed in joggers with greasy hair looking like a state.

His hands had begun to travel upwards, seeming unable to get enough. I wrapped my arms around his neck and my legs tighter around his waist, allowing him to have as much of me as he wanted. With my legs like a vice around his waist, my hands were crawling under his t-shirt,

exploring the places I had only dreamed of. It seemed that no matter how close I was to him, he wanted me closer, and I wasn't one to protest.
"What took you so long?" I asked him, breathlessly, I craved to know what had caused him to make this decision, why tonight? Why the hell not sooner? I needed to know, I needed to know what had caused this change. "Clearly I've been out of my mind for far too long, it's like I've been fighting through fog all my life," he confessed. "Thank god I finally saw clearly." Instead of replying I just nodded and kissed him again, knowing that anything I'd say would betray how deep my feelings truly were, and I wasn't ready to go there just yet.

I was addicted to him, his lips, his smell, his touch. The kiss had been taken to a whole new level now and I didn't want to stop, I rocked against him not wanting to stop.
"Woah, hey Lex." He said against my lips, but I just kept kissing him. "Sweetheart, hold on."
"What?" I asked breathlessly, and slightly dazed.
"I want to take this slow; there's no need to rush right?" He asked.
"You don't want to go further?" I asked. Had I made a mistake? Maybe he didn't want me as much as I thought he did.
"Lex, you have no idea how much I want all of it with you. I've tried to fight it for so long feeling like I had to, that I couldn't feel how I did. But with you here? I could

never have imagined this in my wildest dreams, but I don't want to rush anything. Tonight sweetheart, I just want to lay down with you, hold you in my arms and remind myself how lucky I am that you gave me the time of day in the first place."

I looked at him, searching for any dishonesty in his words, but I could see how pleading his eyes were and I knew he meant every word. I nodded softly and got off him, he stood and grabbed me one of his tops to wear. I shuffled underneath the duvet with him and could feel him wrap his arms around me and pull me tight against his chest.

That night I stayed over at his place, not because I was worried about him being alone, but because he asked me to. He pulled me in closer to him so I was laying right against him. I could feel his breath tickling my neck and his touch all the way down my body.

"Goodnight Jake," I whispered.

"Goodnight sweetheart," he murmured with a delicate kiss against my neck and within ten minutes I could feel the rhythm of his soft breathing indicating that he had settled into a calm sleep. His arms were wrapped around me protectively, keeping me close to him. I knew I was safe in the comfort of his embrace.

Chapter 18: Lexi

Oh. My. God. I thought I'd endured bad hangovers in my life, but this one was truly a winner. My head was throbbing beyond belief and my eyes were blurry and all over the place! But with Jake's soft breath tickling my neck and his hand resting on my thigh under the covers, I couldn't bring myself to care about anything else. True bliss. His scent was all consuming and I couldn't get enough of it. I needed to get away, work through everything before he woke up. I lifted his strong, heavy arm and slid out from underneath. I didn't want to just leave so I found a scrap of paper from his desk and scribbled a note for him. I slipped on my trousers and left his shirt on, simply tucking it in so it wasn't as much of a dress as it had been during the night. Once I had combed my fingers through his hair and looked more presentable, I grabbed my shoes and crept out of his room before slowly making my way out the house.

After getting a safe distance away, I slowed down and let myself register what had actually happened last night. Everything with my parents, me drinking beyond belief, Jake coming to save me, us in his car, his room, his bed. Last summer was repeating itself and all I could think was that *I hope it doesn't end like before,* but I guess only time will tell… I hated that.

I decided to prolong the inevitable a bit longer and took the long way home, desperately worried about getting home and dealing with my parents. Mum would usually just blame me, but dad? Well, that was a bit more of a concerning factor in all honesty.

I arrived at my front door all too soon and fled to my room before I could be stopped. Once I was in my room, I cleaned my face off, grabbed some new clothes, put my clothes in the wash basket and threw Jake's top to the back of the wardrobe.

"Alexis." My dad commanded from his office. Once I had finished getting ready and looked as I usually would, I slowly crept to his office.

"Hello father," I said as I stood on the threshold of his office. He didn't turn around immediately, rather finished work on his laptop before he decided to look my way.

"Why did you not come home last night?" I demanded.

"Mum told me not to come home," I explained.

"Don't blame your mother for deciding to stay out all night!" he shouted.

"Sorry father." I murmured.
"We need to discuss what we will do about your university work," he stated.
"Yes father." I replied.
"Your results were completely shameful and you have disgraced the family, Alexis."
"Yes father, I am so sorry, I will do better next year." I explained.
"DO NOT INTERRUPT ME!" He screamed. "NOW YOU WILL TURN IT AROUND AND DO BETTER."
"I'm sorry father, I tried as hard as I could this year-" I tried to explain before I felt a hot sharp pain in my cheek. He hit me. While I was aware of the stinging, I felt numb. Tears pricked my eyes, but I refused to show him that weakness. He had never once hurt me that bad, I turned to him and once I looked at him stunned, I saw his whole demeanour change.
"Oh Alexis, look what you made me do, I just want the best for you. Can't you see that? I just want to help you."
"Yes father, I know. I am going to get some ice for my face if that is okay." I asked him, still keeping my hand against my face.
"Yes, you should," he straightened, his anger had vanished but there was no remorse or sympathy in his eyes.
"Thank you," I turned out of his office, shutting his door behind me and starting downstairs. Mum was in the kitchen cooking when I walked in. I went to the freezer

and grabbed an ice pack and placed it gently against my face.

"Alexis." my mother said tightly, not even looking up from the stove.

"Good morning mum," I said to her, "I am just going up to my room." she simply nodded, not stopping her actions once. I walked out once again and walked quickly past my dad's office to my room, shut the door and sank to the floor. Now I was in the safety of my room, there was nothing stopping the tears from streaming down my face, it was all I could do to not let out the wail that was lodged in my throat. I stayed there for longer than I could even remember, staying until no more tears were able to be released. I've never been able to please my parents and would never be good enough for them. I needed to get out of here, I needed to escape. Even just temporarily. I grabbed my phone from my pocket and messaged the girls.

Lexi: Who's around to do something?

        Connie: Absolutely! What did you have in mind?

    Cassie: I'm so sorry I'm still away with Noah, can come over tonight?

Lottie: I'm so sorry, I have loads of work to do, I'll see you next time.

Lexi: Okay just us Connie? Coffee?

Connie: Perfect, meet you in 20 minutes?

I sent a thumbs up and then messaged Cassie too saying we'd come over later and wanted to hear all about her trip with Noah. I checked the time while I had my phone out and noticed it was nearing lunch and I realised just how long I had been sitting on my floor. I needed to get out! I quickly fixed my makeup, made sure that my face looked normal and calm, ensured there were no signs of the redness at all, brushed my hair again before grabbing my bag and leaving.

I arrived before Connie so I stood outside waiting for her and calming myself from the events of this morning. My mind was spinning so much I was afraid of getting whiplash, I needed some time with my friends to be able to calm myself. I stood there scrolling through my phone until I heard the familiar voice of my friend yelling and bounding towards me.
"Hey!" Connie called cheerfully while she was still several metres away, earning a few unapproving looks from those around her.

"Hey Con, how are you?" I asked her with my arms open and she accepted the hug straight away.
"Ah, exhausted and needing caffeine, let's go." she said and grabbed my arm before heading inside. We joined the queue, which thankfully moved rather quickly, and then quickly ordered. I didn't get food; I'd lost my appetite after this morning.
"So, what's been going on?" I asked Connie, "How's Ryan?"
"Oh yeah it's great, I've been focusing on my painting and things this summer, enjoying the sun and just having a chance to pause from uni. I'm not ready at all for our second year." she admitted.
"Oh no, me either!" I agreed, "this year actually starts to count and I can't deal with it!"
"I needed a break from it all." Connie agreed.
"But how is everything with Ryan?" I asked.
"It's fine," she said flippantly and speedily before changing the topic, "but that's old news now, what's going on with you? How is everything with Miles, that was his name right?"
"Yeah, it was so good, I did actually end things with him, but he was so nice."
"Wait, why?" she asked, clearly disappointed.
"I mean I think it was just too different; we got on well, but I just didn't feel anything with him, I wanted something else." I admitted.
"Something else? Or someone else?" she asked.

"What?" I replied.
"Don't play dumb, Cassie isn't here. Jake?" She stated. "I know you've liked him for years; you're not still holding out hope with him, are you?"
"Ha, no Connie come on, you know that was just a childish dream," I told her, hoping I sounded convincing. Clearly, I wouldn't be telling her about last night.
"Are you sure? You know it won't happen with hi-" she started but luckily got cut off by the waitress appearing at the table with the food and drinks.
"I have a sugar free caramel latte and a hot chocolate." she said as she sat the tray down on the table, "is that everything?" We both thanked her and Connie quickly went for her stuff.
"I've been needing this coffee all morning." Connie moaned as she reached across the table to grab her cup off the tray.
"Why's that?" I asked.
"Oh, I was up until 3am designing something. I've got this new idea and I just couldn't stop so I'm exhausted." While she was talking, I felt my phone vibrate in my pocket quickly grabbing it to see who it was, desperately hoping it wouldn't be either of my parents.

Unknown: I can't wait to see you later. Very interesting conversation to be had... xx

I still hadn't saved his number, but I knew exactly who it was and that blissful feeling returned. Maybe Connie was wrong and this could actually happen this time. I put my phone back in my pocket and smiled back up at Connie as she continued on her chatter about her passion projects.

Connie and I spent three hours sitting in the coffee shop chatting. With that message from Jake, my appetite had started to return so I decided to grab a croissant when we both got our second drink and ate it slowly as Connie mentioned her plans for her second year. She had found out about this art exhibition at her university and was considering entering a piece for it. It was incredible hearing her talk about something so passionately and I knew that one day she would be something big!
"Cassie just messaged about going over, wanna join?" I asked.
"Oh god, I would love to," Connie apologised, "but Ryan and I have plans and he gets so stressed when we're late, I've stayed here too long already, I really should get going."
"That's fine, I'm sure Cassie will understand, she's just been away with Noah, so not one to talk." I replied.
"Okay great, tell her I said hi." She said as we both stood and started out of the coffee shop. Connie and I parted ways at the front of the shop, her returning to her car and me walking quickly to Cassie's house. My legs were bouncing, but I just didn't want to admit that my

excitement was now controlled by my best friend's brother too rather than just her...

Cassie didn't live too far from the high street so I wandered over to her house. I would like to say that I took a leisurely stroll, but the excitement and nervousness that pumped through me made it impossible for me not to rush over there. I knocked on Cassie's door and within ten seconds she swung the door open and launched herself at me.
"Ha, you make it seem like I've not seen you in years." I laughed as I welcomed her hug.
"Dude, a few days for us is like years!" She returned.
"What about when we're both at uni and we don't see each other." I reasoned. She paused for a moment before answering.
"That's different. Shush." She laughed, "Plus I've had too much boy time, I need my girl now."
"Wow, thank you darling, I love you too." Noah said from somewhere in the house.
"I love you baby, but it's true." She shrugged, "now I need my Lexi."
"Of course, I know. Have a good time, girls and I'll see you later babe." He said with a kiss on Cassie's cheek, "Bye Lexi, have fun. Bye guys!" Noah added and called back into the house earning him a chorus of goodbyes from various places in the house.

"So, a good weekend I gather?" I asked. She looked at me and smiled, she was the real-life heart eyes emoji- practically glowing.
"Come on, let's get pizza and head upstairs." She said and dragged me inside, after a few days of such unrest at home, it felt so good to finally feel like I belonged somewhere again.

"Did I hear Noah head ou- Lexi." Jake said as we met him halfway up the stairs. He had his joggers and a plain white t-shirt on and looked truly divine. I had to stop myself from launching at him and attacking his face with kisses.
"Jake," I said and offered him a timid smile, I had no idea how to act around him anymore. I couldn't break away from his gaze and we stood there.
"Cassie," Cassie butted in, breaking the spell I seemed to be under.
"Shut up Cas," Jake murmured, "Move." he nudged past her on the stairs continuing down, evidently able to make his legs move sooner than I could. As he passed me, he grabbed my hand, giving me a comforting squeeze and drawing my attention back to him. With a wink, he let go of my hand as soon as he had grabbed it. Cassie continued walking up the stairs but I could stop myself from waiting for an extra beat to see if Jake would turn back one more time. He did.

"Okay so what is going on?" Cassie questioned as soon as the door was shut, she flopped onto her bed and I followed suit.
"W- what do you mean?" I stuttered.
"Well mum said you seemed pretty down over the past couple days and she was worried there might have been an incident with your parents." She mentioned, I shuddered really not wanting to go into too much depth about anything that happened over the past few days.
"Well, yeah there was a little incident, I guess," I started and she stared at me expectantly and patiently so I explained (minus the time with Jake).
"Lex, I'm so sorry. I knew things were bad with them, but this is something else. You know I love you and will do anything I can to help." Cassie said and reached over to give me one of the tightest hugs I've ever had. At that point I broke down in her arms, knowing I was safe. After 5 minutes of me sobbing into her shirt I pulled away.
"Ugh, okay, enough of that. I want to hear something happier." I told her and sat back against her headboard and calmed myself. "Tell me about your weekend away."
"Are you sure?" She asked, clearly worried about changing the topic when I wasn't okay.
"Yes definitely. I need a distraction and I want to hear about it." I assured, wiping my eyes.
"Okay, okay. As long as you're good."

"Absolutely, but ice cream is needed. I'm going to go and raid the freezer," I told her and climbed off the bed. "Want some?" She nodded.

I started downstairs and went into the kitchen, opening the freezer and breathing deeply when the cold air rushed over my face offering a sense of calm. I dug around for a second before I heard someone clear their throat behind me and I realised I wasn't alone. I quickly straightened and twisted, shutting the freezer door behind me.

"Woah you okay? Your face is red and a little puffy." Jake commented, I could see the concern on his face, even from across the kitchen.

"You do know how to charm a girl." I teased.

"No, no- that's not what I mean. I just- It's just-" Jake stuttered, he wandered over and tenderly brushed my face.

"I'm teasing you honey. I'm all good. Just filling in Cassie." I explained, as his expression changed, I could tell he knew exactly what I was talking about.

"Ah." I placed my hand over his where it rested on my forearm.

"It was good," I assured him. "It's Cassie so she was so supportive and said I can stay here as long as I need to. I may find myself needing to stay here a lot…" I said, he grinned. He stopped for a minute and just looked at me, his head tilted slightly to one side simply watching. I waited, growing nervous at his silence. I was so tempted to turn away under the intensity.

"I want to take you out." He announced, his grin deepening.

"Like on a date or with a gun?"

"Don't be smart." he gave me a warning squeeze at my waist.

"I thought you liked my smartness, one of my countless appealing attributes."

"I want to take you out. On a *date*." Jake qualified, more insistent this time.

"Jake, we can't," I painfully admitted, it was exactly what I wanted, more than anything, "what if someone sees us or Cassie catches on? We can't risk it."

"Lexi please, I don't want to just sneak around with you, hidden moments in the car or stealing a minute when you're away from Cassie. Please, I want to go on a proper date with you. I messed this up last summer, I won't do that again. I want to show you off, please let me take you out." He insisted.

I had been waiting so long for him to finally share my feelings and I wanted to start things with him now, we'd already wasted so much time.

"Jake…"

"Okay look, what if I organise it so that it's not nearby, I'll come and get you or even meet you somewhere so that your parents don't see either. You can decide what you want to tell Cassie and I will go along with whatever you want to say." He said, clearly trying to convince me.

"Cassie can't know." I insisted.

"I won't push it. If you don't want to-" he continued, his face now full of doubt at what he said.

"Oh, Jake shut up, of course I want to, I have for years, but it's Cassie, I don't want to risk it."

"I don't want to mess things up with you and Cassie so it's up to you," he assured me, "I just want to spend time with you."

"Okay," I sighed and nodded, I couldn't stop the smile spreading over my face, "I want to see where this goes, so if you can work out where we can go, then I'll work out what to say to Cassie."

Without a further word, he took my chin with his finger and thumb before bringing my mouth to his and giving me a soft sweet kiss. His other hand moved from my forearm and snaked around my waist, I let my hands travel up his chest until they linked around the back of his neck. I began to lose myself in his kiss until I heard a shout from upstairs.

"Oi Lexi, where did you go?" I leapt away from Jake and I slammed my hip on the side of the cabinet, the pain immediately spreading through me. Jake reached out to comfort me, but I could see the laugh he was suppressing. I thumped him on the chest and went to the freezer to grab the two pints of ice cream and two spoons, before racing away from Jake.

"Coming!" I yelled and rushed upstairs. As I left the kitchen, I could hear Jake no longer be able to withhold his laughter and his deep chuckle echoed around me as I made my way back to Cassie's room.

"What took you so long? I am *starving* and in desperate need of an ice cream fix!" She said so very dramatically. I saw no point in lying to her about what had kept me.

"I bumped into Jake in the kitchen," I explained, "he was just getting some food and I didn't want to get in his way."

"Oh ew. Just push him out the way next time. It's only Jake who cares?" She replied and I laughed along with her, saying I would next time. Cassie grabbed the sweating ice cream from my arms and began to dig in, I promptly followed her and settled in beside her. She already had Grown Ups lined up; classic comedy was exactly what I needed. We fell into a comfortable silence watching and munching. I was incredibly lucky that I had people that could take the worst day of my life and turn it joyful.

Chapter 19: Jake

I was finally getting a chance to go out with Lexi, the girl that had been at the back of my mind for years. The girl I never thought that I could have, I couldn't believe it! I guess miracles do happen. I had followed her to the kitchen and being able to sneak a kiss had me floating on air. I had felt her warmth against me down the whole length of my torso. I'd been desperate to lift her to the counter, position myself between her legs and show her how excited I really was about this date. But before I had the chance to close the distance, a shout echoed from upstairs.

"Oi, Lexi, where did you go?" Cassie's voice seemed to shock her out of our little kiss bubble and bring her back to where we were. Panic set in her face and she sprang away from me as quickly as she could, as a result she banged her hip against the cabinet and I could barely suppress my laugh. She shot me, what she thought was, a threatening glare but she was just too cute to take seriously.

"Coming!" She called back and I watched her flee from the kitchen up the stairs, shooting me one more scathing, yet adorable, look before she vanished out of sight.

I'd done it! I had finally gotten up the confidence to ask her out and she had actually agreed! Now I just needed to make sure that I made her mine. I needed to make this date perfect.

I arrived home earlier that evening, soon before Cassie and Noah had come barrelling in the front door. I knew that as soon Cassie was home, Lexi would soon follow, and I was right. Not twenty minutes since Cassie had been back did the doorbell chime and Lexi walked in. I felt like a child on Christmas morning, waiting to see the incredible present that Santa had bought. And there she was. Standing at the front door looking insanely gorgeous. I wanted to snatch her away at that moment and steal her away to my room, but she wasn't mine. Yet. That time with Lexi in the kitchen had just been a sweet and brief insight into how it could be between us, how it could have been *last* summer, if I hadn't been such an idiot with her. So scared of what was developing between us. I wouldn't be making the same mistake this time round, I knew Lexi wouldn't be giving me another chance if I messed it up this time too.

After she left the kitchen, I gave her enough time to get back to Cassie's room and then I followed up to my room. I settled into my work, just looking through paperwork and different, extremely dull, parts of the job. I changed into some shorts and a top before grabbing my gym bag and heading out, I would be back in time to cook everyone dinner before they got back.
"Bradley, I'm going to the gym, I want you in your pyjamas when I get back, I'll cook dinner when I'm home." I received a non-committal grunt in response but I knew that he would get it all sorted. I called goodbye to everyone else in the house and set off. I immediately started into the weights section when I arrived and began to run through my regular routine. Those moments that I could steal to myself were so relaxing, my parents were still rocky after only reuniting recently. All through my workout I was unable to stop my grin, thrilled at the prospect of my date with Lexi, to get as much time with her as I could as possible.

"I'm back!" I called out when I got back home and was greeted to laughter and music flowing out of the kitchen.
"Hey brother? How was the gym?" Cassie asked as I walked into the kitchen and saw her, Bradley, Lexi and Hailey all in the kitchen. There were pizza boxes sitting on the island and they had just begun to tuck into the food. Hailey sat with Lexi at the table munching on her

margarita pizza and both her and Bradley were already in their pyjamas.

"Yeah, it was good." I told her, "I was going to cook dinner when I got back."

"I know, but you've been so busy lately and mum and dad felt bad so they let us order pizza." Cassie explained as she chewed on her slice.

"Yeah, come on Jake, be happy you don't have to cook and join us." Lexi said from where she perched at the table with her own food. I didn't need to be told twice; I grabbed the last plate on the island and piled some food onto it. Cassie was sitting on the other side of the table along with Bradley, so I slid next to Lexi, squashing her between Hailey and me. It seemed that I would be fighting for her attention with all my siblings.

"So how are we all doing?" I asked as I sat down. Bradley jumped into what he had been doing and how school was going and once he was done it seemed it was now Hailey's turn. This gave me the opportunity to, innocently, get even closer to Lexi and place my hand on her leg, brushing her thigh. I could feel her tense from the shock of the touch but soon settled in and shifted her leg towards me. I knew it was dangerous, sitting opposite Cassie while my hand was on her best friend's thigh. I've used my restraint for so long with Lexi, that now I was allowed to touch her, I never wanted to stop. Nothing went further than my hand resting gently on her leg with my thumb rubbing small circles, but I could feel Lexi lean in.

The rest of the evening passed in a wonderful haze of laughter and Lexi. Bradley and Hailey wanted us to all watch a film together before they had to go to bed so we all filtered into the living room after we had finished our pizza and tidied up the mess. Badley chose the film and gestured me over to sit with him creating a guys and girls sofa. Lexi and Cassie had situated themselves on the longer sofa with Hailey tucked in between them and us on the other. It was impossible for me to ignore the presence of Lexi. She seemed to have borrowed Cassie's clothes and I love how relaxed she looked in my home. I only wished she was wearing my clothes instead. I wanted her here all the time, just maybe a little closer to me.
About three quarters of the way through the film I heard a soft snoring beside me and Bradley had fallen asleep. "I'm going to take him upstairs," I whispered as I grabbed him, the girls nodded and I wandered out with him in my arms sound asleep. I put him to bed and he immediately rolled over and settled down. I wandered back downstairs and saw all the girls settled down. I was so tempted to leave a kiss on Lexi's head that I knew I had to leave before I did something that would get us caught. I left them to it and wandered upstairs, settling down I could feel the exhaustion hit me like a wall, sleep didn't take long to follow.

The next day felt full of possibilities. I had a day off work, giving me ample time to plan my date with Lexi. Sort some work and then chill with Bradley this evening when he got home to make up for all the time I had spent working lately. With work not really having any strict times, I could have the day off mid-week and then have some days where I worked on the weekend. Bradley and Hailey were in their last week of school and they were itching to be done. It was even worse for them to see me at home all the time and Cassie completely free, seeing as her university finished for summer a month prior to the schools. This was Cassie's mini summer at home before she was leaving for her summer camp again. I was looking forward to spending more time with Bradley, I knew I hadn't spent much time with him recently so it would be really nice. But for now, I had coffee to make and a date to plan, with the plans in mind I grabbed my phone and then started down to the kitchen. I was scrolling through my phone and noticed a message from Millie that had come through last night and I had totally missed it.

Millie: Hey stranger, are we going to get that date?

I'd forgotten about the date we cancelled and I never followed up after. In all honesty, after everything happened with Lexi, I didn't feel the desire to message

Millie let alone meet up with her. I knew I had to cut this off quickly and make sure that there was on overlap with Lexi.

> **Jake**: I'm sorry but I don't think it's a good idea for us to go out.

Millie: what?

> **Jake**: I'm just not really interested and I don't think it's fair for us to go out.

Millie: Is there someone else? Are you rejecting me?!

Jake: Yes, I'm sorry, there is someone else. I'm not rejecting you, but I just don't want to go on the date.

Millie: I can't believe you! You are making such a mistake.

Jake: Look, you were lovely, but I'm not interested. I'm sure there'll be someone else. I'm sorry for wasting your time.

Millie: You will be, don't worry.

I felt terrible, I didn't realise there would be such a problem since we had only been on one date. But at least it was sorted now and I wanted to focus on Lexi as much as I could. She was what mattered to me after all. I was wracking my brain on where I could take her that would be deserving enough of her. I was coming up empty so far... I couldn't ask anyone, no one could know about us yet, that was one way this would be ruined before it even started. I needed to come up with something on my own, easier said than done. I wanted to get it booked in as soon as possible so there was no way she would have any second thoughts. After around an hour, I had searched up countless different date ideas, countless options and ideas but none of them felt right. None of them seemed good enough for Lexi and I didn't know what to do, I would start with the day first.

Jake: So, when are we booking this date in?

Lexi: Not wasting any time, are you?

Jake: I've waited long enough for this date; I'm not messing it up now by putting it off.

Lexi: Okay, fair enough I am glad I must say, I was worried you'd change your mind.

Jake: Absolutely not, you?

Lexi: No way!

Jake: Good, then give me a date and I'll make the arrangements.

Lexi: This weekend?

Jake: Perfect x

She sent a heart in response and I locked my phone. I started up a single player game on my computer and played a few rounds. It was then when it struck me what would be the perfect date for us, a balance between cute and competitive. Romantic and risky. I knew she would love it. Immediately I switched off my game, started researching.

I wanted- no *needed*- this to be perfect, I needed this chance and a way to prove how much I care for her. She was far too good for me and I needed to make sure she never realised that. The morning had already gotten away from me and I could feel my stomach rumbling. I needed lunch! With a groan I stood from my desk, stretched and started downstairs.
"Oh, you're still here." Cassie commented as I wandered into the kitchen.

"Yep, as I do live here." I reminded her and she rolled her eyes. I was standing by the cupboard getting a glass when I heard that luscious caramel sound.
"Hey Cas, where are the…" she started, then stopped.
"Oh Jake, hi." Lexi said as I spun and our eyes collided.
"Lex," I murmured before recovering, "how was last night?"
"Oh fine, we just stayed on the sofa with Hailey and slept. Hailey woke up early today to get sorted so we went upstairs to be more comfortable and here we are now for some lunch." She replied and smiled at me.
"Ah nice, I've been working all morning." I explained. My eyes were glued to her and I had to fight every instinct to turn away. I was desperate to stay there and just watch her, but my stomach reminded me of my original plan so I turned to the fridge. I grabbed the bread and ham to make a sandwich. Lexi had made her way over to the table, where she and Cassie were already settled with their food. They returned to their conversation.
"What were you saying when you came in?" Cassie asked her.
"Oh no it doesn't matter, I've forgotten really." Lexi said.
"Hmm, okay." Cassie continued, "anyway, we need to sort out our plans tonight."
"Oh, Cassie do we have to." Lexi moaned. I was desperate to turn my head around and watch her, but I needed to make sure that no suspicions were raised. I

couldn't be seen to care in front of Cassie, I know that Lexi didn't want that. I kept my head down and focused intently on my sandwich.

"Lexi come on, we need to get the logistics of the double date sorted, Tate is really excited you know." Cassie replied. My head snapped up at that point, my hand clenched.

"Huh?" Lexi said, I was trying not to immediately turn round, grab her and kiss her. Show Cassie that Lexi wouldn't be going on a date with anyone except me. But I couldn't.

"Tate. Noah's friend. Come on Lexi, you really need to remember this guy's name if you're going on a date with him." Cassie moaned. I couldn't help but smile at the fact she couldn't even remember his name. She was mine; I was the only name I wanted her to think about.

"Cassie, do we have to?" She asked.

"Yep." Cassie snipped, "we already agreed and there is no way you're bailing now, you need a date after Miles. It'll be good."

"Fine," Lexi replied, "I'll go." With that last confirmation, I finished making my sandwich, if you could call it that, looking down at the destroyed mess on my plate. I had to eat something but this will have to do. I threw the items back in the fridge and slammed the door.

"Woah, what do you have against the fridge?" Cassie asked. I turned around, she looked curious but Lexi just looked guilty.

"Nothing. Work is annoying me." I explained. I glanced at Lexi again and she was still watching me. "I need to go."

"Okay…" I heard Cassie say as I left the kitchen. I went upstairs with my ruined sandwich and went back to my room.

"Hi." I heard from behind me. She stood in the doorway of my room; she looked incredible and still had the look of guilt on her face.

"Uh-" I stood speechless.

"I told Cassie I was going to the toilet, so I don't have much time." She explained and moved into my room slightly. I was unable to contain myself and within no time, in two large strides, I walked over to her, shut the door and pushed her against it. I took her head in my hands and pulled her lips to mine. I needed her to know I belonged to her. I wanted her to be mine. She quickly flung her arms around my neck and her hands found their way into my hair, tugging it gently. I moved my hands down to her hips and pulled her closer to me while covering her with my whole body and keeping her flush against the door. Her tongue pushed into my mouth and I groaned at the new sensation. Both fully sober, during the day. This was new and addictive. She pulled away far too soon.

"Just for the record, this wasn't what I came up here for." she explained while I leant down and my lips explored her neck, her smell was intoxicating.

"Uh huh, of course." I murmured against her skin.
"I wanted to explain the double date." she continued. That sobered me very quickly.
"Right." I said to her and pulled away to look at her.
"So, ages ago Cassie wanted to set me up with one of Noah's friends. This was before I even met Miles, but after that she wanted to go on the double date even more. Obviously, I couldn't tell her about us, so I had to agree." she swallowed, her look of guilt returned, "I don't want to go, there's only you. But I couldn't let her get suspicious. Plus, I-" I placed my finger over her mouth and she stopped talking. Looking up at me now with those gorgeous eyes.
"Sweetheart, it's alright. I know, I know the situation." I reassured her, "I'm extremely jealous and I hate the idea of you spending any time with anyone but me but I understand. It's okay."
"Jake, I'm yours. Okay?" She told me and all I could do was look at her, stunned. I knew my words wouldn't do my feelings justice so I just leant down and kissed her once more. Pulling her closer to me again. I moved away slightly, putting mere millimetres between our lips.
"I'm yours," I said against her lips. "Always will be." I could feel her smiling against my lips and my heart warmed once again. I pulled away from her and looked down once again.
"I should go." She whispered, I could see the hesitation in her face, I smiled at her not wanting to leave. I nodded

and moved away from her and opened the door for her. She darted out and into the bathroom, quickly flushing and washing her hands before going back downstairs. She looked back at me and shot me a wink before she disappeared.

Chapter 20: Jake (One year ago)

Lexi was in my bed. She was in my bed wearing my top. Wearing my top and nothing else. What the hell had I been thinking? I crossed a line yesterday, and it was something that, if I wasn't careful, could derail everything. There was already so much going on at home with mum and dad, I needed to be here for Bradley and Hailey and if I became too swept up with Lexi, I knew I wouldn't be able to be there for them the way I needed to be.
I'd wanted this moment with Lexi all summer, the chance for us to finally have something, but now? Well now my family needed me and I knew I couldn't fully commit to Lexi and be there for them, particularly while Cassie was away too. They all relied on me.

Lexi was laying on her side facing away from me and my arm was currently draped over her hips, our legs tangled together. I wanted to stay here forever, enveloped in her warmth, her luscious curves sculpted to my body. She fit like the puzzle piece I had been missing all my life. The longer I stayed here, the harder it'll become, I needed to detangle myself and get my distance from her now before it became too hard to say goodbye to this part of her. Lexi deserved better than I could offer her right now, and maybe one day I would be deserving of her. But that day wasn't today. With extreme caution, I managed to extract myself without stirring her. I'm sure that after keeping her awake yesterday, she was deeply out of it.

Once out of bed, I made my way down to the kitchen, luckily I was alone and I got straight to making a pot of coffee. I was sure the others would be awake soon and looking for coffee too.

"Hey," I heard softly from behind me, Lexi had appeared at the door as I was finishing making my cup of coffee from the pot. She looked irresistible in the morning, her hair piled on her head, still wearing my top but she had tucked it up and slipped on the joggers she had been wearing yesterday.

"Hi," I replied, "The kettle boiled, you want tea?" I asked knowing she didn't like coffee, desperate to break the tension. I could see the questions from last night and the hope she wore on her face.

"Yeah, thank you." She replied and reached to grab the cup, being sure that our hands wouldn't touch. "You weren't there when I woke up?" She questioned, clearly trying to keep the hurt out of her voice.

"I'm sorry, I thought I heard my mum and I came down to grab some coffee and chat to her quickly." I explained, the lie burnt as it escaped but I needed to diffuse this.
"Thank you for coming to get me last night and making sure I was okay." I continued.
"Er yeah, it's fine. Of course I came, I'll always help you." She explained and took a step forward.
"Yeah, I know I really appreciate that." I replied and took a step back. "I was in a really bad place last night and you really came through."
"About last night..." Lexi started, but I jumped in before she could finish what she was saying.
"Look Lexi, I can't do this. Last night was a mistake, I was a mess because of my parents and I'm at such a weird point, I don't know what I'm doing. I'm sorry." my heart clenched with the lies I choked out.
"So last night didn't mean anything to you?" She questioned, "all those things you said to me. It was all just lies?"
"I wasn't lying, but it just wasn't what you wanted it to be Lexi." I swallowed, "it can't be." I said more to myself.
"I get it, you just needed comfort and I was the one there right?" She asked incredulously. I started to open my mouth to respond but she just held up her hand and stared at me.
"Lexi-" I started.
"No Jake, don't. I can't do this, you've said how you feel and you've shown me what that was. You were upset and

I was a distraction. Fine." She stated, she put her tea on the island and turned away.
"Don't go." I pleaded; I needed her. Even if she hated me, I needed her around.
"I'll be back later," she replied and my heart began to fill, *"but not to see you Jake, I can't talk to you right now. I promised to spend time with Hailey and I'll be back to do exactly that. But nothing more."*
"Okay." I replied. Not trusting myself to say anything more.
"I'll bring your top back then too. I just need to go home and change." She explained, I was about to say that she didn't need to but I knew that anything more would just hurt her. I nodded and did the worst thing I've done in my life. I let her walk away from me. She didn't look back once.*

Two hours later the doorbell rang. Bradley and Hailey were up and had been running around the house. Mum hadn't surfaced yet, but that wasn't surprising, she spent most of her mornings in her room now. Since dad moved out, mum has been a wreck. It was Lexi who usually came over and helped me with breakfast and then would spend some time with Hailey while I usually did some work or occupied Bradley. Today breakfast was on me.
"Lexi!" Hailey called from the hallway where she greeted Lexi. Hailey pulled her into the kitchen and I saw

her smile fall as she saw me flipping pancakes at the stove.
"Hey Lex," I said to her, her shoulders were tense but she still managed to turn to me and offer a tight smile.
"Good morning, Jake," she said to me and then immediately turned to Hailey. "So have you had breakfast?" To which Hailey replied with a very enthusiastic nod.
"Jake made us pancakes and chocolate milkshakes," she explained.
"I can see, you still have some over your face." Lexi laughed and grabbed a wipe to clean her face. She was so good to them and my heart clenched once again watching them. Even after the way I was this morning she was still there for them and I couldn't ask for anything more, she was perfect.
"It was delicious!" Hailey declared and jumped up and down in front of Lexi, earning a small giggle and a smile from Lexi.
"So, what are our plans today?" Lexi asked her.
I watched Hailey ponder for a moment before shrugging her shoulders and pointing to the garden.
"Pool and trampoline?" Lexi asked and checked to which Hailey nodded vigorously. "Sounds amazing." Lexi was dragged out the back door, the sound of her laughter echoed in the kitchen as she followed Hailey outside. All I could do was watch her walk away and remind myself that I never deserved her in the first place.

Chapter 21: Lexi

"Ugh my feet are killing!" I moaned as Cassie, Lottie, Connie and I wandered around the shopping centre. Cassie had demanded for a girl's day so we could catch up. Apparently, she needed to get out of the house too.
"Well, you should've chosen better shoes." Cassie replied, she looked down at my terrible footwear choice. I bought these gorgeous new, leather boots and they looked amazing! But they were still so tough that they were killing my feet. They had a heel too so not the best for an intense shopping day. I wanted to wear them on my date with Jake so I knew I needed to break them in a bit first, but now as we were walking around the shopping centre, I was desperately regretting my choices.
"I know that, but they're new and I need to break them in, so this is my life today." I complained. We continued walking and I could feel my feet stropping with every

step, I needed all of my girls today so I would continue to endure the pain so I to enjoy the day.

We'd gone to a few different shops and my bank account already felt the struggle. Cassie had found a cute dress she had been looking for and Lottie had, of course, found a new book. We started towards the Starbucks to get a coffee and refuel before we did the rest of the various shops.

"There is nothing better than an iced coffee in the summer." Connie sighed as she grabbed her iced white mocha and took a seat.

"You're addicted." Connie laughed.

"I don't get it frankly," I shrugged, "Iced tea is much better."

"Agreed." Lottie smiled.

"Iced coffee and books, what could be better?" Cassie laughed. She had bought a book with Lottie too and was now flicking through it excitedly.

"I'd rather watch TV." I chimed in. I'd always been more of a comfort show watcher and scroll through Pinterest rather than sit and read.

"I love Pinterest, there's so many cool art things on there." Connie added. We jumped into a debate about what was better, it didn't last for long before we all decided we'd rather be shopping. Continuing our shopping trip, we made our way to Hollister and began spending even more money. A few hours later with my feet in agony and my bank account moaning, we made our way home. Cassie dropped off the girls before taking me home, despite it being the last thing I wanted to do.

My night consisted of TV, girl dinner and bed. It was the most relaxing thing ever and desperately needed after the events of the past days. My parents didn't come home last night and I wasn't sure when they would be home, but this was expected. I would take full advantage of the freedom and relaxation and get prepared for my date with Jake that was quickly approaching. My anticipation was bubbling and I knew that it would soon be here.

"Are you seriously not going to tell me where we're going?" I asked Jake. It was two days later and he picked me up from my house this morning. We were driving to the apparent first location of our date, yes there were multiple parts. Jake refused to utter any type of hint as to where we were going and I was itching to know.
"Absolutely not! This is our first date and I want to surprise you. Develop some patience, woman." He replied, I was staring daggers into the side of his head but he was paying no attention to me, jut grinning.
"Jake, you want to date me so you should know this by now. I have no patience and I hate surprises." I moaned. in all honesty the surprise was actually really cute. I was just so nervous.

"I *do* know you and you love surprises, shut up." He laughed, "Just wait a little longer and then you'll find out."
"Are we nearly there then?" I asked him, now bouncing in my seat. Finally he turned and winked.
"Haha, yes sweetheart, a few more minutes and we're there." I could hardly contain my excitement. I couldn't wait to see what Jake had in store for us.

After another five minutes, we arrived at an adventure place. I still couldn't work out what we were doing as there were so many different activities advertised. We walked towards the front office, there were both inside and outside areas and I was just looking at Jake. Inside there were signs for darts, an arcade, axe throwing, snooker and loads of other games. While there was another sign that pointed outside for climbing, paintball, shooting and archery. Jake continued up to the front desk.
"Hi, I have a booking for 2 under the name Jake Bailey." He informed the worker. The guy simply nodded and started looking at the computer.
"Right this way." He said after a moment and started walking away. We followed closely behind him.

He led us down a narrow corridor that had doors on both sides. They had no windows and gave away no signs as to what was going on behind them. He gestured to one of the doors on the left for us and Jake stepped in front to open the door for me before walking in.

"Hi there, you must be Jake and Lexi." A voice thundered from the other side of the room, "I'm Russell and will be your instructor for today to make sure that everyone leaves with their fingers intact."

"Hi, great to meet you." Jake replied and reached out to shake his hand, I reached out to shake his hand too. The room was full of different lanes with targets at the end of them, along the other wall were axes of different shapes and sizes.

"Hi," I said. Jake's face had changed, no longer with his stereotypical grin, but laced with nervousness.

"Hey, you okay?" I ask him. He turned to me, chewing his lip.

"Yeah, yeah. I'm fine, so what do you think?" He asked.

"What do I think?" I paused, finding his nervous face quite cute, "Jake this is amazing! I've never done this!" At that point he let out a nervous breath.

"Oh good, I just thought that after everything you've had going on recently, this could be a good bit of a release of anger and we can have a competition too." He said nervously. I leant up and kissed him.

"Jake, this is perfect. Thank you." I assured him.

"I just want to make this special for you sweetheart, however I can You deserve this and so much more." He replied and leant down to kiss me again.

"Well come on then!" I was bouncing with excitement. He nodded and we walked across the room to where Russell was standing with the axes to get us sorted

I was trying to get the hang of the weapon, but everything I was doing was falling. No matter how strong I threw it, nothing stuck into the targets.

"Are you kidding me?!" I moaned, I was desperate to do this well and it was going terribly, Jake had gotten a bullseye twice and my competitive side was roaring.

"Okay, sweetheart, can I help you?" Jake asked me, I admitted defeat and nodded. With a chuckle he picked up another axe and came over to me.

"So, first your stance, you need to have your hips like this." He explained and rotated my waist to reposition me. I nodded and let him move me.

"Okay," I replied. I adjusted my stance and got used to the new angle.

"Then your throw," he started and held the hand that was holding the axe, "You need to release it here, not lower down." He explained, but with his hands on my body I couldn't hear a word he was saying. I nodded again.

"And then," he continued, he was so close now that I could feel his lip against my ear. "You, release." I hadn't even realised but the axe had left my grasp hit the target, extremely close to the bullseye. I screamed and jumped, full of joy at the unfolding of events. I leapt into his arms; he immediately wrapped around me and lifted me up.

"Well done sweetheart." he murmured against my ears and a feeling of warmth flooded through my body. Jake's praise is something I'll never get tired of.

Our time flew by and to our dismay Russell came back telling us it was time to go. After Jake had explained everything to me, I had actually managed to hit the target a few times. My anger had subsided and I was so satisfied with how it went. Jake had done really well too, which was to be expected. We thanked Russell and started out.
"Jake, that was incredible, I don't know how to thank you."
"I can think of one way." he said with a growing smile. He slowly leant down, took my face in his hands and kissed me, I drew my arms around his neck and he pulled me closer. It was an excellent way to thank him. Once we drew apart, I just stood there and smiled.
"This has been perfect." I told him.
"It isn't over yet…" he said with a knowing smile, he grabbed my hand and started pulling me to the car.
"Where are we going now?" I asked.
"Hush, you'll find out soon. Just let me spoil you sweetheart." he complained and I rolled my eyes but agreed. He opened the door for me and we settled into the car and started onto part two of the date.

"Oh god I am stuffed," I groaned as I finished up the main. Jake had ended up taking me to this gorgeous little restaurant for dinner. I was thankful my dress was so stretchy as I felt like I could explode. It had gone perfectly with my boots and the look from Jake had confirmed how hot I looked. There hadn't been a single moment of silence, the conversation flowed so easily. We had managed to skirt around Cassie and that whole situation. In all honesty we avoided discussing both of our families, which I think was safe. I could actually enjoy the evening; we had turned off both our phones for a while so that Cassie couldn't locate us and we didn't have to deal with distractions.

"Me too," Jake agreed.

"Would you like any dessert?" asked the waiter as he approached the table to collect our plates.

"Oh um?" I paused, sending Jake a questionable look, I mean I always wanted something sweet but I had just said I was stuffed, as did he, so I don't know.

"Yes, we'll have dessert please." Jake confirmed.

"Great, I'll bring some menus," the waiter said and turned away.

"I thought you said you were stuffed?" I asked him.

"Yeah, I kind of am, but I know how much you like your sweet stuff and knew you'd want a dessert," he explained.

"Wow." I said and had a look at the menu when the waiter circled back round to the table.

"What can I get for you?" the waiter asked.

"We'll take one brownie with ice cream, a hot chocolate and a cappuccino please." he said looking at me and I nodded.

"Great, I'll put that through for you." the waiter said and turned away.

"Brownie's okay right?" he asked me when the waiter had gone, "I know that chocolatey stuff is your favourite."

"Yeah, it's great," I assured him, "but I thought you wanted one too."

"Well yeah, I thought we could share." he said, "or is that not okay? Sorry I thought it would have been nice for the date, I didn't think about how possessive you'd get with your chocolate."

"No, no I'm happy to share, I'm just shocked about you. I thought you didn't share your food."

"I thought I'd make an exception for you," he winked as he reached his hand across the table to take mine in his.

"Wow, making me feel special." I said to him and took his hand.

"You certainly are," he agreed.

"And thank you for the hot chocolate," I added, squeezing his hand.

"You don't like coffee so I thought that would go well if I was having a coffee."

"Thank you," I told him. "This date has been amazing."

"Thank you for agreeing to give me a chance," he teased.

"I'm just glad you picked somewhere where we didn't need to wear a silly disguise or hide away somewhere."

"I never want you to hide Lex," he told me.

"But what about Cassie?" I asked him, the sense of worry starting to bubble up.

"We'll tell her at some point, but for now, let's enjoy tonight together. I've been waiting for this for so long and I don't want it overshadowed by worry." He insisted.

"Yeah," I said slightly non-committal, I could see that he could sense my doubt and he shot me a stern look. "Fine, fine, I'm forgetting it. Let's enjoy our evening."

"Thank you," he replied and lifted my hand to his lips and gave me a light kiss on my knuckles before releasing my hand as the waiter walked over with the tray of food.

"And here we are, one brownie, one hot chocolate and one cappuccino." the waiter said and placed everything on the table, "please enjoy."

"Thank you." we said in unison and I immediately dug into the brownie, not waiting for Jake to start.

"Hey!" he complained and quickly dived in and took an enormous spoonful of brownie and ice cream. The brownie stood no chance, it was soon devoured by the both of us.

"Go on, you have the last bite." he said and pushed the plate over to me.

"No, no, you planned this whole date. You at least deserve the last bite of brownie." pushing it towards him.

"Ah no, but the reason this date took so long was because I was an idiot for so long. So, you have the brownie." he said to me and pushed it back.

"But I want you to have it, and surely you should listen as it's your fault this date took so long so you have it." I said and pushed it back.

"Fine. I won't say no to an extra bit of brownie." he finally conceded. He scooped up the mouthful that was left onto his spoon and lifted it to his mouth.

"Ha, I knew I would win," I started but as I opened my mouth to continue talking, he quickly shoved the spoon into my mouth and grinned in satisfaction.

"What was that?" he asked. I tried to stare him down as maliciously as I could with a mouthful of brownie, but it soon dissolved into a smile when I realised how foolish I must look. He laughed at me and leaned over the table kissing me sweetly. This was truly the best date of my life.

Jake called for the bill and there was a slight battle with our cards when the waiter came over but Jake knew how stubborn I was so had managed to swiftly pass his card to the waiter, who promptly fled.

"I wanted to pay!" I demanded.

"Hush sweetheart." he said and leant over the table to give me a swift kiss, "let me spoil you. I've waited long enough for this."

After another five minutes, the waiter came back with the receipt, we thanked him and left the restaurant. As we were walking back to Jake's car, Jake hesitantly grabbed my hand but I held tight reassuring him. He stopped us where we were and pulled me to him before moving his other hand to hold my face and leant down to kiss me. I tilted up on my toes and deepened it, he let go of my hand to snake his arm around my waist instead. He pulled me against him and slowly started to walk me back until I was pushed against the wall of the shop nearest us. His other hand moved into my hair and tugged gently. The whole length of our bodies was now touching and I felt like I was about to go up in flames, I was desperate for more. But in that moment a passing car honked his horn and Jake jumped away.

"Haha okay, maybe we shouldn't be doing that on the street." He chuckled and made sure I was steadied before fully moving back.

"Maybe not," I agreed, but part of me wanted to get back to it.

"Come on sweetheart, let's get you home." He said and pulled me along with him again.

"Ow!" I exclaimed, I had tried to wear-in my boots, but I hadn't done the best job and they still killed my feet.

"What? What is it?" Jake asked, his face full of panic and worry. I could see his eyes scanning my body trying to find any injuries.

"No, no it's fine. It's my shoes, they're really hurting. They're new and just not the comfiest to walk in." I admitted. Jake looked at me with a more amused expression now and looked as if he was trying to calculate something in his mind.

"Right." Jake stated, "we can't have that." Before I could register anything, Jake swooped me up into his arms like a fireman and continued down the road.

"Woah, wait." I exclaimed, "Jake what are you doing?"

"It's not comfy for you to walk, so you don't walk." He explained.

"No, don't be daft, I can walk." I assured him.

"Does it hurt?" He asked, I simply nodded with my arms still around his neck, "Then you aren't walking."

"But Jake-" I tried to say, yet my words were promptly cut off by Jake's lips on mine. I giggled against his lips and all complaints were silenced. There was no place I would rather be than in Jake's arms. I nestled into him, scattering kisses all over his neck earning me a small moan from him as he walked.

"Lex you're killing me." he murmured, I smiled knowing my goal was achieved. Jake carried me back to the car and I settled into the seat after the most perfect date of my life.

"So back to mine or do you want me to drop you home?" Jake asked.

"Well mum and dad aren't home so maybe we could go back to mine for a little bit." I suggested, the idea of having time with Jake just the two of us sounded irresistible.

"Let's go," he said and we started off to my house.

We pulled up around 10pm and, as expected, my parents were still absent. It had been two days now and I hadn't heard anything from them.

"Parents on business again?" Jake asked as we sat in the car for a moment. I just shrugged and got out, I heard another car door shut behind me and Jake followed. His hand snuck around my waist and squeezed me softly. I couldn't help but lean into him and he took that as an invite to plant soft and light kisses on my neck. After a slight delay from the distraction, I managed to open the door and we both stumbled through the door giggling. We discarded both our jackets and shoes and wandered through to the kitchen.

"Coffee?" I asked to which I received a nod. He stood behind me as I filled the coffee pot and got the cups together. Jake returned to decorating my necks with kisses and moved his hand round so it now sat on my stomach. I turned to him and captured his lips with mine.

"Do you really want coffee?"

"I hate coffee," he replied with a laugh. I turned fully in Jake's arms and met his kiss as deeply as I could.

His hands were frenzied as he explored my body. I looped mine behind his neck and weaved my hands through his soft hair. I had always been obsessed with his hair, ever since I was twelve and I would see him joking around and running his hands through his hair. I had always wished I would be able to do that instead, and now I actually can.

"What's on your mind?" He said as he pulled away slightly, as if he could sense that I was thinking about something.

"Hmm," I said and paused looking up at him, "just how long I have admired your hair and wanted to do exactly this." I explained as I ran my hands through it, he closed his eyes and groaned. I gave it a slight tug which elicited a soft moan from him and it excited me even more. His hands reached under my thighs and lifted me up so that my legs were wrapped around his waist. He carried me out of the kitchen and into the living room. He settled onto the sofa with me on his lap. Each time I felt Jake's touch on my skin I was set aflame, I could feel my excitement growing in the pit of my stomach and I soon felt like I was going to combust.

All of a sudden, my phone rang like a bucket of water to extinguish the flames inside me. We broke apart like opposing magnets, I pulled my phone out of my pocket and saw who was ringing.

"It's Cassie," I explained and showed him the screen, "I should pick up in case something is wrong."

"Yeah of course," Jake agreed, I clicked to answer and put the phone to my ear.

"Hey," I said to the phone and tried to keep my voice as level as possible, which was extremely hard seeing as Jake was running his hands up and down my thighs.

"Lexi! This is really important and it can't wait." Cassie tended to over exaggerate. Jake has now turned to give attention to my neck and laughed when he heard his sister's tone.

"Right, Cassie what's up?" I asked, now beginning to feel breathless as Jake started to nibble my neck.

"Well, I was talking to Noah…" she started slowly, "and we need to solidify plans for this double date."

"What?" I asked her, Jake's movements seemed to slow as he listened to Cassie.

"The date with Noah and Tate, remember?" She asked me and I felt Jake's movements cease entirely. He stopped his kisses and looked away trying to hide his hurt.

"Cassie, I agreed to that ages ago," I reminded her, "Things have changed now." I said more for Jake's benefit than hers.

"What do you mean?" She replied confused now, "Come on, you're not seeing Miles anymore. And you're single so why not."

"Well…" I knew full well I couldn't explain that I was falling in love with her brother all over again. I stayed silent and wished I could do something about the hurt in Jake's eyes.

"Exactly, it's settled. We're going out together and you can finally meet Tate." Cassie announced and then hung up before I could protest any further. All I could do was stare at Jake, trying to work out what I could even say.

"So... The double date is still happening then?"

I couldn't tell what was going through his mind at that point but I just wish I could have told Cassie then and there why there was no way in hell that I would want to go out with Tate.

"Yeah. I'd forgotten about it to be honest. She sorted it when Miles and I had stopped seeing each other. Since things started with us, I hadn't thought of anyone else." I tried to explain.

"Right." He replied tersely. He slowly pushed my hips and I took that as an indication to get off him. I sat on the sofa and Jake stood and started to pace the living room.

"Jake, I don't want anyone else. I just forgot."

"Yeah or maybe you were worried I would ditch you again the same way I did last summer and you wanted to have a contingency plan in case that happened." He voiced, his tone now becoming irritable.

"Wha- what are you talking about?!" I replied and stood to go to him. I tried to take his hand in mine but he batted me away and continued to pace.

"Come on Lexi, I know I broke your heart last summer. Even when you tried to hide it, you changed after our night together and you never forgave me. Admit it."

"Jake I was hurt, you know I was, but I trust you. I want to trust you and I want to be with you." I tried to assure him, to no avail.

"Lexi please, I can't deal with being left again. Dad left last summer and I dealt with everything alone."
"You weren't alone Jake! Even after everything you put me through I was still there for you. I still helped with Bradley and Hailey. I did *everything* I could. You were the one that abandoned me and yet I still opened my heart to you again this summer and now *you're* going crazy on me!" I snapped, I couldn't believe what he was saying.
"Lexi… you have to understand my side." He replied, now seeming quieter, but the damage was already done.
"No, I don't Jake. I have waited for you my whole life; I have wanted you since I was 12. Now you're looking at me and doubting me. Do you know how much that hurts?" I told him.
"I- I can't do this." He replied. Not even acknowledging or trying to understand what I was saying.
"Fine." Was all I could say. We stood there facing each other in the living room, neither of us saying anything and unable to take back what had been said.
"I think I should go." He grumbled, grabbed his jacket and slipped his shoes back on before walking out. I didn't move until I heard the front door shut and saw his headlights drive away. I sunk to the floor and couldn't stop the tears that fell.

Chapter 22: Jake

I raced out of Lexi's house even though every bone in my body was screaming at me to turn back, pull her into my arms and tell her that I'm just jealous. It was too late now, I had already done the damage and I knew I needed to redeem myself. I *knew* she was being honest and I *knew* Tate didn't mean anything to her, but I just saw red as soon as she mentioned anyone else. I needed a minute and I should give Lexi some time.
I got to my car, started it and drove off before I could change my mind. I drove home on autopilot, pulled into the driveway and finally let myself breathe. I took a minute to myself in the car before heading inside.
"Hi darling, you're back late." Mum said, I could see her pop her head out from the kitchen, I walked over to greet her and gave her a quick hug.
"Yeah sorry, I was out with some of the guys and time got away from us," I explained.
"Ah sounds lovely, how was your night?" She asked.

"Oh, it was great. We went to the pub for a few pints and just caught up." Mum started making a drink alongside hers and handed me the tea she just made.
"That should help," She replied.
"Thanks," I feigned a yawn, "I'm sorry to cut this short, but I'm going to head up and get some sleep."
"Okay sweetheart, don't stretch yourself too thin." She said, her face showing her concern.
"I'm okay," I assured her with a light kiss on the cheek. "I'll see you in the morning."
"Goodnight." She called as I started upstairs. I got to my room, changed from my date outfit and flopped down onto my bed. I settled down, already dreaming about how I could make it up to Lexi.

The sun was shining through my window when I peeled my eyes open the following morning and I could hear the grating whine of my alarm clock reminding me that I had to get to work. I hauled myself out of bed and started the morning.
"Out the way." Cassie moaned as I was walking towards the bathroom. She slipped into the room before me and slammed the door on my face.
"Cassie, come on!" I yelled, "I need to get to work."
"Well, be faster next time." She yelled back through the door. "I won't be long, be patient."

"Fine." I grumbled, I leant against the wall outside the bathroom and waited for her to be done. Five minutes later she finally revealed herself again.
"All yours." She said and waved her hand as if to usher me into the bathroom.
"Wow thanks." I replied sarcastically and rushed into shower and get ready for work. Fifteen minutes later I was finished and downstairs, made myself a coffee, said goodbye to my mum and dad before rushing out the door.

I pulled into the car park at work just before 9am and rushed inside. Patrick was waiting for me in the lobby, no doubt with an excessive list of things that needed to get done today. Things that would mean I would be busy all day, not having to think about the destruction of my relationship until I get home tonight.
"Hi Pat, how are you?" I asked cheerily as I walked in the door.
"Jake, morning! Great to have you in today, I'm doing good, doing good. How are you?" He asked.
"I'm great." I told him with as much enthusiasm as I could muster. "What have you got for me today?"
"So, not too much." He explained, "I've emailed you a copy of the stuff that needs doing and preferably today please. It needs to be finished in good time as we have got *so* much going on."
"Okay, great. I'll go and get settled and get started on the list right away." with a brief smile I started over to my

desk and got situated. I logged on and rolled my eyes at the list Patrick had given to me. There was so much on here that it would be a miracle if I got it all done today, I got started straight away before I could dwell on just how overwhelming it all was.

I thought I would reward myself with a coffee a few hours into work. I stood from my desk and stretched my back. Walking to the break room I started the coffee machine and stood waiting.
"Hey honey," Sheila said, Sheila was the receptionist at the company and she was the most wonderful person ever. She was so kind and lovely and was always so caring, even though I hadn't known her for very long. She was practically the mother of the office.
"Hi Sheila, how are you?" I asked.
"I'm fine, slowly getting through everything."
"Same here." I agreed.
"Are you okay?" she asked me, a look of scepticism on her face.
"Yeah, I'm fine," I assured her, "just tired."
"Okay, well if you need me honey then I'm always here."
I nodded and smiled, something about her just feeling comforting.
"Thank you, I've got enough work and coffee to stop me thinking today," I told her but I was halted by her look, "I promise you I'm okay."

"Good." She replied and nodded. I grabbed my cup, added some sugar and started back to my desk. I sat down and checked my phone. My stomach dropped and I released a series of curses under my breath at the message waiting.

Millie: Hey babe, miss me?

Jake: Why are you messaging? I thought we said we weren't going to see each other anymore.

Millie: No you said that I don't like that.

Jake: Wait what?

Millie: Well, I don't want to be done with you so.
Millie: When are we going to see each other?

Jake: Look fine, maybe we can meet tonight once I've finished work and clear this up.

Millie: We can meet up and see what happens. Sure babe.

Jake: No, just to clear things up.

Millie: Okay hun. Tonight. The Modern, just past the high street. 7PM.

Jake: I'll be there.

Millie sent another message but I couldn't deal with anything else she had to say so I just pocketed my phone and continued to tackle Patrick's list. I was far too irritable to deal with this. I just wanted Lexi. I want her back in my room, smiling and laughing with me. This whole Millie situation would push me to be able to resolve things with Lexi, once I had finally sorted things with her then I could move on with the girl I truly wanted.

By lunch time I had finished all of the emails I needed to and had written up some of the website work and articles that Patrick wanted me to get done. Now I had tables and statistics to look at, certainly not something that was my specialty, but I needed a break before I could get started on that.
"I'm going for lunch," I called to Patrick as I walked past his office, he nodded at me and I took that as permission and I walked out of the building. I started towards the Subway down the road to the offices to satiate my craving.

"Jake!" Andy called from behind the counter, Andy was the regular worker on my office days so I usually bumped into him when I came in for lunch during the week.
"How are you man?" I asked, he was a good guy and it was always nice to have a brief chat with someone outside the office. He was a bit older than me, mid-thirties and I think he was married too.
"Not bad, not bad. Been a slow morning." He explains. "But anyway, what can I get you?"
"I'll go with a footlong BMT on Italian herb and cheese please." I asked. Andy got on with the order and as he was assembling the sandwich we chatted for a little longer.
"Right, I need to get back," I told him as I started out of the store.
"No proper lunch break? You've been here for like ten minutes." He protested.
"We're getting everything up and running and we have a launch coming soon so things are all over the place. I'm mostly working from home for very long days or eating from my desk." I explained.
"Don't work yourself too hard." He warned.
"I won't, I promise, it *is* a lot but it'll be rewarding." I assured him and with a wave goodbye I headed back to the office. I took ten minutes to inhale my sandwich at my desk and took a quick break before starting my work again.

In the afternoon I shockingly managed to get through the write-ups and tasks that Patrick has dumped me with. By 6:30 I was able to pack my stuff up and head home. Compared to other days, this wasn't too bad. I said goodbye to Sheila and Patrick, started back out of the building and on the way to my car I pulled out my phone to message Millie back.

Jake: Finished work, will be there soon.

Millie: Perfect xx

I rolled my eyes, and drove to the address Millie had given, knowing it would be painful. I had punched the place into Google Maps and within ten minutes I pulled into the car park. It looked like a very glamorous bar, there was a sparkling sign with an array of coloured lights. Exactly the thing that Millie would like and exactly my type of torture.

I wandered through the door, headed to the bar to grab a cider and found a table in the back. I pulled out my phone to see if there was anything from Lexi and of course there wasn't, but I couldn't stand the silence from her for any longer.

Jake: We need to talk. I'm coming over to yours in an hour.

Lexi: Fine.

At least she was going to talk to me, I could work with that. I could go over and explain everything. Beg even if I need to. I'd confess I was jealous and I know that she wants to keep up the pretence for Cassie. She's too important for me to give up, I won't walk away from her.
"Hey babe," Millie's shrill voice cut through my thoughts, now there was a girl I would happily walk away from.
"Millie, hi." I replied, not getting up when she came over to the table and winced when she leant over to kiss me on the cheek. Her top gave me a full view of her cleavage and I averted my gaze. She raised her hand and clicked her fingers, signalling for the waiter to come over. She ordered a Martini then turned back to me.
"So have you missed me?" she asked flashing me her pure white smile, it seemed like she was baring her teeth now rather than being sweet.
"Well not really, seeing as I told you this was over." I explained.
"Ah don't be daft babe," she laughed, "we're not done until I say so, no one dumps me."
I took a swig of my cider trying to keep my annoyance at bay, I needed a way to get rid of her and keep her gone for good.
"Millie, I'm not dumping you," I said and paused, she looked at me with a triumphant grin before I leant

towards her and lowered my voice. "I'm not dumping you, because we never started. It was a trainwreck, and only one date. Now leave me alone." silently revelling in the look of shock that took over her face. I leant back, downed the rest of my cider and walked away. There was a girl waiting for me who I truly wanted to be with.

I raced over to Lexi's as fast as I could, without breaking any speed limits. Knowing her parents were probably home; I didn't want to risk ringing the doorbell so I instead messaged her quickly and then waited. After a few restless minutes of waiting I saw Lexi scurry up her driveway and glance either side for me, the minute she recognised my car she rushed over and slid into the passenger side.

"Lexi I'm so-" my words were halted by her grabbing my face and pressing a desperate and fast kiss to my lips. I grabbed the back of her head and deepened the kiss, my hands weaving into her hair and tugging slightly. I pulled away with a gasp and looked at her, her eyes were glazed with lust and her breathing was hard.

"I'm so sorry," I managed to get out, "I didn't mean what I said yesterday, I was just mad with jealousy and I let that ruin something amazing. Please give me another chance, let me take you out tomorrow and make up for what happened."

She shrugged, "I had a minute to think about what you said and actually it was hot to see you jealous and I completely understand what you said." I tried to jump in but she held her finger up, "Which is why I'm going to let Cassie know tomorrow that I won't be going on that double date. You're the only one I want to be with and the only one I want to go on *any* dates with."

"Oh god, thank you sweetheart." I leant in and kissed her again quickly. "But I want to take you out tomorrow, make it up to you."

"I won't complain about going on a date with you," she teased.

"How about dinner?" I asked her, I could see her thinking it over.

"How about lunch and something in the afternoon?" She bargained, "I want to talk to Cassie and that way I can come back to yours after and talk to her about the double date."

"Perfect, mini golf?" I asked her.

"Absolutely, as long as you're ready to get beaten." She replied.

"By you? Anytime. But I doubt that is going to happen." I leant in once again to kiss her. She met my lips with equal enthusiasm and in no time our argument and Millie was all forgotten. Everything faded away while I was with Lexi and this was what I wanted for the rest of my life. My hands had a mind of their own as they traced up and down her back and around her hips. Her hands trailed up my chest and rested on my bicep, I could feel the goosebumps decorating her skin as my hands traced up

and down her arms. I could hear her sigh against my mouth as I squeezed her thighs. All too soon she pulled away, I followed her as she moved back, protesting at the sudden space between us.
"Oh god, how could I have been so stupid to not see what was right in front of me all these years," I said. "All this time you were right there."
"And I'm still here, Jake, I'm not going anywhere."
"Good because I'm not letting you go," I insisted.
"You'll have to right now, because if I get caught I won't be able to see you tomorrow."
"Ah come on, ten more minutes," I tried to convince her, I didn't want her to leave my sight.
"I'm sorry. I *really* must go now," she confessed, "I snuck out of the house to talk to you but I need to get back before they realise I'm not there."
"Okay sweetheart," I replied and ran my hands up and down her arms. I would protest but I knew what her parents were like and they didn't need much to make her life hell. I would not be responsible for that.
"You called me sweetheart again," she repeated.
"Is that okay?" I asked and scattered kisses on her neck.
"Absolutely, I love it."
"Now go, I'll come and get you at 1 tomorrow for our date." I said and with a final kiss she launched herself out the car and snuck back to her house.

Our Summertime Secrets

I woke up the next morning barely able to contain my excitement. Today was a work from home day, so I woke up and immediately started on my work. I knew if I worked now, then went on my date, I could do the last bits when I get back. After I had rushed downstairs, said a brief good morning and hello to my mum and dad before they went to work and Bradly before he went to school, I grabbed a coffee and rushed back upstairs to start my work. I was able to get straight into it and pushed through a lot more work than I expected to. When I shut my laptop off at midday, I was feeling satisfied and ready for my date with Lexi.

I knew I was running early, but once I had finished my work, I couldn't wait to see Lexi again. I had a record fast shower and changed into a nice pair of trousers and a shirt. I turned up to Lexi's ten minutes early and just waited in the car until she was ready. I knew not to knock on the door and I didn't want to rush her. When her parents weren't away they worked from home a lot, so I didn't want to risk it.

At 1.05pm, Lexi rushed out of her house and slipped into the passenger seat, just as she had last night, she reached over and gave me a kiss as soon as she was in the car.

"I missed you," she said once we pulled apart.

"I missed you too sweetheart." I replied with a chuckle, "you ready?"

"Absolutely." she said, showing her keenness. I pulled away from her house and we started towards *'Sunny Side Up',* one of Lexi's favourite brunch places. She turned and smiled at me when I pulled into a parking space outside and started bouncing in her seat. Practically pulling me through the door, she requested a table for two and the hostess sat us before taking our drink orders and leaving us there.

"Did I make a good choice?" I asked her.

"Amazing choice." she confirmed. I reached across the table and took her hand in mine, relishing in how natural it felt to sit here with her.

"Good, I wanted to make it up to you after everything that happened with that double date drama. I'm so sorry about all of that sweetheart."

"Uh, no apologies please, there's no need to be sorry." She assured me, "it was hot to see you jealous."

"Good, because you're mine. And if another guy dares look at you, then I can assure you, you'll see the jealous side again." I replied with a squeeze of her hand.

"Is that a promise?" She asked coyly.

"Oh yes." I responded and she leant back and laughed, that melodious sound was musical. I'd never get tired of that sound, and I would spend the rest of my life making sure that the only tears that flowed were from laughter, not pain. At that moment the waiter returned with our drinks, a Diet Coke for her and a Sprite for me. We thanked him for our drinks and ordered our food before he left us again.

"I'm just going to go to the bathroom." She said, "I meant to go before I left but I could hear my dad coming and I wanted to get out of the house before he stopped me."

"Lex, it's fine. Go before the food arrives." I told her. She nodded and wandered over to the bathroom, I pulled out my phone to check if I had anything important, luckily there was nothing.

"Well fancy seeing you here." her sickening voice shocked me back into focus and I saw her leaning down against the table.

"Millie." I growled glancing over to the bathrooms watching for Lexi. She didn't need to see this.

"Hey baby, who are you looking for? That little tramp you walked in with?" She asked.

"Don't you dare talk about her!" I hissed, trying to keep my voice down, even though I was about to burst.

"Oh come on." she said and slid into Lexi's seat.

"Go away." I demanded.

"But it's so fun Jakey!" She said and her smile seemed more like a snarl now.

"Please just go away," I glanced back to the toilet and saw Lexi appear. I was desperate to get Millie away before she said or did anything to Lexi. There was no way I would let that happen. I watched Lexi as her eyes met mine and she smiled, then noticing the blonde now in her seat a look of confusion passed over her face before it seemed to be quickly replaced by a look of determination. She marched over and instead of giving Millie any attention, her eyes didn't leave mine as she walked over to me, grabbed my face and pulled me into a deep kiss right in front of Millie. Lexi had my attention, all my attention, I grabbed her head to keep her against me and as desperate as I was to pull her onto my lap right here, she pulled away before I could.

"You're in my seat." she spun to face Millie; in the sweetest voice I had ever heard her use. Clearly, I had underestimated my girl and clearly didn't need me to rush in to protect her.

"I'm sorry?" Millie stuttered, clearly shocked by Lexi's brazen behaviour.

"Apology accepted. Now move, you're crashing my date and you know what they say, three's a crowd." this time she paired her words with a quick sweeping gesture as if batting Millie off. Stunned into silence, Millie clearly realised she had lost and she stood and stumbled away.

"Uh-" I started but couldn't get any words out.

"Could you explain why that blonde bimbo was sitting here drooling over you?" she asked, completely composed as she lowered herself into her seat.

"Uh-" I cleared my throat, "that's Millie, she's the one the guys set me up with. I ended things when I realised I couldn't ignore my feelings for you, apparently things don't end until she says so."

"Right, well I think I've just ended that one, if she dares come near you again, I'll be doing a whole lot more." she replied, that sweet smile still on her face.

"I can see what you mean about that jealousy thing," I said to her, "you are so hot right now." She looked away and I captured her hand in mine on the table again, she shook her head at me, but her smile was just growing larger. I knew that if I hadn't fallen for this girl already, then I was on my way to being head over heels for her.

Chapter 23: Lexi (One year ago)

I can't believe he said last night meant nothing to him. It had been everything, something I would remember and think about for the rest of my life. But clearly it wasn't reciprocated. Cassie was away for another week and I wanted to be there for Bradley and Hailey. I knew Jake was doing well but I wanted to help. It wasn't fair for it to fall on him and I knew how it felt to feel isolated. As painful as it was, I wouldn't leave him alone. I would pretend nothing happened, I'd return his top and simply focus on Hailey and Bradley.

My parents were away at the moment, each on their own business trips and my house felt far too large, too quiet, too isolating. Cassie's house was the total opposite, even with their dad moving out still looming over them all, there was so much love and laughter in this house.

Our Summertime Secrets

I was out in the garden playing with Hailey, Jake was gaming with Bradley in the living room and for the first time all summer I was glad that Bradley wanted to stay inside rather than us all playing together. I was trying to be as calm and composed as I could manage, but the way that Jake made me feel was killing me inside. I gave myself away to him in a way I had never imagined ever happening and now I wish it never had. I knew Jake was playing the game and paying me no attention, but even his presence felt suffocating now, at least before I was able to hope there were feelings, now I knew the truth and it was too difficult to accept.

"Hey! How about we go to the pool?" I asked Hailey, desperate to get out of the house.

"Yes, yes, yes!" She answered and started jumping around.

"Okay, okay." I laughed at her enthusiasm, "Go and get your swimsuit on and get what you want to take and we'll walk over." Hailey nodded and ran inside to get ready. I wandered in after her aiming to head to Cassie's room and borrow a bikini.

"I want to go swimming too!" Bradley called and scrambled up from where he was sitting. Jake paused the now discarded game and stood too.

"Of course, buddy, you can come with us, get changed and we'll go." I told him with a smile.

"Jake you'll come too, right?" He turned and asked his brother.

"Uh." Jake stuttered and looked at me questioningly.
"Yeah, we can all go together." I kept the most genuine smile on my face as I could muster. He stood silently trying to read how I felt, I was hoping he couldn't see how I was dying inside.
"Well okay then," he finally replied, "I'll go and change." I tried to calm my thumping heart. I trailed up the stairs and shut myself in Cassie's room to change, and to prepare myself, this was going to be fun...

"Lexi, Lexi hurry up!" Hailey moaned as she practically pulled my arm out of its socket to get me to the pool. I let her drag me across and we quickly snagged a few sunbeds and laid out our stuff. Jake and I on either end with the little ones in between us. Hailey ran and jumped straight into the pool and I followed suit, she surfaced and spluttered in the water before she found her footing and we started playing volleyball.
"Wait for me!" Bradley called and jumped in to join us. Jake jumped in too and we all played for a while, luckily I was able to avoid any contact or interactions with Jake.
"Okay, time out, I'm going to sit down." I said in an attempt to get away from Jake, there was only so much I could handle being surrounded by his wet topless body,
"No, I want to play with you." Hailey protested.
"Leave her alone," Jake grunted.
"Why don't you practise your water handstands." I suggested it and went to sit down and check my phone.

Our Summertime Secrets

There were the usual messages from my parents, telling me the jobs they expected me to have done by the time they got back and a message from Cassie on the group chat. I placed my phone back in my bag and laid back, enjoying the sun and the peacefulness. A splash of water on my legs caught my attention and I briefly opened my eyes before closing them again quickly when I realised it was just a couple of guys playing in the pool. My attention was drawn again when I noticed it had gone a lot darker than before, I opened my eyes and one of the guys that had been playing in the pool now stood before my lounger.

"Can I help you?" I asked.

" Uh, the ball went under your bed." He explains while pointing down.

"Right," I stood up from the lounge chair and bent down to grab it, "There you go." I said and handed it over.

"Thanks," he said but didn't leave, "So do you come here often? I haven't seen you before."

"Er, yeah I guess a few times before." I replied, crossing my hands over my chest and waiting to see what he said.

"Ah right, that's cool. I mean if you're here again, maybe we could hang out?" He asked, I took a moment to look at him, he was tall and had a swimmers body. I would say he was a little older than me. His hair was dark and had been pushed back with the water.

"Yeah, that would be nice, I'm Lexi by the way." I stood and extended my hand towards him. He could be a good distraction for the summer.

"Great, I'm Josh." He flashed a charming smile.

"Everything okay here?" Jake thundered behind me, I felt rather than hear his voice due to his proximity. He was practically pressed up behind me, I could feel his chest against my back.

"We're fine," I snarled, not trusting myself to look at him.

"Yeah, all good man. I was just making conversation." He replied, starting to back up now.

"Right well if you don't mind, we're having a day out here." He replied and gestured between Hailey and Bradley in the pool.

"Woah, my bad. I didn't realise." Josh now said moving further back, "I'll see you around Lexi." I smiled and waved as nicely as I could and once he was far away enough, I spun to Jake and gave him the most malicious look I could muster.

"What the hell is wrong with you?" I whispered to him, no wanting Hailey and Bradley to notice.

"I'm trying to look after you! That guy was a total creep." He scoffed.

"No he wasn't! He was pleasant and interested, which is more than I can say for you."

"Lexi-" Jake started.

"No. Don't 'Lexi' me, you had no right to do that. We aren't together, I'm not yours, you don't get to control who I do and do not speak to." I hissed and turned away before he could reply. I bent down to my bag as an excuse to compose myself before rising, taking a deep breath and jumping in the pool to play with Hailey. I peeked back at Jake, but he was now sat hunched over on his chair staring down at his phone. I guess this was how it was going to be now.

Chapter 24: Lexi

I don't think I'd stopped smiling since our date. After the brief disruption with Millie, everything had gone smoothly. Our food arrived shortly after the scene, I had a BLT while Jake had a burger and chips. *'Sunny Side Up'* did gorgeous food and I loved that Jake remembered it was my favourite. We chatted about everything and nothing. He asked about how my parents had been and in turn he told me all about his job and how things had been going. He seemed overwhelmed but had been doing so well with it all, I squeezed his hand in what I hope was a reassuring way. Once we had finished eating, Jake paid the bill, refusing to let me pay for anything. He even went so far as to go up to the counter to pay instead of waiting for them to come over.

The mini golf course was zoo themed and while lots of people probably found it ridiculous, I had always loved this place. My parents had never let me come here when I was younger as they had never seen the point of it. Everything always had to be educational with them. As a result, my childhood was full of museum and gallery visits instead of cinemas and mini golf. Cassie had mentioned it to her mum once and since then, they had always invited me to their fun days out. It was her family that took me to the zoo, the theme park and so many other amazing places. Jake had done so well with this date and it had made me like him even more. Possibly even love him.

Our round went so quickly and Jake even pretended to help me after I had made an atrocious shot on the second hole. He rested his head on my shoulder and his lips brushed against my ear as he explained what to do and he scattered light kisses along my neck. It was pure bliss, even with Jake's heckling. I made sure to repay his distraction later on round the course. As he was about to take his shot, I wandered around him and traced my hand over his stomach and rested on his back. It worked far better than I expected as his ball ended up in the water. From then we both conceded and ended up sharing my ball for the rest of the round.

We started back to his house once we finished, of course with Jake winning, but with me getting the only hole-in-one. He dropped me off a little down the road from their house so he was able to pull straight into the driveway and ensure we didn't get caught coming back together. I

called Cassie to let her know I was on my way and she said she would be back soon. I knocked on the door, it was Hailey at the door this time, she gave me a wide smile and an excited hug, I returned the hug with as much gusto.
"Hi missy," I said to her, a nickname I often used with her, "how are you?"
"Ugh, okay I guess," I looked quizzically at her from her response. "School is just a nightmare." she confessed with a grimace, as if the mere mention of it was too much.
"Oh no, what's going on?" I asked with genuine interest, causing her to erupt into a monologue about everything that was wrong at school. Her friends being mean, teachers being harsh, work being too difficult.
"Okay, come on Hailey, let her in the door before you start attacking her." I heard Jake say as he walked downstairs. He smiled at Hailey as she stuck her tongue out and stormed off to the kitchen. I could hear her mumbling as she went but couldn't make out anything she said.
"Hi," I said to him as he reached the bottom of the stairs and Hailey was in the kitchen and out of sight.
"Hey," he reached out and brushed my hand, our fingers briefly linking before he let go and walked into the kitchen. Even the smallest touch lit my body on fire and made it impossible to think straight. I could tell that he knew what he did to me too, he was too smug as he

walked away, my breathlessness was obvious. I just needed to keep it under wraps when I saw Cassie.

As per her usual entrance, Cassie came blowing in the door fifteen minutes later. She seemed determined and as soon as she walked into the kitchen and saw me, she dragged me out again and to her room.
"Okay so the date with Noah and Tate is going to happen this weekend. We'll get dinner and then go for a walk, okay?" Cassie said. I bit back my eye roll and braced myself for the backlash of telling her I wasn't going.
"Listen, Cassie about the date…" I began.
"Yes! I am so excited, I can't wait to introduce you to Tate, he's looking forward to it too according to Noah." she said and I knew I needed to tell her before it went any further. It wasn't fair to him or Jake for this to happen.
"Ah, right." I said.
"I was thinking of wearing my new denim skirt with a white blouse and some cute sandals, what about you?" She asked.
"I can't go," I blurted out.
"Sure you can, we can find you something to wear."
"No Cassie, I don't *want* to go." I emphasised.
"Wh- What do you mean? This has been in motion for ages, everything's sorted." She rebuked.
"Cassie, I love that you care so much and I really appreciate what you're doing, but I just don't want to." I told her.

"Why not?" She asked.

"I just don't want to deal with all the stress of boys and things at the moment." I tried to justify myself.

"It won't be stressful; I'll make sure it's all okay and that nothing hap-"

"No! Casse please, I just don't want to. I know you and Noah are all loved up and I am so happy for you, but I don't want that. I have a degree to focus on and work to do." I told her.

"As if I don't?" she asks as if she's offended.

"No, I'm not saying that."

"No I get it Lexi, your degree is harder and you have no time for menial things like boys, that's just for us people that have time to throw about." She retorted.

"Cassie," I started.

"No, it's fine. Consider the date cancelled and don't worry about *boy stuff* at all." she snapped and stormed out of her own room and by the sounds of it, into the bathroom. Here I sat in my best friend's room, unsure of what to do.

After ten minutes of Cassie not returning, I stood from her bed, offered a hollow goodbye through the bathroom door and wandered downstairs. Jake was on the way up and he could tell from one glance that something was wrong. He stopped me, with his arm on the wall blocking my way, giving me a quizzical look and waiting for me to explain.

"I told Cassie I wasn't going on the double date," I confessed and the smile that spread over his face was dazzling.

"Lex, you don't understand how happy that makes me." He said and I could feel him lean closer before he stopped and pulled away as if he remembered where he was.

"Me too," I told him weakly.

"Lex, I have wanted to do this for a while and it's far overdue, but will you be my girl-" Jake started, but I raised my hand to stop him, I couldn't answer right now.

"Jake, no." I slapped my hand over his mouth.

"What? Why?" he spoke between my fingers, I could see the confusion and hurt on his face. I let my hand drop and glanced to the bathroom where Cassie had locked herself in, Jake understood straight away.

"I can't do that to Cassie." I told him.

"But-" He started.

"She's my best friend and I've already kept so many secrets from her. A secret boyfriend, let alone her brother, isn't something I could do to her right now." I explained.

"But like you said, she's your best friend, she'll be happy for you when she realises." He assured me, and while I hoped he was right, I just wasn't sure.

"Yeah, well right now Cassie isn't exactly happy with me." I explained. But he just waved his hand away.

"It'll be okay sweetheart, you know what she's like sometimes, she just needs a minute to get over it then she'll be fine." he said reassuringly, but inside I knew that wasn't all. He knew Cassie like a sister, I knew her like a best friend and things with her were never that simple. I feared it would take a while before she forgave me properly. I wouldn't share that with Jake, he was so happy and I couldn't take that away from him.

"I'm going to give her some space," I explained. "I'm going to head home." At that Jake's smile vanished and was instead replaced with furrowed eyebrows.

"Are you sure? Cassie will be fine, you don't have to leave." he replied, my hand still firmly clutched in his.

"No, I do. I need to get home and Cassie deserves her own space." I assured him.

"Okay, I understand, but please think about what I said," he said, "I don't want to keep this a secret anymore, I've made too many mistakes when it comes to us Lex, I don't want to hide what I feel."

I couldn't think about what to say to him at that moment and I knew my words would fail me, so I did all I could think to do. I kissed him sweetly and squeezed his hands, I slid away from him and once I could hold onto him no longer, I turned away and walked downstairs. I didn't know what would happen with Cassie now, particularly when she found out about Jake and me. I pushed that thought away and with a wave goodbye to Hailey, I left their house and started the walk back to my own.

I walked home but chose a brief detour past Connie's before dealing with what waited for me at home. I arrived at her house after a brief fifteen-minute walk and knocked sharply on the door. Her mum, Anna, opened the door, greeted me and invited me in.

"Do you fancy a drink?" She asked me. I smiled and nodded.

"A glass of water would be wonderful, thank you." I replied, she smiled in response and turned to the kitchen, I followed behind her as she called up to Connie to tell her I was here. Anna was a lovely woman, she had always been so kind to me and while we didn't hang around Connie's house particularly often, Connie's mother was always straight to offer to give us a lift or to take us somewhere when we were younger, before we learnt to drive.

"How are you?" She asked me.

"Not too bad," I replied, "Getting through uni work and trying to enjoy the summer."

"You are such a hard worker, even into your holidays you are still working hard." She smiled in approval, "You could teach Connie a few things." She laughed.

"Yes, thank you mum," Connie said from the doorway, she had suddenly appeared, neither of us had even heard her enter.

"Hi honey," Her mum said, "Drink?"

"No thanks," Connie replied.

"Hey," I said and gave her a small and hopefully reassuring smile.

"What are you doing here?" She asked.

"I wanted to come and see you, just wanted to catch up."
"Oh right," She replied. There was a brief pause, it was as if no one knew what to say. Anna cleared her throat and shifted.
"Okay, well I'll leave you girls to it, just let me know if you need anything." Anna said and she wandered out of the kitchen towards the living room.
"Do you want to sit outside for a bit?" I asked her.
"Sure," was her only reply. I let her lead the way and followed out to the patio, she sat on the rocking seat they had right outside the door so I went and sat next to her, "So, how are you?" I asked.
"I'm doing good, loving my free time."
"That's good…. And how's Ryan?" I asked her.
"Yeah, he's great." She replied, "we're going on holiday soon and I'm so excited to have a few days away."
"I'm so jealous. Greece will be amazing."
"I know! Five days on an adorable island!"
"You can live your Mamma Mia dreams." I teased; she had an odd obsessed with that film.
"Except for the three different men, I'll be sticking to just the one."
"Probably a good idea." I laughed.
"How are you?" Connie asked.
"I'm… good?"
"That's super convincing." She replied sarcastically.
"No, it's just my parents being insane and I feel like my emotions are all over the place." I admitted.

"Anything you wanna talk about?"
"At the moment? Not really. I feel like I'm still trying to make it all make sense in my head at the moment."
"Well don't suffer in silence. The worst thing you can do when you're struggling is push away the ones that love you." Connie reached out her hand and took mine.
"I know, and I'm so glad I've got you girls to support me. You have no idea how much it means to me."
"As long as you know you can talk to us." she insisted.
"I do. And I will."
"You better." She squeezed my hand. I stayed there for a little longer and we visited safer conversation topics before I made my excuse and headed home. Connie gave me a tight hug at the door before letting me go.

Returning home had never felt so isolating. Arguing with Cassie, the uncertainty with Jake, the disappointment of my parents. It was all so much and I hadn't even started to think about everything I needed to do for university. To my relief, the house was peacefully quiet when I returned. I rushed to the solace of my bedroom in the fear that my parents were in fact home, I couldn't face them right now, it was all too much.

Once in my room, I collapsed onto my bed and could feel the tears spring from my eyes. Why did everything have to be so complicated? Things were finally happening with the boy I have been dreaming about forever, all of my fantasies were coming true! But I was just laced with fear. There were too many components to worry about, too many obstacles to deal with. The fear of things not working out plagued my mind, would Cassie and I still be friends? Or will it just be too awkward for everyone, would I ruin everything? Cassie always used to tease me about liking Jake, but I knew when it came down to it, she was worried about me pushing her aside and spending all my time with Jake. I felt like I had hardly been honest with her at all. Couldn't tell her the real reason Miles and I broke up, couldn't say why I couldn't go out with Tate, couldn't talk boys with her at all. I was stuck, going round in circles about what to do. I couldn't see a possibility where I didn't lose either of them, I knew I wouldn't be able to bear that.

In a vain attempt to distract myself I climbed off of the bed, settled into my desk with full intention to get on with my university assignments. My workspace was minimal, my desk was simple and white, simple photo frames hung above the desk, some of me and Cassie, others with all four of the girls in it, one of Cassie's family and I from four years ago. It was my 16th birthday and my parents had done nothing for it, but Cassie must have told her mum as when I went around to theirs the day after and they had organised a surprise for me. They cooked my favourite meal, decorated the kitchen with balloons and streamers and had even made me a birthday cake. It was

one of the happiest memories I had and one I would never forget, something that I never wanted to lose. There were no photos of my parents on the wall, I couldn't even remember the last happy memories I had with them.
I grabbed my laptop from my bag and logged on so I could get started on my work. I had always been expected to work during the holidays, since primary school, while other children were able to sit and relax in the sun. I was working. My parents thought there was always more to do, if you felt bored then you could do some work, it had been drilled into me since I was 6 years old. So here I was, while the glorious sun shone down and the echoes of laughter from others outside danced around, I was sitting at my desk. Sweat gathered underneath my thighs against my wooden desk chair, and I was working on assignments that hadn't even been set yet. It was the safest way to avoid my parents' rage and disappointment. I had a reading list to begin, which would mean a visit to the library to grab the various books, tasks to start before my lectures and practice essays to write, plenty to keep me occupied and distracted.

By the time three hours had passed, I'd started on the tasks and had even found copies of some of my books online, which I had downloaded onto my iPad and began annotating. I heard the front door open and slam shut, I couldn't help but flinch at the sound, it meant that dad was home, and he certainly wasn't happy. I feared going downstairs, I knew that whatever I would do would be the wring thing, but at least being in my room was a slightly further sense of protection. There were countless crashes and shouts from downstairs, he was in an extremely foul mood today, one I had not seen in a very long time. I knew that there would be nowhere I could avoid him for long but I could at least try.

The last time I had seen him like this, he had been consumed by his anger and had left the house in a true state. He had struck mum and then left the house, expecting mum and I to clean the carnage he had left behind. That was when I was 14, nothing like that had happened before, and nothing like that had happened since. Until now.

I tried to distract myself in my room, staying quiet and staying away. It was the best way to cope when he was like this. After another five minutes of crashing and shouting from downstairs, I could hear his thunderous steps up the stairs. I braced myself at my desk, wishing he would leave me alone, but my wish was futile my door swung open and slammed into my wall. A push so fierce that it had probably left a dent. I sprung up from my seat and turned to him, he just stood there and stared at me, rage filling his eyes.

"Good evening father," I said as politely as I could manage, I was wringing my hands together so much that I could see my knuckles become white.

"SHUT UP!" He demanded. His hands kept clenching and unclenching by his side.

"Sorry father," I whispered.

"DON'T YOU DARE MUMBLE." He continued and at that I simply nodded, unable to say anything else.

"WHAT THE HELL DO YOU THINK YOU'RE DOING UP HERE?" he asked.

"My university work father," I stated.

"THERE IS PLENTY OF WORK TO DO IN THE HOUSE, WHAT MAKES YOU THINK YOU CAN SIT UP HERE ON YOUR OWN WHEN THERE ARE THINGS TO BE DONE. YOU NEED TO EARN YOUR RIGHT TO LIVE HERE."

"Yes, of course, I will go down and get started on it." I walked towards my door nearer him, he stunk like a distillery. He was always the worst when he had been drinking and it took a lot to drive him to a drink.

"ABSOLUTELY NOT," he shouted and shoved me back into my room, "I AM TIRED OF YOUR CONSTANT INSOLENCE AND YOU THINKING YOU CAN DO WHAT YOU WANT."

"I'm sorry," I replied, I knew at this point I just needed to agree, he could make my life hell, or more hellish than it already was.

"YOU ARE SUCH A DISAPPOINTMENT TO US, YOUR MOTHER AND I HAVE TRIED SO HARD TO HELP YOU, BUT THERE IS REALLY NOTHING TO BE DONE FOR YOU." His screaming had grown hoarse,

but he wouldn't stop on any account. He stepped further into my room and began pacing, he was mumbling to himself but I couldn't tell what any of it was. My heartbeat was thumping in my ears.
"Father, is there something I can do?" I asked him.
"As if there was anything you could actually help with." He snarked.
"I just thought I could assist in some way, you seem…" I started.
"I SEEM WHAT?" He roared, I gulped and stepped away from him. With every step I retreated by, he advanced.
"N- nothing father," I stuttered.
"NO! Please continue." He said and at this point I was now forced back to the wall while he stood mere centimetres from my face.
"I thought you were stressed." I told him.
"You would be too if you had people like yourself around you. With a daughter like how, how could I not be stressed." he sneered.
"I'm sorry." I told him.
"WHY NOT ACTUALLY DO SOMETHING RATHER THAN JUST BE SORRY." he screeched and before I could react his hand rose and struck me so hard I was unable to keep my balance. I hit the floor and thought it was better to stay there. After a few minutes with my father screaming at me, he soon seemed to grow tired and he left my room, slamming the door behind him.

Once he was gone, I stumbled to my feet and checked the door, it had been locked behind him. I spun around to my desk to find my phone and call someone, but both my laptop and phone had gone. He took them both and locked me in here. I couldn't help the sob in my throat, but in fear of my father hearing I collapsed on my bed and allowed my pillows to silence my sobs.

Chapter 25: Jake

I'd scared her off, maybe she wasn't ready to be official, I'd rushed it, maybe she felt like she couldn't trust me. I couldn't work out why she had been so quick to turn me down. All I wanted to do was to be able to call her mine, I just hoped she would feel the same way soon. I hated hiding her, she's perfect for me, the most gorgeous girl I ever met and with the biggest heart I'd ever known. I had always been curious about her, but never really questioned why, I just thought it was because she was important to Cassie, but it was because she was the missing part in my life. When I realised that last summer I got scared and ran away from her, now was my time to show her what she truly meant. Cassie wouldn't be *that* mad about it would she?

After Lexi left I wandered upstairs to talk to Cassie, the bathroom door was open and she was back in her room, sitting on her bed on her phone.

"Hey," I said timidly as I knocked on her door.
"What," she replied glumly.
"You okay?" I tested.
"Fine."
"Come on Cassie, what's going on?" I ventured.
"It's just Lexi," I said and thumped her phone down onto the bed next to her.
"What about her?" I asked cautiously.
"She's just been so distant and secretive with me lately, I don't know what is going on with her." She sighed. I knew Lexi was being distant because of what was going on between us but I couldn't tell Cassie that.
"Cassie, you know Lexi loves you, you're her best friend, I'm sure there is a reason for how she is acting. Maybe there's just something going on." I suggested.
"Maybe, but I don't know what it is, and what if it is the same as dad last year, what if she decides she doesn't want to be around us anymore and she just leaves?"
"Cassie, Lexi won't do that, it's different to dad, he was working through some things, he and mum had been together for so long. It is completely different." I tried to assure her, but her question brought forward the fear that had been growing in the back of my mind since. If my dad could leave so easily, what was stopping Lexi from doing the same.
"I'm just scared Jake; I can't lose her." She said.
"I know Cassie, I know." I moved towards her to give her a hug. "It'll be okay, everything with Lexi will be

absolutely fine and dad's back now, he's here and he's okay."

"Thanks Jake," she replied and returned the hug. It had never occurred to me that last summer with dad has caused the same insecurities for Cassie as it had with me. We stayed there for a little longer, not talking but thinking.

I left Cassie in her room, needing time to myself too. I went into my own room and grabbed my phone. I hadn't heard anything from Lexi yet and I was getting worried.

Jake: Hey please just let me know you're okay, I'm sorry if I scared you with the questions.

I waited for her response, Lexi was a fiend on her phone and usually replied immediately, but no response came through. I pocketed my phone and turned to my computer, hoping my games would offer some sense of distraction. It did wonders to relieve the overthinking, at least for the brief time I was able to play. It was a perfect few hours where my worries about Lexi just seemed to fade and my brain switched off.

"Jake, Cassie, dinner!" My mum called from downstairs. I hadn't realised how much time had passed, but as I left my room I could smell the food and my hunger hit me like a wall. I wandered downstairs and into the kitchen, mum was standing by the hob stirring something.

"Smells great mum." I told her and wandered over to her to drop a kiss on her cheek. She turned and smiled at me. "Thank you darling," she replied. I grabbed the cutlery to lay the table for dinner.
"Hey dad," I said as I approached the table where he was sitting. He was looking through the paper and briefly looked up as I walked over, grunting in acknowledgment.
"Hi," Cassie said as she joined us all in the kitchen, she seemed in much higher spirits than she had earlier, but I knew she was very good at hiding her feelings.
"Hey honey," my mum greeted her and opened her arms as Cassie walked over to embrace her. The hug seemed a little tighter and longer than usual and I knew Cassie needed it.
"I invited Noah over to join us if that's okay." Cassie informed us.
"Of course, it'll be lovely to catch up with you both before you go to camp." My mum answered.
"Great! He'll be here in about ten minutes." She informed us and came to help finish sorting the table. Hailey and Bradley were out in the garden playing on the trampoline, clearly trying to expel some energy before dinner. Mum called them in to join us for dinner. Noah arrived shortly after and we soon settled at the table while mum plated up the food and it was all brought over. She'd made chilli served with nachos and rice. One of my favourites. None of us stood in ceremony as we all dug in as soon as the plates touched the table.

"So how have you been Noah?" Dad asked, breaking the silence that had fallen over the table as we all ate.
"Good thank you, I've been enjoying a nice break from uni," he said.
"And you're in?" My dad inquired.
"Oh dad, how have you forgotten?" Cassie playfully scolded. But my dad just grinned and shrugged as if it couldn't be helped.
"Over in Nottingham, studying architecture at the moment. Just finished my first year." Noah replied.
"It's where I'm heading in September, dad." Cassie added. She looked at Noah with such affection, it was beautiful to see her so in love she truly deserved it.
"Yes of course." He nodded.
"Are you enjoying it?" My mum chimed in.
"Oh absolutely," Noah confirmed, "It is so interesting and actually enjoyable."
"I'm so glad to hear it. I know Lexi has had her mix of horrible lecturers this year." Mum added. My head snapped up at the mention of Lexi, I hadn't heard anything from her all day and I was starting to worry.
"I'm surprised she isn't here." I mentioned nonchalantly, "she's usually always at family meals."
"I haven't heard from her since she left," Cassie said and I could hear the bitterness lacing her voice. My worry grew with there being no contact.
"I hope she's okay," my mum commented, her face growing concerned and it grew silent again. Bradley

decided to fill the silence by rambling on about school and telling everyone about what he had been up to recently. The rest of the dinner passed in an easy peacefulness with simple conversions and light-hearted chatter. We tidied our plates away and mum brought dessert to the table, a raspberry pavlova.
"Before you all dig in," my mum began, "I have some news I want to share with you all."
"*We* have some news." My dad added. They were looking at each other and smiling.
"Okay?" Cassie said, "what is it?"
"Well, your dad and I have booked a cruise for this summer, we're going to go away together and have some quality time together." she told us.
"When?" Cassie asked.
"The end of August," My dad said, "we'll be gone the last two weeks of the month."
"Ah that's amazing!" Cassie replied.
"We thought that this has been a really difficult year for us and we have been working hard on communicating. I think it's time we have a moment to ourselves to celebrate how we've done." mum explained.
"What about Bradley and Hailey?" I asked, I glanced at them on the other side of the table and while they seemed happy, they seemed equally confused.
"They're both in their holiday clubs this summer and you'll be here to take them to and from when it's needed right?" Dad asked me.

"But I have work," I explained to them, "I can't look after them all on my own again."

"What do you mean again?" my dad replied incredulously.

"I mean *again* as in last summer it fell to me to look after them all the time and keep them busy. Thank god I had Lexi because without her it would have been impossible." I tried to keep my voice as even as I could.

"You weren't on your own last summer Jake," My mum muttered, but her face clearly showed her guilt.

"Yes. I was." my voice raising, "Dad stropped off to wherever he went and you were so miserable that you barely came out of your room. I had to look after them last summer, make sure they did their work, keep them busy and get them to their camps and activities. Me." I can hardly hold in my emotions now and it all starts flowing out of me. "I was all on my own last summer, save Lexi, and now you want me to do it again?"

"Only for two weeks Jake, there's no need for this reaction." My dad reasoned.

"What do you know?" I turned to him, "you go to work, come back and sit and watch TV. When was the last time you played with Bradley? Or took Hailey swimming?" I waited for his response but he sat there in stunned silence.

"Jake, please." Cassie said, I looked at her and could see her desperate face. She wanted things to work for mum and dad so badly and I could tell that I was shattering her excitement, but there was nothing I could do, this was all too much for me.

"I'm happy for you both, and I hope you enjoy your cruise. Of course I'll look after Bradley and Hailey and I'll make it work. Congratulations." I said to them and after excusing myself from the table I walked out of the kitchen, grabbed my keys and stormed out of the house. I needed a drink.

Sitting at the bar in the White Lion didn't make me feel better. I always came here knowing I could trust the cheap pints and lack of questions. But as I sat there, I'd never felt lonelier. Lexi still hadn't replied and I'd probably messed it up at home too. I was truly happy that my parents were making things work and that they had come back together, but part of me couldn't help but resent them for leaving it all up to me, again. They neglected us all last summer and by the sound of it they were to do the same thing again. This time I wouldn't have Lexi to help by the way things were going, I messaged her a few more times and still hadn't heard anything from her. I decided I would bite the bullet and call her, see if she answers, if not then clearly she needs more time. I pulled up her number on my phone and dialled. It didn't even ring, the call failed and when I tried once more it did the same. I grabbed my pint on the bar and downed the rest of it.

"Oi." I heard behind me; Cassie has clearly found me.

"What." I replied.
"Are you okay?" she asked me.
"Eh," I replied and ordered another pint.
"What was all of that about Jake?"
"I was just so tired of mum and dad always leaving things to me." I confessed.
"Come on, surely it's not that bad." she tried to reason.
"Cassie, I love you, but you weren't here last summer. Mum hardly did anything and dad was nowhere to be seen. I had to do it all."
"Why didn't you ever tell me?" she asked.
"With your panic attacks being what they were, I didn't want to make it worse while you were away. You needed time too."
"But I could've helped Jake."
"No," I said, "it wasn't for you to deal with, it was mum and dad that needed to sort it out and I wouldn't let their problems affect all of us."
"But why do it all on your own." she pleaded.
"I wasn't really alone." I whispered more to myself than her, remembering what happened last summer.
"Lexi." Cassie said, my eyes catching hers as she said it, "I didn't realise how much she helped."
"She didn't want the acknowledgement or the gratitude, she was just doing what she thought was right. Doing what she could for our family." She wasn't mine but my heart filled with pride.
"Damn, I had no idea." Cassie said.

"She never told you?" I asked her, I was surprised Lexi never said anything, she was at our house almost every day while Cassie was away and the little ones were off from school.

"No," Cassie replied, "I mean she mentioned she came over to check on things, but she never mentioned the apparent extent of time she was at ours."

"I guess she didn't want you to worry, if you knew how much time she spent at ours and what she was doing then I'm sure she knew you would catch on to things not being okay." I reasoned, looking down at my drink and again realising how selfless Lexi truly was.

"I need to talk to her," Cassie murmured to herself and I just nodded. I couldn't tell her that Lexi wasn't answering her phone without raising suspicion. "Jake?"

"Yeah?" I looked at her.

"Things *will* be okay with mum and dad," she told me, "They just need to discover their new normal and work out how they fit with each other again."

"I guess."

"They will, and I know things have been weird lately with them and this year has felt super weird sometimes. Dad being stuck in a rut and mum trying to pretend everything was how it was before they separated. But I can see the love between them, the way they are together, they'll make it work, they can't be without each other. They just need time, that's why I think they need this cruise." she explained.

"Yeah." They needed to find themselves together again and they couldn't just fall into everything again
"They'll get back to it." She reassured me.
"When did you get so smart?" I asked her. Cassie had grown up in front of me, she had flourished this year and I hadn't even realised, her gap year had done her a world of good and now she was ready for the next step of her life and I couldn't be prouder.
"I love you Cas," I told her, "You are such an incredible woman."
"I love you too, big brother," she replied, "You've always done so much for me and I'm so thankful to have you."
"Always." I said to her and slid off the stand to hug her. I held her tighter and longer than usual and was hesitant to let her go.
"Are you coming home?" she asked. I looked back at my pint thinking I could sit here and wallow a little longer, feeling bad for myself. Or I could go home to the people that loved me and spend time with my family.
"Yeah little sister, let's go home." I told her. I settled up the bill, grabbed my phone and left the pub making our way back home. Cassie spent the whole way home talking about uni and all of her plans, I just listened.
At home, dinner had been tidied up and Bradley was already in bed, Hailey wouldn't be too far behind. Cassie said she was going to head up, say goodnight and chill in her room. Once she had gone upstairs, I wandered towards the kitchen.

"Mum?" I called as I walked through the hall.
"She's gone to bed." I heard from the living room; dad was sitting on the sofa in the dark.
"Oh right." I replied.
"You really upset her." he said.
"I know and I am so sorry. I was completely out of line-"
"No, you weren't." dad interrupted. "You were absolutely right and that's why it hurt so much."
"Oh," I couldn't think of anything else to say.
"Jake, we are so sorry for how much we put on you last summer, you've always been so strong and I guess we never considered how much this affected you. Just because you're the oldest doesn't mean you should have to do everything." Dad explained, "you were right, I did just leave, and I can't speak for your mother but she has mentioned how she was last summer. You had to deal with all of that, at 21, it wasn't fair for you. You had just finished University and you should have been able to enjoy your summer, instead you had to play parent to your siblings."
"It was okay," I said.
"No, it wasn't, we never should have done that to you," I heard my dad's voice break and his eyes began to glisten as if wet with tears. "I'm so sorry son."
I couldn't think of anything else to say, so instead I just hugged him. Tight. I put all of my feelings into that single hug, to show him that it hurt, but I understood and that I missed him.

"Thank you," I replied.
"I don't think I tell you this enough Jake, but I am so proud of you." he said, now sniffling.
"I know dad," I assured him, "thank you."
We pulled apart and looked at each other, an understanding between us.
"I'm going to bed okay. Don't be too late to sleep." I simply nodded and collapsed onto the sofa when he had left. I was so emotionally drained that I made myself a cup of tea and promptly went upstairs. Sleep took me far sooner than I expected and I fell into one of the deepest sleeps I have had in a long time.

The next day I woke feeling refreshed, the memories of yesterday were still with me, but I was feeling much better now. It was already 10am and I had slept in far longer than I had planned but I clearly needed it. Mum would have already left for work and the little ones already at school. I leisurely got up and wandered to the kitchen, made myself a coffee and some toast before settling at the dining table.
"Morning," I heard as Cassie walked into the kitchen. There were a lot of days that me and Cassie were both at home as she was on her gap year and I worked from home a few days a week.
"Hey, I made a pot of coffee if you want some."

"Amazing thank you," she said and nearly dove over to the counter to get herself a cup of coffee. "What are your plans today?"

"Oh, I just have a couple things to sort out," I told her, "Possibly a meeting later. What about you?"

"Packing and then work later." she told me, I nodded and went back to scrolling on my phone. She came and joined me at the table with her coffee and a doughnut that mum had bought recently.

"Really?" I asked her with a smile. She looked at me quizzically and I gestured to her doughnut she was holding, it was one of those heavily decorated and filled ones, it was one of the Nutella ones.

"What? I wanted one." she defended, "You know what the little ones are like, they'll be scrambling for them when they get back from school, I wanted to get in first."

"You have a point there," I told her and copied her idea by grabbing myself a doughnut from the box on the island and settling back into my seat.

"Exactly." she laughed.

"Cheers," we tapped the doughnuts together in fake cheers. We both turned back to our phones and enjoyed our doughnuts and coffee.

Once Cassie had finished, she started to think of all the little things she needed for camping and began asking me where a number of items were. Things I had no clue about. I put my phone down to help her look for some stuff under the stairs, but after a while I heard my phone vibrating on the dining table.

"Oh, one second." I told her, pausing her questions, and wandered back to the table and grabbed my phone. It felt like a volt of electricity shot through me as I saw Lexi's name on my phone. I turned the screen away so Cassie didn't see and answered.

"Hey" I answered.

"Jake?" I could hear the shaking of her voice and the way she was whispering.

"What's wrong?" I asked her, my heart was thudding now, after not hearing from her all day yesterday.

"I need you." she breathed.

Chapter 26: Lexi

My sleep last night was restless, I was so scared that dad or mum would walk in at any point and I didn't want to be asleep when they did. I didn't know what they would do. I flinched at every noise I heard. Mum and dad locked me in my room all night, they hadn't even let me have dinner. Rather unlocked the door for a brief moment, dumped a tray with a sandwich on the floor and slammed it once again, locking it behind them.

This morning when I woke up, my eyes were puffy and red. I cried myself to sleep last night and each time I woke up I would start crying again, the cycle continuing all night. To make matters worse, my face had swollen up where my dad had hit me and it was too sore to touch I didn't even want to look in the mirror, horrified by what

I'd be met with. This morning I didn't even bother getting up, I had no way to escape and no way to contact anyone either. My bedroom window was too high for me to climb out of and there was nothing below it or around it for me to cling onto. I was trapped. Completely alone.

My bedroom door opened around 11am, at that point I was starving and was desperate for some sort of sustenance. My mother walked into my room and stood at the end of my bed, she was poised and her back so straight I thought she would snap at any moment.
"Your father and I need to go out," she told me, "As I believe you learnt your lesson we are allowing you out of your room."
"Thank you," I croaked, I had sat up and was staring at my mother. If she noticed the way my eyes looked or the bruise that was on the side of my face, she showed no reaction to it at all.
"But you are not to go outside, you are not to use the television and you must focus on your work and your work only." She told me, "If your father and I catch wind of anything else then there will be consequences."
"Yes mother," the way she said it seemed calm, but I knew better than that. With a curt nod, she left the room without saying anything else. I didn't see my dad at all that morning.

Our Summertime Secrets

I waited until I heard the front door shut and then I waited a further ten minutes until I was sure they wouldn't be coming back before I raced to my parent's room. I put my hunger aside instead desperate to find my phone. I needed to get out of here. I scanned their room and saw nothing so I started looking through their drawers, shelves and cupboards, desperate to find anything I could use to contact someone. When I came up with nothing, I went to dad's office. I followed the same steps I had in their room and just as I was about to give up, I found it, thrown into the bin. Clearly he had no intention of returning it, just something else he would happily take away from me. I grabbed it and raced back to my room. The screen was smashed but luckily it turned on and had enough charge to make a call, I was unsure who to call first, I knew Cassie would freak out too much. I was worried her parents would call the police, so I knew there was one other option that would take care of me.

I found his contact and pressed the call button; he picked up after two rings. My heart was thudding at the fear of my parents coming back.

"Hey," he said, he seemed cheerful.

"Jake?" I couldn't help the shake of my voice, I kept it quiet in fear of anyone hearing, even though no one was here.

"What's wrong?" he asked me, his voice now changing, becoming serious and concerned.

"I need you." It was all I could get out, and all I could say in the moment.

"Lex, you're scaring me." he sounded panicked now and I wished I could reassure him, but I was about to crumble and Jake was all that could put me back together.

"I'll explain it all, but not over the phone, how soon can you get here?" I asked him.

"You want me to come over?" He asked, clearly confused.

"Yes."

"I'm on my way," he told me, "Do you want me to stay on the phone?" I could hear him moving around on the other end of the phone.

"No, it's okay. Just hurry." I said to him and then hung up. I sat back on my bed, my hunger vanished, replaced by fear. I sat on the edge of my bed, unable to think of anything else and waited.

Fifteen minutes later I heard a bang on the front door. *Thump thump thump.* I raced downstairs and opened the door a crack to peep out, once I saw who it was I flung it open the rest of the way.

"Jake," I sighed, "you're here." Relief washing over me as he stood in front of me. I leapt into his arms and he caught me easily. His arms tightened around my waist, holding me to him.

"You needed me." he said "You're okay. You're okay." I couldn't tell if he was reassuring me or him. He placed

me down gently and scanned me over, his eyes landed on my face and I could see anger flare up in his eyes.
"Who did this to you?" He took my face in his hands and searched me. I could see he was trying to remain calm but his anger flamed behind his eyes.
"My dad," I choked out. "He was angry when he got home from work yesterday and usually I can hide and avoid his lashings. Normally my mum manages to calm him down. But she wasn't here and I didn't know what I could do. He came into my room and after he spent time yelling. He hit me."
"Oh sweetheart." he soothed.
"Then he took my phone and my laptop so I had no way to contact you. I wanted to call you as soon as I got home yesterday but I couldn't." I explained and he just stood and listened, "I only managed to call you today because they went out and I managed to find my phone in the bin."
"What?" he said.
"He threw my phone in the bin in his office, I found it and the first thing I did was call you." I explained. I felt so detached from it all that it felt like it had happened to someone else.
"Come on, where's your room?" he asked and took my hand.
"Upstairs," I pointed, "door to the left."
"Right," he said and we walked upstairs.
"What are you doing?"

"Getting you out of here," he explained like it was the most obvious thing in the world. He went to my room and he stopped at the doorway.

"I've never seen your room," he said and he looked around, "it doesn't suit you very much." I looked around trying to see it the way he did. It was all very clinical, white painted walls, nothing except for a few pictures. A simple desk, bed and chair, all white too.

"My parents chose everything," I explained, "it took me months to convince them to let me put the pictures up." He walked in and looked closer at the pictures.

"I remember that day," he said as he pointed to the birthday picture of me with his family.

"It was one of the happiest of my life." I told him.

"I had a present for you, you know," he admitted and turned his attention to me and away from the picture.

"You did not." I replied.

"I did," he insisted, "a little bracelet that had a star on it, I saved my allowance for three weeks to buy it for you."

"Your mum gave me that," I said as I reflected, I remember that bracelet, it was the first piece of jewellery I'd ever received.

"I chickened out from giving it to you, so I asked her to give it to you instead." he explained, "I just wanted to make you happy, even if the present wasn't from me. I knew you would love it."

"I did. I do. I still have it." I said and rushed to my jewellery box to get it. "It means even more now I know it was from you." I couldn't help myself anymore, I walked back to him, reached up to wrap my arms around his neck and pulled him to my lips. I put all of the emotions into that kiss, but I could feel his hesitance and worried I had read it all wrong, I pulled back.

"What's wrong?" I asked.

"I'm worried about your face; I don't want to hurt you." he told me.

"I'm not as fragile as I look," I told him affectionately.

"I know, you're one of the strongest people I know." he said and leant down once more to meet my lips. The kiss was a gentle and kind one, full of emotions and feelings. "I was foolish to think I could ever walk away from you. I tried to get rid of you, but you're rooted in my mind, my life, my heart." I smiled and shook my head.

"Sweetheart, you've been my oxygen for longer than I ever realised. I guess I only realised when you weren't in my life and I felt like I was suffocating." He stroked my cheek tenderly.

"Jake, I love these words and you're saying all the right things, but I don't want to hear them here."

"I know sweetheart, I'll save the wooing for later then." He dropped a kiss on my lips and my heart hummed at the final sweet moment replacing the shitty ones from this room.

"We can't stay here long," I told him as I pulled away from the kiss, stopping before it got too heated.

"When will your parents be back?" he asked, his anger returning, I shrugged.

"They never said."

"Okay, well let's get going. The sooner the better." He said, "grab what you can and try and get everything you need."

"Okay, thank you." I told him and kissed him quickly once more before grabbing my overnight bag and shoving in as many clothes as I could. I made sure to slip the bracelet on. I decided it was my favourite piece of jewellery. I grabbed my chargers and skin care, getting all of the essentials I could.

"Done." I told him and started to hoist my bag on my shoulder.

"Let me," he said and he grabbed my bag easily. We made our way downstairs, Jake first and me following him behind. I heard the lock in the door turn, then my mum walked in and gasped at what she saw, with my dad close behind.

"What is this?" My dad asked, he tried to keep his voice level but I could hear his anger.

"Lexi's coming with me." Jake stated, "you treat her like a piece of dirt and she's not staying here."

"I don't think so," My dad said.

"Alexis…" Mum whispered from next to him, he had pushed into the hallway now and he and Jake were staring each other down with such fury that I thought they may combust.

"You attacked her, you abused her. She isn't safe here and I won't let her stay." Jake's voice had begun to rise now.

"She is my daughter and that is none of your concern," my dad growled, "Now get out."

"Not without Lex," Jake demanded.

"Dad, let me go." I told him his eyes turned to me and I could actually see him snarling.

"You're *my daughter* he said, I won't just let you leave."

"You can't make me stay." I told him and he knew I was right. Jake went down the rest of the stairs, making sure to keep one of my hands firmly in his. He shoved my dad out of the way, he slammed into the wall and the exit was clear for us.

"Alexis!" my dad demanded, he reached out to grasp my forearm but Jake pulled me out of his grasp before he could.

"You touch her again and I will end you." Jake hissed.

"Is that a threat?" Dad scoffed.

"It's a promise." Jake's voice was dripping with venom. Dad was speechless, something I had never seen in my life before.

"Dad, let me go." I told him and pushed past Jake to get out of the house, I rushed to his car and got in the passenger seat. He put my bag in the backseat and climbed in next to me.

"It's okay," Jake said and he rested his hand on my thigh, rubbing soothing circles on my leg. "You're okay."

I nodded at him and looked back at the house, it had never been my home, dad stood in the front garden and the sight was enough to turn my stomach.
"Let's go." he put the car in first gear and drove away. I watched my house shrink behind us and the sight of my dad disappear. I took a deep breath and I focussed on the feeling of Jake's hand on my leg.

Chapter 27: Jake

The ride back to my house was spent in silence. Lexi hadn't said anything since we left her parents' house, she just stared out the window. I didn't want to push her but I couldn't stop worrying about her, I had never truly understood how malicious her parents were. I can't even fathom it. I wanted to make it all better for her, to take it all away from her and never let anyone hurt her again. I left her to think and to hopefully calm down after what she had gone through, it wasn't a long drive to my house and we soon pulled into the driveway. As I was getting out of the car, I saw Cassie run towards us. Once I had gotten that call from Lexi I'd raced out of the house so quickly that I hadn't had a chance to explain anything to Cassie. She halted in her movement as she saw me open the passenger door and Lexi got out of the car.

"Lexi!" She called and ran over to her.

"Hi," Lexi said weakly in response.

"What the hell is going on?" she demanded, "what the hell happened to you?" she asked, looking at Lexi's face. Her already puffy eyes looked as if they were about to flood with tears and the bruise on the side of her face was a painful mix of brown, blue and purple.
"My dad." was all Lexi said and Cassie seemed to understand immediately.
"Come on," Casie said softly and with a guiding arm around Lexi's shoulders they wandered inside, I locked the car and followed behind.

Cassie led her straight into the kitchen and boiled the kettle.
"I won't push if you don't want to talk but you know I'll listen to anything you want to say." Cassie said. My heart hurt for Lexi and it killed me even more that there didn't seem to be anything I could do for her. I couldn't bear to be separated from her but I knew I couldn't embrace her the way I wanted to with Cassie around, so I leant against the door frame and watched, waiting in case there was anything I could do.
"My dad got back from work yesterday, earlier than I expected. And he was his usual angry self, only this time he had been drinking too. He doesn't tend to drink much but when he does it makes everything worse." she paused, she seemed to be getting up the courage to go through everything that had happened. "I tried to stay in my room and away from him, hoping he would avoid me.

But he found me and started screaming at me, just the usual stuff he always says." she chuckled rather bitterly. "I knew that anything I said or did would only cause more harm, but nothing changed it. He hit me."
"Oh Lexi," Cassie gasped, her hand rising to cover her mouth.
"I fell to the floor from the impact and just stayed there until he finished shouting at me. After he got bored, he left. He locked me in my room, this morning mum said they were going out. As soon as they left I found my phone and called Jake." she said. At the mention of my name, Cassie swivelled from where she was sitting at the table and looked at me.
"And he came and got you?" she asked and Lexi nodded.
"He came over when I called him, I packed a bag and before we left my parents got back, he stood up to my dad and got me out of there." Lexi explained and I might have been reading into it, but I was sure I could hear the affection in her tone.
"Right, well done Jake." Cassie said to me.
"Anyone would have done the same," I shrugged.
"No, not that much. No one has ever done anything like that for me," Lexi said, "You stood up to him and took complete charge."
"I wasn't going to let him hurt you again." I said to her; I wouldn't let *anyone* hurt her like that again.
"He could have hurt *you*." she said and I could tell she was worried.

"Nah, I would have taken him if he tried anything." I joked, but secretly I had been worried about the same thing, Lexi's dad really wasn't anything to laugh at.
"Good thing you were there." Cassie noted.
"That's why I called him," Lexi started, "I knew if I called you then you could get hurt, but Jake would have been okay."
"Uh huh," Cassie said but I could hear a sense of humour in her tone, I knew she didn't believe Lexi. Her gaze kept flickering in between the two of us and I knew her brain was currently churning.
"What can I do Lexi?" Cassie asked.
"Let me stay here?" Lexi replied, there was no way she was going anywhere else. I didn't want her more than 5 feet away from me, she was my life and I would do anything to keep her safe.
"Obviously." Cassie said as if it was even an actual question. "You stay here all the time anyway; you can stay here as long as you want. Noah and I are off to camp next week, but you can have my room and stay here as long as you need."
"You don't need to check with your family?" She asked.
"You're practically a third daughter to them already," Cassie laughed, "they won't mind."
"Okay, that would be great." Lexi replied thankfully.
"I've got work this afternoon, but I'm thinking that we need a rom com and some ice cream?" Cassie said.

"Absolutely," Lexi replied. They both stood up and Cassie went to the freezer to grab the ice cream.
"Okay let's go," she said and wandered out the kitchen.
"I'm just going to make myself a hot chocolate and toast if that's okay." Lexi said.
"Sure! But I'm picking the movie if you're not there." Cassie replied.
"That's fair." Lexi laughed and it was so relieving to hear her happier. The kettle had boiled earlier so she didn't need to do that, but I watched her as she grabbed the bread and popped it in the toaster. She belonged in this house and she belonged with me.
"Come here," she whispered to me and I moved from where I had been leaning against the doorway and I walked over to her. She was leaning against the counter looking at me, I placed my hands on the counter either side of her waist.
"Hi," I whispered as I leant my face closer to hers.
"Thank you again for today," she said, "I wouldn't have got through it without you."
"I'm sure you would have, you're so strong." I replied. She looked at me and shrugged.
"It would have been harder without you," she told me, "I guess you're right in some ways and I didn't need you for today. But I wanted you, through everything I wanted you by my side more than anyone."
"I'll stay by your side as long as I can," I told her, "There is nowhere else I'd rather be."

"You're incredible Jake, having you is greater than I ever imagined." she replied.
"Lexi, you have no idea what you mean to me. I could have missed out of the greatest thing in my life if I had continued to be so thick." I chuckled.
"At least we're here now." she whispered. I leant down and closed the small gap between us. I met her lips gently, still worried about the mark on her face but unable to resist kissing her. Her hand came up and rested on my chest, gripping my T-shirt to keep me close, my hands moved from the counter and came up to hold her.
"I'm not going to break Jake, kiss me."
Her lips parted and deepened the kiss, my tongue sliding into her mouth and a moan escaped her throat. I moved my hand to the back of her head, tilting her up and allowing me to deepen the kiss even further. I was addicted to her lips and I could happily spend the rest of my life with her like this. The toaster had other ideas however as it popped up and caused us to spring apart like opposing magnets.

She straightened down her hair, turned to the counter and started applying butter to her two slices. I came up behind her, snaking my arms around her waist and rested my head on her shoulder. She leant her own head back against my shoulder and we stood like that while she buttered and cut her toast.

"Do you have to go and watch a film with Cassie?" I asked her, I didn't want to let her out of my sight.
"Yeah, I want to spend some time with her." Lexi replied, "But she's going to work this afternoon, so we can have some uninterrupted time together before the little ones get back from school." she said.
"I like the sound of that," I told her and sprinkled soft kisses all over her neck, she giggled and squirmed in my arms. I pulled back from her and let her finish making her drink. I leant against the island with my arms crossed and just watched her, how much more relaxed she already seemed.
"I'll see you later." she said to me and leaned on her tiptoes to kiss me once more.
"I can't wait sweetheart," I replied and winked, seeing her face glow at the nickname reminded me how much I loved it. She already owned my heart so it seemed apt. Lexi deserves so much and I wanted to give her everything in life. It killed me that I couldn't sweep her away from everything that was wrong and keep her safe.

After I calmed down from what Lexi had told me, I wandered to my room and started on some work. There were a few tasks I needed to get done today and if Lexi and I were going to be able to spend time together this afternoon I knew I needed to get it done now. I sat down at my desk and started with the emails from Patrick that were waiting in my inbox. I spent an hour working hard and managed to get through most of the emails, they were all pretty trivial, asking for certain data to be logged or asking me for little errands that I could do in no time. Once I made my way through all of them, I moved onto the write ups that I needed to do. I had great incentive to get it all done and shockingly by 2 o'clock I was finished. The plans of the afternoon had me bouncing with uncontained excitement. Doing nothing with Lexi was greater than anything with anyone else.

I wandered downstairs to grab some lunch, I made a quick sandwich with some crisps and sat down with a Diet Coke.

"Lexi! Do you want some food?" Cassie called up as she wandered down the stairs.

"Yeah, I'm coming. One second." Lexi replied.

"Hello brother," Cassie said coyly as she entered the kitchen.

"Alright?" I grunted, not looking up from my food.

"You were quite the hero to Lexi earlier." she said.

"She called." I shrugged, trying not to be too defensive.

"And you were there." It wasn't a question.

"Would you rather I wasn't?"

"I'm glad you were, you were quite the knight in shining armour…" She paused. "Is there something I should know about?" My head shot up at the accusation.

"What? No! Of course not. What are you talking about?" I uttered.

"Why did she call you instead of me then?" Cassie asked, "She always calls me."
"She explained that to you." I told her.
"Like I believed that." She scoffed.
"Cassie, come on."
"Fine, fine. I won't push anymore." She surrendered, "But I am warning you, whatever is happening, if you hurt her even slightly. There will be hell to pay brother."
"Right." I told her and started her down. At that moment Lexi finally made it to the kitchen.
"So, what are we eating?" she asked and she looked between Cassie and I, "everything okay here?"
"Perfect." Cassie said and smiled, "I was thinking toasties?"
"Sounds good," Lexi replied slightly suspiciously, she looked at me questioningly but all I could do was smile. Did Cassie suspect something between us? Would it be long before her suspicions finally came out?
Cassie had work at 4 o'clock, so she and Lexi spent the final time relaxing on the sofa in the living room and watching The Office before she had to go and get ready. I stayed in the kitchen, desperate to be near Lexi if she needed anything, ready to spring into action. It also meant I could subsequently spy on them and hear what they were saying. At around 3:30 just before Cassie was about to leave for work, I could hear her talking.
"You'll be okay here?" Cassie asked.

"Of course I will, I'll be fine. I feel safe here, happy." she replied.

"Okay good, my parents will probably be back before me but I've messaged mum and told her you're here."

"Did you tell her why I'm here?" Lexi asked, now seeming anxious.

"No, I didn't feel like that was my place, I did tell her not to ask too many imposing questions so it'll be up to you how much you say and what you say." Cassie assured her.

"Thank you," Lexi sighed, "what about…" she trailed off, I assume she was referencing her face.

"Ah yea, that might be an issue, all I said was something happened at home and you would be here for the foreseeable." Cassie explained. I wandered into the kitchen, desperate to see her.

"Okay," Lexi replied.

"Lex, she won't say anything. She won't push you until you're ready to speak." I reassured her. I glanced at Cassie and saw her eyebrows rise at the nickname, I was never affectionate with names and the nickname was clearly noticed, I'm just glad I didn't slip and call her sweetheart.

"I can call in sick for work if you want me to." Cassie offered, but Lexi shook her head.

"No, you need to go about your life, I'll be okay. I just want to sit and watch TV." Lexi replied.

"Okay, but call me and I'll come home immediately." If Lexi needed it Cassie would walk through fire to be by her side. I was surprised she was even leaving for work now, but I feel there was a lot of back and forth between them upstairs about it all. Lexi would never let Cassie do too much for her, especially miss something important like work.

"I promise, I'll call you if anything happens." Lexi promised. Cassie sized her up once more and then nodded when she was satisfied Lexi would be okay. I stayed by Lexi's side while Cassie sorted herself out and called to say goodbye. I looked out the front window and watched Cassie disappear from sight before walking into turning to Lexi. She was laying on the sofa, her face propped on a pillow, the bruised side of her face away from the pillow and her legs curled up underneath her.

"How are you?" I asked Lexi, at the sound of my voice she sat up and looked over at me.

"I'm... getting there." she told me.

"Is there anything I can do?" I asked, desperate to be useful.

"Just a cuddle would be incredible, and maybe a hot chocolate?" she laughed and smiled.

"Coming right up," I said and went back to the kitchen to make her drink, I made myself a coffee too and five minutes later I wandered back into the living room, placed the drink on the coffee table and sat on the sofa,

Lexi has her feet pulled underneath her on the other end of the sofa.

"Come here," I murmured and gestured her over. She quickly scrambled over to my side and tucked herself underneath my arm. I pulled her close and she draped her legs over my lap, I placed my hand on her thigh and rubbed my thumb soothingly, hoping it brought her some comfort.

"This is all I need." she whispered as she buried her face into my chest and let out a sigh.

"Then this is what we'll do," I said. We stayed that way for ages, watching episode after episode of The Office. I felt her soft snoring and realised she had dozed off, I just relaxed with the comforting weight of her against me and enjoyed the moment.

At around 5:30pm I noticed mum's car pull into the driveway and Lexi shot awake at the sound of the doors shutting. Bradley and Haiely had been at after school clubs so mum must have picked them up on the way home. Lexi twisted her legs off of my lap and sat up.

"Morning sunshine," I told her and smiled.

"That's a nice way to wake up." she replied.

"To the sound of *The Office* playing?" I asked, I was sure I knew what she meant but part of me wanted her to hear it. She smacked me on the chest.

"No. Next to you, dummy." she laughed and leant in and placed a quick peck on my lips before the front door swung open and the sound of the little ones streamed in. We both stood up and went into the hallway.

"Hey!" I said, making my way to hug mum and grab the bags from her. Lexi stayed at the threshold of the living room clearly trying to stay out of the way. Bradley and Hailey saw Lexi stood to the side and went bounding over.

"What happened to your face?" Bradley asked her, I tensed as I watched her, her smile slipped momentarily but she immediately recovered.

"And hello to you," Lexi teased.

"Yeah, hi. What happened to your face?" he asked again and this time he pointed up at her too as if to make his point. She bent down and gestured for him to come closer.

"I got in a fight with a ninja." she whispered to him.

"Yeah right," Bradley scoffed.

"What, you don't believe me?" Lexi gasped and I just watched and smiled at her.

"No way, ninjas don't exist!" Bradley declared.

"How do you think I got this then?" she asked him. Bradley stared for a moment and then shrugged before running into the kitchen.

"Did you really fight a ninja?" Hailey then came up and asked.

"Oh yeah," Lexi said, "and if you think this is bad, you should see the other guy." Hailey giggled at her and ran

into the kitchen after Bradley. Lexi straightened and looked over to my mum.
"Hello honey," she said and walked straight over to Lexi embracing her in a tight hug. She whispered something to Lexi, but I couldn't hear. I just noticed Lexi's eyes become glassy and she nodded. My mum pulled away from her and led Lexi into the kitchen too.
"Are you going to help me make dinner or what?" She asked Lexi.
"Absolutely, you need to teach me your ways with food." Lexi smiled, I followed quietly behind.

Bradley and Hailey were set up at the table doing their homework while Lexi and mum were in the kitchen cooking dinner. Mum had decided to make tacos, one of Lexi's favourite meals and I knew it was no coincidence. Lexi was so loved by this family and I don't think she even realised, I was going to make it my mission to show her how much we all truly loved her, particularly me. Lexi excused herself briefly and I wandered over to mum.
"How is she?" mum asked as she watched Lexi wander out the room.
"She's doing well considering."
"What happened? I don't want to push her but I want to know how to handle it." she said to me.
"I can't tell you mum; it's her story she needs to share but just be gentle with her. Don't mention her face and she

just needs some comfort and love now." I told her and she just nodded.
"Have you been with her?" she asked.
"Wh- ah yeah, I mean we've both been hanging out today I didn't want to leave her on her own." I stuttered.
"Good, that's good. She shouldn't be on her own." Mum nodded, there was a brief pause.
"Mum, I just wanted to say I'm sorry and I really love you." I told her.
"Sorry?" she asked.
"For what I said about the cruise, I didn't really mean it, I lashed out in fear. Last summer was tough and I didn't know how to deal with it." I told her.
"Your dad told me about the conversation you had last night and I just wanted to say that I'm sorry Jake. We put so much on you at such a young age and we shouldn't have relied on you like that." mum replied.
"It's okay." I told her.
"I promise you; it won't be like that again. Your dad and I are working on it." she told me, "We're getting there."
"Good, I just want you to be happy." I told her.
"I want that for you too honey," she said to me. "Be brave."
"I love you mum." I replied, I came closer and wrapped her in a tight hug.
"I love you too honey," she said. "Oh the food!"
"Right, yes." I said and we broke away from the hug, she got back to preparing dinner and not ten minutes later, my

dad was walking in the front door and dinner was ready to be served.

"Jake, would you mind going to grab Lexi please?" my mum asked, "if she isn't hungry then don't push her, but food's here."

"Yeah sure," I told her and wandered upstairs.

"Lex! Dinner." I called up but got no response. "Lexi?" I called again.

"Here," I heard her trembling voice from Cassie's room and wandered over. I stopped briefly on the threshold and saw her sat on the bed; her eyes glazed over with tears.

"Hey, hey what's wrong?" I rushed to her and knelt in front of her so I was eye level with her. I brushed the tears that had trickled down her cheeks and waited for her to reply.

"Your family is just so amazing," she sniffled.

"And that made you cry?" I asked her, slightly confused.

"I just don't understand why I got dealt such a crappy hand when there are parents like yours out there? Why don't my parents like me? What did I do?" she asked.

"Lex, you didn't do anything. You're an incredible person and a wonderful girl, anyone who has you in their life is incredibly lucky. I don't know what's wrong with your parents and frankly they're just assholes for making you feel this way." I replied.

"I just want to be enough for them." she choked out and right at that moment I wished that I could take any insecurity that she had and destroy them.

"Lex, you are more than enough. You are so intelligent, incredibly gorgeous and you are full of so much love that I don't know what I did to deserve being this close to you." I paused and looked at her, "you are the single greatest thing in my life and I hate myself for not realising it sooner."
"Jake…" she started.
"No, let me finish. You are the single most amazing person I have ever met and I will spend the rest of my life trying to prove that to you if that is what I must do." I told her. She just looked at me and her eyes had softened, her tears subsiding.
"How did I get so lucky to have you in my life?" she asked and smiled.
"I'm the lucky one." I told her, "Now time to go, our tacos are getting cold and if we're not quick Bradley will try to steal them all."
"Ha you're right." she laughed. "Do I look like a mess?" she asked me.
"Ummm, sort of." I laughed, "but you're my mess and I wouldn't have it any other way." She smiled sweetly and kissed me before she moved to the mirror to wipe her eyes quickly and she took a deep breath.
"Let's go." she said and I let her lead the way to the kitchen.

No one said anything about her appearance as she sat down at the table but I could see the silent questions

floating around the room. Luckily, my parents did excellent work in keeping the conversation light and playful and there were no incidents through dinner.
"That was incredible darling thank you," my dad said as we cleared up the plates.
"Yeah mum, that was delicious, thank you." I said to her and Lexi agreed.
"My favourite," Lexi added, "it was perfect."
"I'm glad you all enjoyed it." she replied, "now Bradley you're on dishwasher duty please. Hailey, can you finish cleaning the table please."
"Ugh," They both groaned, but still got up and went about their duties.
"Let's go into the living room," mum said and she linked arms with Lexi pulling her along. Dad and I followed behind and as my parents settled into their usual seats and my dad switched through the channels, I made my way to the seat next to Lexi. It was the most uncomfortable one, the middle seat on the sofa of three, but I wanted to be close to her. Mum noticed the choice, but she just flashed a knowing smile and continued watching the TV.
I sat as close to her as I could. Our thighs brushed against each other, our arms touching their whole length. I was desperate to pull her into me again, the way she was earlier, but I knew it wasn't the time or place. I'd take what I can for now. Cassie wandered in and joined us ten minutes later.
"How was work?" mum asked her.

"Exhausting." she said and sighed, "but I got free dinner so I'm not complaining."
"Well, that's what matters." my dad added with a laugh.
"Precisely," Cassie grinned at him.
"Shift okay though? Many annoying customers?" I asked her.
"Na not too bad, the later shift is quieter so I can't exactly complain." She said, "But I'm ready for bed."
"Me too," Lexi chimed in.
"Yeah, I think we all need to hit the hay really," my dad said, "we were just waiting for you really."
"Oh great," Cassie said, "well goodnight, all. Lexi?" Lexi nodded and stood up, brushing her hand across my leg as she stood, something I'm sure was not accidental.
"Coming," Lexi said, "good night, all."
"Good night darling," my mum said, "let us know if there's anything you need." she nodded and with one more glance to me she left the room.
"Good night," I called as they left, and then she was gone. Exhaustion hit me like a brick wall and as soon as they left me and my parents followed closely behind, all of us headed to our rooms. I went into my room and slumped down onto my bed, already missing Lexi and dying knowing that she was so close to me but just out of reach.

Chapter 28: Lexi

Cassie and I wandered up to her room and we were sitting on her floor both doing our skincare before we got into bed.
"So how was dinner with everyone?" she asked me. I could tell she had been worried about me and how her family had treated me.
"Yeah, it was really nice actually," I told her, "Bradley asked what happened to my face. I told him I got in a fight with a ninja and he quickly lost interest."
"Haha that's a good one," she told me.
"And your mum just gave me a hug, a proper hug," I told her and I could feel my eyes begin to fill just at the thought of it. "I hadn't had a hug like that in years."
"Well, I'll happily give you a proper hug any time you want." and as if to prove my point she leant over and squeezed me tight. I hugged her back and she didn't let go of me until I finally loosened my grip.

"Thank you, Cas," I told her, "Not just for letting me stay here but for everything you do for me. For always being an incredible friend and such a wonderful person."

"Lexi, you're my sister, I would do anything for you and I hate to see you like this." Cassie replied. At this point we were both sniffling and I could feel more tears begin to fall.

"Come on," I said, "I don't want to cry again, let's chill and get back to The Office."

"Haha okay, deal." Cassie replied. We both finished our nighttime routine and got into bed. After a couple of episodes of The Office Cassie drifted off clearly exhausted from work. I continued to watch as I heard her soft snoring next to me and saw my phone light up on the nightstand next to me.

Jake: Come to the kitchen.

I checked the clock and saw that it was coming up to midnight then turned to Cassie to be sure she was asleep and wouldn't notice me. I snuck out of bed, grabbed my slippers and snuck out of the room. I knew where the creaky stairs were as I went down and was sure to avoid them. As I turned the corner and wandered into the kitchen, I saw Jake sitting at the table with hot chocolate, cookies and marshmallows around him.

"I wondered if you fancied a midnight sweet treat?" He whispered. His hair was ruffled and he had on his

checked pyjama trousers and a plain white top, he looked divine and I knew at that moment that I loved him.
"That sounds perfect." I crept over to the table, as I neared, I noticed he had one of those portable flames and had managed to collect all the necessary supplies to make s'mores. He smiled even wider as I sat next to him, he lit the flame and skewered a marshmallow before handing it over to me. I hovered it over the fire and watched as it started to brown and crisp up. Once it was the type I liked, I swiped up two cookies and placed it between them, taking an enormous bite and enjoying the sugary bliss on my tongue.
"This is perfect," I told him once I had swallowed my mouthful.
"I'm glad you liked it; I wanted to do something for you." He said, "I just want to make you happy."
"You always make me happy, even when we were kids you made me happy." I told him.
"Really?" he asked me, looking oddly surprised.
"Absolutely," I said to him, "I think my favourite memory of us was when I was around ten so you must have been about 12 or 13, I think, it was in the summer and I was really upset because my parents were being their usual disagreeable selves and they wouldn't let me go swimming. I remember coming to your house and crying about it while you were all having fun and your mum was trying to comfort me. You made everyone stop playing in the pool and we had an enormous nerf gun war

in the garden instead. You gathered all the guns for it, convinced everyone to join in, after that I didn't even think about not being able to swim."

"I remember that." he told me, "You just looked so sad and I couldn't bear it, I had to do something to make you smile."

"And you did, that and my party your family threw me are some of the sweetest memories I have of my childhood." I replied. "Practically every good moment I have is from my time here, and most of them have you in it too. You and your family, especially Cassie, are some of the best things that ever happened to me."

"Lex, you are family, you have basically been a part of this family since we were children." He told me and reached over to take my hand.

"Your family has always given me a sense of belonging." I replied and squeezed his hand, I loved this family, I loved Cassie and I loved Jake.

"Good," he said, "I hope you know how much you are loved."

I raised my hand to my face and just thought how little love I felt as my dad hit me, but sitting here with Jake. I felt nothing but love.

"Lex, please don't focus on that." Jake said and he shook his head, "That was nothing about you, and much more about what your dad is like, not you."

"Maybe," I replied, but not wanting to dwell on that anymore I turned back to the delicious treat Jake had

sorted out, "anyway enough about that. I hope one of those hot chocolates are for me?"
"Indeed," he said and pushed one of the mugs towards me, "extra marshmallows and whipped cream."
"Why thank you," I replied and lifted it to my lips, it was gorgeous and Jake had managed to make it exactly how I liked it. We stayed up a little longer and I managed to get through three more s'mores. Like the flame on the tale, things never dwindled with us and even as things had changed from platonic to romantic, we still maintained the ease and playfulness we always had.
"I think we should get back to bed." I told him. "I'm worried about Cassie waking up."
"Yeah I guess," he replied, "you know she asked me about us."
"Wait what?" I was sure calling Jake was going to raise some questions but I just needed him, "what did she say?"
"Well not much really," he shrugged like it wasn't a big deal, "just asked what was going on between us and that if I hurt you then there would be consequences."
"Classic Cassie," I said, "I knew I wouldn't be able to keep this a secret anymore. Maybe I need to talk to her."
"It's up to you; I won't push you as you already have so much gone on." He said, "but I don't want this to be a secret, I want to be able to tell everyone that I have this amazing girl that actually seems to like me."

"I want that too Jake, I want to be able to tell everyone and not hide how I feel, particularly with Cassie."
"Then we will, but you can do it in your own time." And that was the best thing he could have said. I wanted to tell Cassie and wanted it out in the open, it just meant I had one more thing to lose. With everything going on now I could turn away from it and while it would kill me, no one would know about it. But as soon as I put it out in space, there would be something else I could lose and everyone would know. It would be worth it to be loved out loud, but that didn't stop the fear I felt.
"Okay, I'll tell her, I promise." I assured him, "I just need the right time."
"I know sweetheart, we can take it slow, we've got plenty of time." he assured me.
"I will, soon I promise. I have a few things I need to sort out, and I promise I will." He was my person; I had kissed enough frogs and finally found my prince.
"Let's get back to bed, we need to get at least some sleep." Jake said and I looked at the clock and realised it was already nearly 2am.
"Yeah you're right," I agreed. "Let me finish this and then we can go." I said and I polished off my hot chocolate before Jake collected everything up and put it all in the dishwasher.
"Let's go," Jake said as he stood at the kitchen door. He held his hand out to me and I walked over taking it, at the top of the stairs he pulled me to him and kissed me.

"Goodnight sweetheart, I'll see you in the morning."
"Thank you for the little midnight snack," I told him.
"Anytime," He replied, "anything I can do for you, you know that." He kissed me once more before he went to his room and I went to Cassie's. Luckily as I settled back into bed, she was sound asleep and in no time I was fast asleep next to her, the Office casting light into the room.

"Oi," Cassie poked me early a couple days later.
"What?" I asked as I woke up from my sleepy haze, I checked the clock and it was only 8:30am. "Why are you waking me up so early?"
"You were snoring, it's annoying." She teased.
"Shut up," I replied and threw my pillow at her, "You should hear your snoring." I replied.
"I do not snore." She gassed.
"Oh yes you do, now let me sleep." I groaned and rolled over.
"No way, we're going out this morning," Cassie said, "you need to get out of the house for a bit and actually do something."
"Cassie, I don't want to go out when I look like this." I said and gestured to my face, while the bruise had gone down you could still see there were signs of it and I didn't want anyone staring.
"No one is going to say anything, I promise, why don't we just go for a walk and grab a coffee?" she asked.

"That does sound really nice, I would love to get out of the house really." I admitted. Cassie smiled at me.
"Perfect. Do you want to invite the girls?" Cassie asked.
"Can we leave it this time?" I asked her, "I just want it to be the two of us."
"Of course, that sounds good, we can have some quality time." Cassie said. We both got up and dressed, I grabbed one of my summer dresses and trainers. Cassie was dressed in her signature converse, denim shorts and a top.
"You ready?" Cassie asked. I checked myself over in the mirror and had managed to cover my bruises slightly with my makeup, it only seemed noticeable if you were looking for it.
"Yeah, let's get going." I said to her; we wandered downstairs and into the kitchen where Nora was making pancakes for everyone.
"Morning mum," Cassie said as we walked in. Bradley, Hailey and Jake were sitting at the table while Nora was in the kitchen.
"Hello girls, did you sleep okay?" she asked us.
"Yeah, great!" Cassie said.
"Yeah, yeah all good." I said but I couldn't stop my eyes flitting to Jake at the table, he was sitting there smirking as he looked down at his plate.
"I thought I felt you get up in the night," Cassie chimed in.
"Oh yeah, I just needed the bathroom." I mentioned, "it was hard to settle."

"Ah okay, if you need anything sweetie then let me know," Nora replied. I nodded and thanked her.
"So Lexi and I are going to go out for a walk and a coffee," Cassie told everyone.
"Ah that'll be nice. Where are you going to go?" Nora asked.
"Just to the park, we'll grab a coffee on the way and then just have a wander around. It's a nice day and some fresh air would be good." I added.
"Are you going to be okay?" Jake chimed in from the table, his eyebrows were furrowed in concern.
"Yeah of course," I assured him, "I just want to get out."
"Okay." he replied rather apprehensively. "Call if you need anything."
"Of course," I said and smiled at him. His whole attention was on me and I could see the others around questioning why Jake seemed to care so much, he cleared his throat.
"Uh-I just mean, call any of us, if you need some help or you see anything then just call any of us and we'll be there." he explained.
"Yeah, of course Jake," I replied and laughed at his ridiculous save. Not that it mattered, I wanted to tell everyone tonight if I told Cassie today. Of course, I just needed to make sure Jake still wanted to be my boyfriend.
"Okay, well we're going to head out." Cassie said.
"Do you not want some pancakes first?" Nora asked.
"It's alright, right?" Cassie asked me.

"We could stay for one, I guess. I mean I love your pancakes Nora so it would be a shame to miss them." I said. There were slight ulterior motives of not wanting to be away from Jake too, but that didn't need to be said. We grabbed a couple pancakes from the pan and thanked Nora before sitting down. I sat opposite Jake and next to Cassie, I felt Jake nudge my foot under the table and as I looked up, he was already watching me with a bright smile at me, Jake winked at me and I could feel the blush rise on my cheeks. I tried to just enjoy the pancakes and soon we had polished off our plates.
"Those were delicious mum," Cassie said.
"Yeah, thank you Nora, exactly what I needed." I told her. After me and Cassie had put our plates away, we grabbed our jackets, said our goodbyes and we left. Just as we left the house, I felt my phone vibrate in my pocket.

Jake: I'll miss you xx

"What are you smiling at?" Cassie asked me, she tried to look over at my phone but I twisted it away before she could see who it was from.
"Nothing," I told her.
"Yeah, okay." Cassie laughed and we set off towards Starbucks. After a fifteen-minute walk we arrived and ordered our drinks, Cassie got an iced vanilla latte and I got a chocolate Frappuccino (no coffee of course). It was

rather quiet so we didn't have to wait for long and we started towards the park.

"How's the milkshake?" Cassie asked me.

"Er Frappuccino thank you." I replied, "and it is very good thank you."

"Same difference when there's no coffee in it." she teased. We wandered along with our drinks and soon turned the corner to the park entrance.

"So how are you doing with everything?" Cassie asked.

"Not the best," I offered a hollow laugh.

"What do you think you'll do?" she asked me.

"I considered going to the police in all honesty, seeing what they say and suggest for me. I mean do I file a report? Do I tell them about the attack?" I explained, "But part of me doesn't want to open that can of worms and I really want to just move on with my life, I can't go on living there."

"You've got a new house with us sorted already, my mum said you can stay as long as you need." Cassie said, "As for the rest, I won't pretend like I understand exactly how it feels or that I know what you're going through. But I do know that you need to do what feels right for you. If that is to shut your parents out and allow yourself to have your own life then that's what you should do, if you think you want to report it just in case anything happens then that is a good option too, just so they have it on record maybe. But if you want to put it behind you and focus on the good you have coming your way then I totally support you."

"Thank you, honestly I think I need to talk to them and see what they say." I told her.

"And that's totally fair, you can wait and see what you feel first and then go and speak to them. See where you stand and how you feel around them, but there is no rush for you to do anything you don't want to." Cassie assured me.

"Okay," I said and took a deep breath, "anyway I need a lighter topic."

"Fair enough, umm okay. I have no idea." Cassie laughed.

"There is something I need to tell you," I explained, "I have wanted to tell you for a while and I know I am like the worst best friend for keeping it from you and hiding but I didn't even know what was going on at first and I wanted my head straight before I told you. Given this probably isn't the best time seeing as what is going on but-"

"Lexi, you're rambling. Chill," Cassie said with her hand on my arm.

"Okay, I want to tell you something and I don't want you to freak out or hate me, although you probably will and I wouldn't blame you really." I began rambling again.

"Lexi!" Cassie snapped me out of it. "You hooked up with Jake right."

"Okay I'll just say it- what?" I asked, shocked.

"You and Jake?" she asked slowly.
"How- how did you know?" I asked her.
"Oh please, I always knew you had a thing for him, even when we were kids, always trying to impress him, wanting to play whatever he was playing. It was obvious! And while I knew it faded slightly over the years, there was always something there. I think I saw it from Jake's side too, particularly since you've been back this summer, just the way he got angry and jealous when you were out with Miles and that's not even mentioning when I talked about that double date. Also, you two really aren't that slick, it's been obvious for a while now." She finished and took a sip of her drink.
"Why didn't you ask me about any of it?" I questioned, "you never said anything to me."
"I didn't think it was that serious, until I saw the way Jake treated you with your parents." she explained.
"He was just trying to protect me," I defended weakly.
"It was more than that," Cassie said, "I've never seen him like that about anything before, I knew at that point there was something more."
"So why did you say everything about the other guys this summer if you could see how much it bothered Jake?" I asked.
"Honestly Lexi, I've been scared to lose you. It has always been the two of us, I was scared that if Jake got in there then you would always be with him. Goodbye Cassie." she paused and started wiping at the

condensation on her drink, "I didn't want to be the stepping stone you needed to get to Jake; I wanted you to be my friend, want to be with me. Plus it was kind of fun to wind him up and him not be able to do anything."
"Oh Cassie," I said.
"No look, I know it sounds stupid, but with three siblings I've not had much that's only mine. I'm in the middle, I'm not the oldest doing everything first like Jake, nor am I the cute little ones, I don't want to lose you to him." she sighed.
"Cassie, I can promise you even in a hundred years that you would never lose me, you are my sister, my platonic soulmate, I couldn't do life without you. And I was scared to tell you because I didn't want to lose *you*. I was scared that you would hate me for it and I wouldn't be able to have you both. I love you and Jake, just in different ways and I want you both in my life." I told her.
"Wait, you love him?" Cassie asked me.
"Well yeah, I mean I think I do. It has always been him."
"Oh Lexi, honestly this could take some getting used to, but I am so happy for you. I know how much Jake means to you and I want you to be happy, so if this is what it takes then I guess I will have to put up with it won't I?" She laughed.
"But it won't change anything between us, and you know that right?"

"Don't promise something you don't know." Cassie returned. I stopped where we were and looked at her, grabbing her hand as she focussed on her drink again.
"I can promise it because I do know," I insisted, "There will never be a time that you are not my best friend and where I don't need you. Plus, it could even lead to becoming your sister legally. Then there's no way to get rid of me."
"Woah, okay I am just getting used to the idea of the two of you even being together, let's not throw marriage into the mix yet." She laughed, "although I would love to have you as an official sister."
"We'll take it slowly." I replied and laughed. "I need to make sure he wants to be my boyfriend officially first. I just knew I wouldn't be able to be with him until I knew it was okay with you."
"I, Cassandra Bailey, here by decree that I allow you to date my brother should he be agreeable." she said and reached out her hand to shake mine.
"Splendid." I replied and shook her hand. We both laughed and I truly scolded myself for thinking that Cassie would be anything but okay with it all. Now all I had to do was ask Jake.

Cassie and I finished our lap of the park and our drinks so we began our walk back to the house, it only took us around ten minutes from the park and as we got back, I could see everyone had gone their separate ways I assume

to school and work. Everyone except Jake, who I saw sitting at the kitchen table with his laptop and a coffee.
"How was your walk?" he asked as we wandered into the kitchen.
"Great," Cassie responded, "but I am now going to go upstairs as I have things to do. See you later." She disappeared upstairs but not before winking at me as she left.
"Is she alright? She sounded weird." he asked me. I looked at where Cassie had been and I laughed.
"I told her about us," I said and turned to him to see his reaction, he was already up and right in front of me.
"What?" he seemed in disbelief.
"I told her that we were seeing each other." I admitted, "it was time."
"Sweetheart, that's amazing!" he said and grabbed me into a hug, "so does that mean I can finally call you my girlfriend?" he asked.
"I was just about to ask you." I said and laughed.
"I don't think I want to be your girlfriend, that might be a little confusing." he teased which caused him to receive a whack on his chest.
"I hate you." I laughed.
"No you don't," He said and bent down to kiss me, "I will be honoured to be your boyfriend however."
"Good, then that's settled." I smiled. Life was a wild thing sometimes and some good could really come from all the bad.

Chapter 29: Jake (One year ago)

I knew I had royally messed up. Everything with Lexi was ruined. Over the last couple of weeks, Lexi had barely uttered two words to me, she still came over regularly to help with mum and hang out with the little ones, but as for me, she had clearly decided that I wasn't worth her words. I had no idea how to salvage the situation and I was so distracted that I didn't even know what to do with myself. Cassie was coming back tonight which would give me something to focus on. She had told us about the amazing time and even told us all about a new boy she met. I was stunned to see my little sister so grown up and I couldn't wait to have the family dinner with her when she got home. Family dinners had seemed rather quieter since Cassie had been gone.

Our Summertime Secrets

Mum came back with Cassie at around 6pm, she was tanned and clearly exhausted. We had all decided to get a takeaway tonight, at Cassie's request, and to watch a film together, so that was the plan. Once they got in, she went straight upstairs for a shower and to change. She returned thirty minutes later in her pyjamas; we ordered the takeaway and started a film. The evening was calm and enjoyable, but all I could think about was Lexi. I was surprised she wasn't here to welcome Cassie back after she had been gone so long and the only reason I could fathom was because of me. She would be here for Cassie if I hadn't messed everything up. I wanted to enjoy the time with my family, but as much as I tried my thoughts kept drifting back to her. I didn't know when I would see her again and I just knew I needed to apologise. I turned in after the film had finished and we all went upstairs I quickly went to sleep, hoping that these terrors wouldn't follow me into my dreams.

The following week passed much the same, Cassie was back and forth between here and her new boyfriend's house. Cassie went to see dad and to see what was going on with him. I could tell it was difficult but with Noah she seemed to be able to manage it and I was so happy she had I'm for that. With Cassie home, Lexi didn't have as much of a reason to come over and I noticed how Cassie would often go out to meet her instead, I didn't see her at all that week. Not until her farewell dinner.

Summer was coming to an end and that also meant the start of University for Lexi. Cassie was taking a gap year so she didn't have to worry about that until next summer, but from the sounds of it Lexi's parents were making sure she wasted no time, in her last week before she left my mum hosted a farewell party for her. There were a few of her friends, but I was mostly just the family and a sort of buffet in the kitchen.
"There she is!" my mum announced as Cassie opened the front door and Lexi walked in.
"Hi everyone," she said, seeming shy about all the attention and effort for her.
"Come in, come in. we have lots to hear about." Mum said and she ushered her into the kitchen. Lexi chatted away sharing all the exciting news, even a few people she had got in contact with that would be on her course. She was going to study law and while it didn't seem like her sort of thing, she seemed truly excited for it.
"I mean, I'm really nervous about it all and the fact everything will be brand new, but I'm hoping it'll be okay." She said when mum asked how she felt.
"You'll be fine, trust me." I told her, trying to get even an ounce of her attention.
"Thanks," she said and offered me a tight smile before continuing to talk and pretending I don't exist. It was only when I wasn't getting her attention that I realised how deeply I craved it, and I know how truly terrible that

sounded, but it was true. I really didn't realise what was in front of me until it was too late. I really wanted to make it up to her, but without a moment alone with her I didn't know how I could manage it.

They continued with their chatter about everything that Lexi would do, everyone offering advice about what to do or what she should look out for. I could see her listen to everything intently and truly take note of what they were saying.

"I still have so much to do," she told everyone, "And I leave in a couple of days."

"Trust me you'll never feel fully prepared," my mum jokes, "but you'll have a chance to buy anything you need when you get there."

"I guess. I do think I need to get home, I need to get everything sorted." She said,

"Of course, darling. I didn't realise the time. You leave when you need to." My mum told her.

"Do you need any help-" she started.

"Don't even finish that sentence." my mum scolded, Lexi always asked to help and my mum never accepted it.

"Okay, I'll pop to the loo and then be off." she said.

"Do you need a lift?" I asked, desperate to be useful.

"No. I'm fine." she replied tersely, "Excuse me."

She walked past me to the bathroom and I followed behind with a ridiculous excuse and caught her before she went into the toilet.

"Wait, stop." I said and grabbed her arm to turn her to face me. I quickly dropped her arm when I saw her flinch from my touch.

"What Jake?" she asked and she glanced downstairs to make sure no one was listening.

"Look, I just wanted to say I'm sorry for what happened at the pool and for this summer." I said, *"I don't know what happened to me, I just got really protective."*

"Whatever Jake, it doesn't matter." She said and tried to turn away again.

"I don't want you to be annoyed at me." I said, *"we've had a good summer together, right?"*

"A good summer?" she scoffed, *"you mean where I've been following you around, helping with everything and doing whatever you needed whenever you needed it. Yeah, a great summer Jake."*

"We had fun together though." I replied, surprised that was how she saw it.

"I mean it was fun with Hailey." She replied, *"but now Cassie is back and school is starting soon. I won't be needed. Thanks for the apparent great summer Jake. I'll see you around."*

"Lex please." I tried to say but she had already walked into the bathroom and slammed the door. I wouldn't give up on trying to make things right with her, just right now I didn't know what that would look like. Feeling completely defeated, I went back downstairs and waited for her to return. She came down a few minutes later and said her goodbyes to everyone, she briefly glanced at me*

and offered a quick 'bye' before she turned to the door and left. It felt like part of my heart was leaving with her. Lexi deserved better than I could offer her right now, but I couldn't dream of seeing her with anyone else. I would become the better that she deserved.

Chapter 30: Lexi

Last week after Jake asked me to be his girlfriend, he and I sat down to dinner and told everyone that we were together and the reaction was incredible. Nora acted like she already knew, which she probably did, Bradley and Hailey were over the moon jumping up and down about how I was part of the family. Even Colin, his dad, had a small smile on his face.

"About damn time," he said and laughed.

"Yeah, tell me about it." Jake added and laughed, he had his arm carelessly slung over my shoulders and had moved his chair impossibly close so that our sides were practically touching the whole way down. He had hardly left my side since he asked me to be his girlfriend and we had even snuck away again each night for a hot chocolate and midnight snack.

I feel like we were starting a new tradition for us and I loved it, the time when everyone else was asleep and it felt like the two of us in the world. Since that night life has felt amazing. I hadn't heard anything from my parents, they hadn't tried to reach out or check up on me, I wasn't particularly surprised, our conversations never passed instructions or insults.

For the past week I had been focussing on Jake and Cassie, I had been spending time with both, we still had our girls nights and met up with Connie and Lottie. Cassie was off for her camp in two days so the time we had was sparse and I wanted to enjoy as much of the time with her as I could. Jake and I had an official date night too and each time we all sat down as a family I found myself squashed between Cassie and Jake. Cassie constantly whispered comments about what we were watching and Jake rubbing comforting circles on my thigh. Cassie now had in her head a double date for me, her Jake and Noah. I had also focussed on my university work for September so I was all ready to go back. Everything seemed perfect.

But this morning I had woken up with a completely different feeling, the past week seemed like a dream and now it was time to face reality. I knew I needed to return home to get my stuff and to achieve some sort of closure. I had been wearing the same few things over the past few days and I needed more stuff. Both Nora and Collin had insisted I stay here until my university started up again and had even offered to let me convert the box room into a bedroom, but I had declined for the time being. For now, I was enjoying being roommates with Cassie. There were very few things I was sentimentally attached to in my room at home, but I wanted to at least grab what I could.

"I want to go back to my house," I said as I walked into the kitchen that morning. I was determined to take some of my life back and that meant having a clean cut from my parents.

"Okay," Cassie said apprehensively. She was sitting at the table with a coffee and bagel in front of her, she had let me sleep in this morning.

"Are you sure?" Jake asked. He had his laptop open in front of him and I assumed he was working.

"Yes." I said with a matter-of-fact tone, "There's some stuff I want to get back and I need to face my parents, see what they say." The mark on my face had faded now and while the physical signs had faded, the emotional signs were still there.

"Are you sure it's safe?" Cassie asked.

"I don't know." I said, "I mean I'm not sure what he'll do when I get there really, I guess only time will tell."

"You're not going alone." Jake chimed in.

"I need to do this for me." I explained.

"We can come for backup and just stay outside." Cassie added and Jake stood nodding beside her.

"Thank you, I really appreciate that." I said, knowing I wasn't alone in any of this.
"Okay, let's do this." I said. We got ready silently, grabbing jackets and shoes before starting at the front door. It was unsaid that Jake would drive so we piled into his car and we set off. Jake pulled up in front of my house and I looked out the window, a place I had lived all my life now seemed so foreign and distant.
"We're right here if you need anything," Cassie said from the back seat.
"Yeah, just shout and we're there." I nodded at them both thanking them for their support and got out of the car. Standing on the porch of my house had never felt more terrifying in my life. I didn't know what to expect when I opened this door, but I was sure they wouldn't be happy. With a deep focussed breath, I calmed myself and unlocked the door. It was silent as I walked in, no one in sight and no sounds at all.
"Hello?" I called out timidly, secretly hoping no one would answer.
"Oh, it's you." my mum said from the top of the stairs, I was standing in the hallway once more and she stood and stared at me.
"Hello mother." I said as softly as possible.
"Alexis."
"How are you?" I asked her, but instead of offering a response she turned away from me. I slowly started upstairs, still nervous about what to expect from my

father. As I reached the top I peeked into his office and saw him sitting at his desk.

"Hello father," I said to him. He didn't even turn in his chair but just offered a grunt as a response. I was stunned and unsure how to respond so instead I went to my room, grabbed my suitcase from under my bed and began to pack. I grabbed all my photos from my desk, some of my favourite books as well as textbooks. I grabbed as many clothes as I could, there were some my mum had picked out and I hated so I was sure to leave those behind. After around twenty minutes of packing I had filled the suitcase, I zipped it up and left my room. I took one more look at the stark room I had called mine all my life and realised there was nothing here I cared for. In a matter of days, I'd cut all ties to this house and any sentimentality it had for me.

"What do you think you're doing?" my mum asked. I was halfway down the stairs with my suitcase and she stood and watched me from the landing.

"I'm leaving."

"Why?"

"Are you mad? What do you mean 'why'." I scoffed, "I've dealt with shouting and screaming from dad my whole life and when I was here last week, he hit me and locked me in my room! Why the hell would I want to stay here?"

"Alexis, I don't know what you're talking about."

"Mum, what are *you* talking about? You locked me in my room all night."
"That was because you were misbehaving." she scolded.
"I did nothing!" I shouted, "I have tried to do *everything* I could to please you and dad and to be the daughter you wanted me to be. But nothing I do is ever enough!"
"Alexis, you're being ridiculous." she crossed her arms as she watched me, I wrestled my bag down the rest of the stairs and stood by the door, not even bothering to answer her.
"What the hell is all this noise?" My dad demanded as he now emerged from his office, he shoved my mum to the side and stormed downstairs until he stood in front of me.
"I'm leaving," I said.
"Don't be stupid Alexis, it doesn't suit you. Now take the bag back upstairs and stop this."
"No! I have been gone for a week and did you even notice? Did you call to see where I was or if I was okay?" I asked.
"No, because you were being a ridiculous child and we would not entertain any of your pathetic behaviour."
"What pathetic behaviour dad? You hit me! And I had to get out of the house."
"You got what you deserved," he growled, "that is what happens when you act out of line."
"I didn't do anything! You barged into my room and attacked me."

"You are pathetic," he spat, "you know that. You are a disappointment and you always have been. We would have been better off with no children rather than having you."

I was stunned and I didn't know how to respond to that. He had always been this cruel but before I was able to drown it out. Now it was like a foghorn, blaring in front of me.

"Everything okay here?" I spun and saw Jake standing at the front door. I hadn't shut it when I walked in and I was sure he must have seen me and my dad standing in the hall, perhaps even heard the screaming.

"Nothing that concerns you." my dad snarled.

"If you're hurting Lexi then it concerns me," Jake stared at my dad. "Sweetheart, go get in the car."

"She is *not* leaving this house."

"Do I have to remind you about the last time you threatened to keep her here?" Jake's voice had become extremely low and quiet, his sole fury was focussed on my dad.

"She is my daughter!" my dad burst.

"No one should treat a daughter the way you treated her. If she wants to leave you will let her and you will say nothing about it."

Jake turned his attention to me, checked I was okay, urging me to the car again.

"I will. Just one second." I told him and turned towards my parents, my dad's face had turned red with anger and my mum was still standing at the top of the stairs seeming unbothered by the whole situation.

"You have never treated me the way I deserved," I started, "I have jumped through every hoop you gave me, just so I would have a morsel of your approval and for what? To get shouted at, belittled and attacked? Not anymore. I want more than anything you've given me and you have made it abundantly clear over the years that I am nothing more than a disappointment. So, this is me doing you a favour, I'm leaving and going somewhere where they actually love me. I don't want to be here anymore; this has not felt like a home in years."

"Alexis, if you leave now, you can forget any plans of coming back." my dad said. I looked at him once more and realised how small he really was. Even mum, she didn't even seem like a full person anymore, rather a shadow of another life.

"If you think I would ever want to come back here then you're mad." I heaved my suitcase outside, wheeled it to the car and Cassie leapt out to help me get it into the boot.

"So that's it?" she asked me.

"That's it." I replied, she smiled at me and wrapped me in an incredibly tight hug.

"I am so proud of you." she whispered in my ear; I could feel tears beginning to form in my eyes and I quickly wiped them away.

"I couldn't have done this without you."

"You don't ever have to do anything without me." Cassie looked at me and smiled, her face full of pride. After a couple of minutes, Jake finally emerged from the house. Casie and I were both in the car and waited as he got in. The front door slammed shut behind him and he had a large satisfying smile on his face.
"What took you so long?" I asked.
"Just giving your dad what he deserved." he smiled, I looked at him and shook my head.
"You shouldn't have done that."
"What? Don't act like he didn't deserve it." he laughed. I just rolled my eyes at him, "come on let's get home."
"Yes please," I replied. I hadn't realised how tired I felt but after dealing with my parents I was ready to lay down. Jake drove us home and the conversation was cheerful on the way back. A weight had been lifted off all of us and I was sure that all the issues with my parents had weighed on Jake and Cassie too. I'll go back to university for my second year soon. With a job and my student finance, there was no reason why I wouldn't be able to finish it. This time I would do it my way.

I spent the rest of the day curled up on the sofa, I felt so emotionally drained that I needed some time to refresh. I turned on The Office snuggled under a blanket, a book and my laptop. Jake had managed to swipe it from my dad's office before he left the house yesterday and had returned it to me. I was so thankful to him so I could get some work done. Cassie had plans with Noah and as much as I could tell that it killed her to leave, I insisted she go and spend time with him, which left Jake and me in the house.

I was looking at jobs for when I went back to university and applying for as many as I could. Jake came and joined me too and he sat on the sofa next to me while he worked.

"I need to head into the office this afternoon." he said, "are you going to be okay?"

"Absolutely," I assured him, "some time alone might do me some good. Just to get my mind straight."

"Okay, we still have a couple of hours before I need to go." so we spent it sitting on the sofa, I put my laptop away and instead was leaning against Jake and watching TV while mindlessly scrolling on my phone. Just after lunch Jake went to get ready and headed out to work which left me alone at the house, but I didn't feel scared or lonely at all. I felt oddly happy and entirely relaxed. I spent the rest of the day much the same and once Cassie came back with Noah in the afternoon we relaxed in the garden and caught up, it was probably my last time with Cassie before she left for camp.

"Are you ready?" I asked them.

"Oh yeah," Noah said, "Last year was… interesting to say the least and I'm intrigued at how it'll be as leaders this time instead."

"See if everyone is as dramatic as us." Cassie teased.

"It worked out in the end last year right? Plus, we're looking after the little ones this time so I'm sure they'll be better than the older camp."
"Yeah, I guess it wasn't too bad." Noah agreed and planted a quick kiss on Cassie's cheek.
After another hour or so Collin came back with Bradley and Hailey, they had their last day of school and were incredibly excited for summer. They ran straight into the garden and joined us grabbing their water guns and creating utter chaos. That was how Nora found us, everyone in the garden, our clothes soaked.
"Well this seems fun," she laughed. Everyone's attention spun to her.
"Get her!" Collin shouted and we ambushed Nora with the water guns ensuring she was thoroughly soaked too. Everyone dissolved in fits of laughter and while Bradley and Hailey continued to run around the garden, the rest of us sat down to dry off.
"Well thank you for that, I think I'll start on dinner now." Nora said. She laughed and wandered off, she grabbed some towels and chucked them out to us.
"Dry off before you come in." she called. After a while when we were a little drier, we all wandered inside to get changed before dinner. Jake had arrived home too; he greeted me with a sweet kiss as he wandered into the kitchen. It was so odd that he was able to just kiss me like that, but I loved it. I was loved out loud and I would never get tired of it.

Our Summertime Secrets

We all woke up early on Friday as it was Cassie's last day. She was going to be leaving early on Saturday as her and Noah had a long trip planned so they could stop off at a few places first. Nora had planned a day out for us, at Cassie's request and we all needed to be up early so that we could make the most of the day. Nora had packed a picnic and then planned a hike in the woods. Since last summer Cassie had developed an affection for walking and as it was her last day, we were all roped into it. It was surprisingly fun and Noah ended up staying over so they could be here together to head off on Saturday. I wasn't complaining as it meant I had an excuse to stay with Jake in his room. I got ready for bed as usual and wandered to his door.
"I remember when I was here last." I laughed as I wandered into the room. Jake was sitting on his bed dressed in pyjama trousers and waiting for me.
"Oh yeah, I remember that too." he chuckled. "I never should have let you leave."
"I wish I hadn't." Jake and I hadn't made this whole thing easy, but we had gotten to where we needed to be.
"How are you?" he asked me.
"The whole mess with my parents really wasn't fun, but it was certainly necessary. I think people expected me to be sad about it all, but if anything I just feel free. I don't feel like I'm constantly disappointing anyone or that I owe anything to anyone." I said.

"Are you happy?" he asked, both of us laying down and looking at each other.
"What do you think?" I laughed. I leant forward and kissed him, hoping to show how happy I really was. I wrapped my arms around his neck and he pulled me close against him wrapping his arms around my waist.
"Okay," he said pulling apart, "I just wanted to check."
"Goodnight Jake."
"Goodnight sweetheart." He planted a kiss on the top of my head and then settled down too.
I had always thought home to be a place, four walls and a roof and if you were lucky enough then it would feel comforting. But now I realised that home was where you felt welcomed, loved and accepted. My home was a person now, my home was Jake.

Epilogue- Jake

It was the annual Christmas Eve party and my parents had invited everyone they knew, it was the biggest event they hosted each year. We were all able to invite friends too so Cassie had invited the girls and I had invited the guys. I think back to when I told them about Lexi and I and frankly it wasn't the reaction I thought.
"Why do none of you seem surprised at the news?"
"Mate we knew you guys were endgame ages ago."
"Then my set me up with Millie?"
"To make you get your head out of your ass and finally admit how you felt."
"You lot are twats."
"Nah, you're happy we meddled. Look at you now." And *frankly I had to agree, sometimes you're the person in your own way.* They had been right, I was the person that had delayed the best thing in my life for so long.

Bradley and Hailey were off upstairs with their friends while my parents were entertaining everyone in the open kitchen and dining room. I had been itching for Lexi to arrive; the party was in full swing but Lexi was still stuck at work.

Since moving out from her parents she had been staying with us between term time at university and had found a job to help with bills and rent. My parents had insisted it wasn't necessary, but Lexi hated taking things so she had been paying them rent- something I knew my parents hadn't even been touching. Instead, they were leaving it to the side for her so they could give it back when she left university and could afford a place to live. I was pacing in the kitchen waiting for her to arrive, she had been working every day since she got back from uni so our time had been limited. I was checking my phone every few minutes and finally I got the text I had been waiting for.

Lexi: I'm outside xx

I rushed to the front door and swung it open, there she stood in her supermarket uniform with her winter jacket around her and her hair looking slightly frazzled underneath her woollen hat. I grabbed her and yanked her inside, kissing her hard as soon as she was close enough, I wrapped her in my arms and tried to offer her some of my warmth.

"I've missed you," I whispered against her lips, only pulling away a fraction.

"I saw you this morning," she replied.

"Nope, too long. You can't leave my side now." I told her.

"Okay deal, I won't for the rest of the holidays." she laughed. We pulled further apart but I didn't let her go from my arms.

"Come on, let's get you changed and warmed up." I said, worried about her catching a cold.

"You can warm me up anytime," she teased. I groaned in response and followed her upstairs. She had sorted out what she was going to wear already so she grabbed her outfit and ran to the bathroom.

"One second," she said and locked the door behind her. I loitered on the landing waiting for her to be ready and after fifteen minutes she was back out and looking gorgeous. Even after we had been together for half a year I still had to catch my breath every time I saw her. I couldn't believe it took me so long to realise it, all these years. Wasted.

"You look incredible," I told her and grabbed her hips to pull her closer to me. I captured her lips and showed her exactly how much I loved her outfit.

"Jake, we need to go, people will be expecting us." She said to me trying to pull away as she laughed.

"Ah come on, they won't wonder where we are for five more minutes." I told her and started nipping at her neck, her scent was addictive and I wanted to embed myself in her, never separated.

"Okay well I guess five more minutes wouldn't be too bad." she laughed and I dragged her into my room. I pushed her against the door as soon as it was shut and trapped her in my arms. I didn't want to mess up her hair or outfit so I tried to keep it as respectful as I could while trying to show her how much I truly and deeply loved her. Her hands trailed all over my body, tracing my chest and snaking her arms around my waist to pull me even closer. We were flush together and I wanted nothing more than to throw her onto the bed and to never leave my room. But we were expected downstairs, so with a great amount of effort I pulled away from her.
"Okay, you're right, we need to get going." I told her.
"No," she whined, "you can't do that to me."
"Do what?" I asked, feigning ignorance.
"You know exactly what you did." she replied.
"Yes I do," I told her smugly, "and I'm not apologising at all. You loved it."
"Shut up," We both knew she loved it, I laughed and grabbed her hand to pull her out of my room. We wandered downstairs and Cassie stopped us as she walked through to the kitchen.
"LEXI!" she shouted and pulled her out of my arms and in for a hug. Lexi laughed and returned the affection, then moving on to hugging Connie and Lottie too.
"Hey girls, how are you?" they all replied with a chorus of 'good'.

"Did my brother steal you away?" Cassie asked, narrowing her eyes at me.
"He did, but only so I could get changed." Lexi replied and gestured to her clothes.
"Ugh gross." Cassie commented.
"Shush, she's my girlfriend, I'm allowed to." I told her and smirked, I would never get tired of calling her that.
"Don't remind me, I'm still getting used to it." Cassie said.
"Cass, it's been nearly six months." Lexi chimed in.
"Yeah, yeah. Fine, come on, we're going to get drinks and mum just put out the food." Cassie said.
"Food? Let's go." I said and pushed past them into the kitchen, Cassie rolled her eyes at me but still followed behind.

The rest of the evening passed in festive glee. We sat in the living room and chatted about everything, the girls were all cheerful and I ensured Lexi didn't move from my side, always having some part of us touching. Mum and dad were both in their element, chatting and socialising with their friends. Their therapy over the last few months had truly done wonders for them and they seemed to be going from strength to strength now. Their cruise had been wonderful and it had also given me and Lexi a chance for the two of us to spend time together. Cassie had loved being back at camp and seeing Dean and Emma. Things were good, life was good.

Around midnight the party died down, and everyone left to go home, it was just Lexi and I sitting in the living room. My parents had both gone to bed. Bradley and Hailey had long gone and all that was left was Cassie and Noah wandering around somewhere. Lexi and I had changed into the matching pyjamas I had bought us for Christmas and now we were watching Home Alone, her head was resting on my lap and I playing with her hair.
"Jake?" Lexi said and looked up at me. Twisting where she was and sitting up to look at me, she seemed nervous.
"Yes sweetheart."
"I love you, I mean I've always loved you and you probably know that already. But I just needed you to know officially." she confessed.
"I do know baby, but I'll never tire of hearing you say that." I told her and smiled down at her. I wrapped my arms around her pulling her closely.
"Good, I'll never stop then." she stated.
"Oh, and by the way," I started and leant down so that my ear was right next to her ear, "I love you too."
"Yeah?" she asked and pulled away, suddenly looking shy.
"Lex you have been rooted in my heart since I was a kid and there is no way I'm going anywhere." I told her.
"Neither am I." She agreed, "I'm just glad we realised it before it was too late."

"It never would have been too late, there was always going to be a place for you in my heart, I'm just glad we have the rest of our lives to make up for missed time." I murmured as I closed the distance to her lips.

"I like the sound of that," she replied coyly and tilted her head up to meet me.

"Me too." I whispered and bent down to meet her lips with mine.

"Oh god! Look as much as I am glad, you're happy and whatever, can we please refrain from this PDA, I mean I am eating here! I do not want to see my best friend and my brother making out. Thank you!" Cassie exclaimed as she walked into the living room with a plate of food while Noah followed close behind. We broke apart and looked at each other laughing.

"Ignore her," he said, "she is actually really excited about you two."

"Oi!" Cassie retorted from the other sofa.

"Hmm, well so am I." I agreed with Lexi resting against my side.

"Does that mean I'm officially a part of the family now?" she asked with a grin as she peeked up at me, her green eyes watching me. My hands rested on her hip and I couldn't contain the smile that spread over my face.

"Of course. You've always been a part of this family Lex." I replied. I glanced over at the mantle where our family Christmas card sat, only this year there was an addition. Front and centre stood Lexi, my arm slung around her shoulder on one side and Cassie looping her arm on the other. Right where she belonged, not with the family she was born with, but the family that chose her. "Good, there's no getting rid of me," she teased. I could tell she was joking but nothing had ever made me happier. "You're stuck with me."

"That's all I've ever wanted." I had the rest of my life to prove to her how much I loved her and I would be sure to remind her every day.

THE END

Acknowledgements

I can't believe this is my second book! I have written and published two books, that is wild to me! But none of this would be possible without such a network of people around me that supported me all the way through the process.

I have to say a massive thank you to my whole family and my boyfriend for constantly supporting me and helping me in my writing journey. But most of all I have to thank my brother for helping me with formatting, designing and creating both my first and second cover for me.

Finally, thank you to my readers and followers for being along for the journey and wanting to read all of my stories as well as liking, sharing and commenting and sharing my work. Thank you for giving my books a chance and helping my dreams come true, these stories would be nowhere without you.

About the Author

Victoria Jane is a young author that is passionate about sharing stories that people can relate to and appreciate. She aims to deal with more serious issues while weaving in sweet romances.

For years she has loved reading and losing herself in stories which she wishes to continue for future generation and share new stories with others. She weaves in personal experiences to her stories to add a part of her in every book. When she is not writing, she spends her time with family and friends and her two dogs. Or cuddled up with a book herself.

Also by Victoria Jane

Cassie was never good with attention, but when her parents send her off to camp after she finishes school to distract her from the problems at home, everything she knows is far away from her. Mixed in with new strangers, and a cute new blond she begins to settle down. But with the arrival of a new camper mixing things up, as well as her life at home changing, she must make a choice. Will she stay in the background and hide? Or is this her time to open her heart to new people and new possibilities?

Victoria Jane

Our Summertime Secrets

Printed in Great Britain
by Amazon